DONALD TRUMP
AND
ISRAEL

#1 *NEW YORK TIMES* BESTSELLING AUTHOR

MIKE EVANS

DONALD TRUMP
AND
ISRAEL

TimeWorthy
BOOKS

P.O. Box 30000, Phoenix, AZ 85046

No American President has been a
better friend to Israel than Donald Trump.
In his first term as president, Trump has
recognized Jerusalem as Israel's official capital,
moving the American Embassy to the city.
He has also affirmed Israel's sovereignty
of the Golan Heights. Third, President Trump
has changed American policy regarding
Judea and Samaria, allowing Israel to determine
its own future regarding these areas.
In the United States, he has signed an executive
order to fight anti-Semitism on college campuses.
Further, his "Deal of the Century" has been released,
offering the region's best plan for peace in
the Middle East since the re-establishment
of the modern State of Israel.

In *Israel and Donald Trump*, you'll discover vital
details the mainstream media will not mention
regarding Trump's relationship with Israel.
Further, Dr. Evans offers exclusive personal
insights regarding his role on Trump's team of
evangelical advisors, as well as efforts within Israel
revealing how Trump has made Israel great!

CONTENTS

DONALD TRUMP
HAS MADE ISRAEL GREAT

As I sat in the room watching my friend Benjamin Netanyahu and President Donald Trump announce the Peace Plan, dubbed "The Deal of the Century," I kept thinking about all the president had accomplished in just three years since I put up 220 billboards in Jerusalem declaring "Trump Make Israel Great" when the president first came to Jerusalem. I reached into my pocket and pulled out a pen and held it in my hand. The pen was given to me by the president when he signed the executive order on combating Anti-Semitism on American college campuses on December 11, 2019. President Trump noted at that time, "The vile, hate-filled poison of anti-Semitism must be condemned and confronted everywhere and anywhere it appears."

My mind went back to the first time I met Israeli Prime Minister Benjamin Netanyahu. He was 28 years old, grieving his beloved brother's death. I also thought of the recent Embassy Gala where I hosted Ivanka Trump, Jared Kushner, Steve Mnuchin, David Friedman, Lindsey Graham, Ted Cruz, and several hundred other household names. I also kept thinking about all the presidents, and secretaries of state, and national security advisors that I had appealed to in hopes of recognizing Jerusalem and to do the things that Trump has done, with every one of them coldly ignoring my appeals.

As founding member of President Trump's Evangelical Initiative, I've had the privilege of working closely with President Trump, Jared Kushner, David Friedman, Jason Greenblatt, and Avi Berkowitz. I can say unequivocally that Donald Trump and his team have made Israel great.

When the President visited Jerusalem on May 22, 2017, I had many diplomats say to me, "Donald Trump is not going to recognize Jerusalem. Why did you put 220 billboards up around the city that read, 'Trump, make Israel Great?'"

I replied, "I know Donald Trump, and he will do more for your nation than any American president ever." This has certainly proven to be true.

Not only has the President recognized Jerusalem as Israel's capital and also the Golan Heights, he has also stood up to Iran. He stopped the funding for terror through the Taylor Force Act. He closed the PLO office in Washington, DC and the anti-Semitic consulate in Jerusalem. He moved the U.S. Embassy to Jerusalem and built a Sunni alliance that is creating enormous support for Israel and has passed a historic Executive Order on Combating Anti-Semitism. I know, he gave me the pen.

In addition, President Trump has crafted the most brilliant vision for peace of any president in American history that in time could bring an end to the Palestine crisis. For that alone he deserves a Nobel peace prize.

Jared Kushner and the president are builders; they have laid a foundation that everyone can now build upon. There is no doubt that the foundation will last, and will be the basis for a true and lasting peace. Of course, it will take time; but with this plan, time is not an enemy, it's a friend. Every issue has been addressed.

One of the significant factors in the plan is that it is so extensive, it will help normalize relations between Israel and Arab countries more significantly than those which currently exist. It was astonishing to see three Muslim ambassadors in the White House for the unveiling of the plan and Arab leaders did not reject it out of hand or state direct criticisms of it. The Saudi Foreign Ministry said Riyadh "reiterates its support for all efforts aimed at reaching a just and comprehensive resolution to the Palestinian cause" and "appreciates the efforts of President [Donald] Trump's administration to develop a comprehensive peace plan." It also said the Gulf kingdom "encourages the start of direct peace negotiations."

The plan is a realistic solution for the Palestinians to govern themselves, but not have the power to threaten Israel. It addresses limits of certain sovereign powers in the Palestinian areas, i.e. maintaining Israeli security and control of the airspace. The Palestinians would not be allowed to sign treaties. There would be no recognition of a Palestinian state or any movement in the $50 billion trust fund until corruption and terror have been rooted out, and the Jewish state acknowledged. This also includes the demilitarization of Gaza.

The plan deals with everything. In ten years, it would provide one million jobs for Palestinians, reducing unemployment to 10 percent, and the poverty rate by 50 percent. It's a vision. It reminds me of the "I Have a Dream" speech by Dr. Martin Luther King. I was very close to Shimon Peres, the ninth president of the State of Israel, during the last two years of his life. We met with many world leaders, including George W. Bush, Prince Albert of Monaco, and Pope Francis. Shimon was a dreamer.

To me, this plan is realistic, a wonderful dream like that of Theodor Hertzl. Since 1946, the United Nations has passed almost 700 resolutions and over 100 Security Council resolutions in an attempt to bring peace to the region. All have failed, because they did not understand the core issues that had to be addressed. President Trump's plan does that.

It gives the Palestinians self-determination, but it would not provide them with a government that will compromise Israel's security.

It addresses Israel's geographic challenges, such as the danger of Gaza, and demands complete disarmament of the terror state. Many do not realize that Israel has already given to the Palestinians 88 percent of the territory captured in 1967. The plan does not uproot anyone—not Jewish homes or Palestinians, and provides a brilliant transportation corridor.

Although the plan realistically addresses the refugee problem, it does not begin until the Palestinians prove that terror and Jew-hatred have been rejected. It takes into consideration Israel's valid legal and historical rights and recognizes the Bible and the Bible lands as legal. Neither is mentioned in the plan, but in essence it does allude to them. The commitment is that the Jewish people not be uprooted from their homeland.

Ninety-seven percent of Israelis in the West Bank will, through new infrastructure, be incorporated into contiguous Israeli territory. The recognition of Judea and Samaria is astonishing as is the recognition of the Jordan Valley, an area critical to Israel's security. It commits that Israel would maintain sovereignty over territorial waters and airspace.

The plan designates both East and West Jerusalem as the capital of the Jewish state. In no way does it divide the Holy City. A Palestinian capital would be in an area east and north of the existing security barrier, including Kafr 'Aqab—the eastern part of Shua'fat and Abu Dis—as the capital of al Quds. It does not even acknowledge that the Palestinians can use the term "East Jerusalem" as its capital.

The U.S. plan consents to an embassy in al Quds for the Palestinians. It also contains a strategy to work closely with Jordan and Egypt. There is a five-year provision to allow the PA to have a small airport and utilize Israel's ports in Haifa and Ashdod, but only with inspections and security by the Israelis. Palestinian refugees would not be permitted to return to the territories, but the plan does provide billions of dollars in compensation for them.

President Trump in his speech on January 28, 2020, spoke of the fact that Israel is a light unto the world. Prime Minister Netanyahu said that the United States would recognize Israeli sovereignty over the territory with no incremental security risks to the State of Israel. He reiterated that the plan would be a firewall against political corruption and terror. It would give the Palestinians time to meet the challenges of statehood. The Peace Plan decrees that the territorial allocation of a new state would remain open and undeveloped for a period of four years.

Israel is my life and has been for more than 40 years. That is how long it has been since I first began working with Prime Minister Menachem Begin and Benjamin Netanyahu. I can say that I wholeheartedly endorse this plan and so will my 70 million Friends of Zion followers. It is brilliant, but I do not believe that the Palestinians will embrace it this year or next year; it may take a decade. It will take time for the current population to move beyond corruption and radical Islam and join the civilized world.

To see the ambassadors of the Emirates, Bahrain, and Oman in attendance was astonishing. To realize that finally the White House and the State Department have recognized Judea and Samaria as true Bible Land from Bethel, where Jacob dreamed of a ladder ascending to heaven, to Shiloh, where the Ark of the Covenant held the Ten Commandments for centuries. Unlike all other plans, this one does not trade biblical land for peace. Donald Trump is truly making Israel great!

CHAPTER 1

A JOYFUL NOISE

May we shout for joy when we hear of your victory
and raise a victory banner in the name of our God.

(PSALM 20:5 NLT)

On May 14, 2018, a joyful noise was heard in the streets of Jerusalem as Jews from every walk of life celebrated a long-awaited move. On that day, the 70th anniversary of the rebirth of the nation of Israel, President Donald John Trump had kept his campaign pledge to relocate the nation's embassy from Tel Aviv to the Holy City. The decision was announced by the president in December 2017 and generated a jubilant response from Prime Minister Benjamin "Bibi" Netanyahu and his government.

President Trump was the leader who stood his ground, made good on his campaign promise, and moved the embassy. Why was this move so important? It simply meant that one of the so-called "Superpowers" had acknowledged the Jews' right to the land of Israel. The Jewish people settled in the area in about 1,500 BCE—some 3,500 years ago. Jerusalem was wrested from them in AD 70 when it was destroyed by Roman troops. Despite that catastrophic event, Jerusalem was then, and is today, the capital of Israel.

In *Jerusalem, Sacred City of Mankind*, former mayor of Jerusalem Teddy Kollek and author Moshe Pearlman wrote:

> The spiritual attachment of the Jews to Jerusalem has remained unbroken; it is a unique attachment. Should one doubt that statement, he would have to look long and hard to find another relationship in history where a people, even in captivity, remained so passionately attached to a city for 3,000 years.[1]

The very name *Jerusalem* evokes a stirring in the heart and soul. It has been called by many names: City of God; City of David; Zion, the City of the Great King; but only one name has resonated through the centuries: Jerusalem!

Following the 1948 Armistice between Israel and Jordan, Jerusalem was a divided city:

> Barbed wire and concrete barriers ran down the center of the city, passing close by Jaffa Gate on the western side of the old walled city, and a crossing point was established at Mandelbaum Gate slightly to the north of the old walled city.[2]

In 1967, the Six-Day War dramatically changed that situation. No longer would the Holy City be divided and the Jews banned from celebrating their Jewish heritage; she had become a reunited city whose inhabitants were again joyfully remembering her past and reveling in her future.

In 1995, the 104th United States Congress passed the Jerusalem Embassy Act. It was designed to acknowledge Jerusalem as the capital of Israel and provide for a US Embassy to be established there no later than May 1999. Both Houses of Congress voted overwhelmingly to recognize Jerusalem. However, each year since its passage, presidents Bill Clinton, George W. Bush, and Barack Obama each waived the implementation of the Act. Waivers to forestall enactment of the bill were required every six months. The presidential denials were based on petty grievances over which branch of government had the authority to set foreign policy, and on "national security interests." As a campaign promise, Donald Trump resolutely committed to honor the Embassy Act.

At the opening ceremony on May 14, 2019, Prime Minister Benjamin Netanyahu offered this praise:

> Thank you. Thank you, President Trump, for having the courage to keep your promises. Thank you, President Trump, and thank you all, for making the alliance between America and Israel stronger than ever. And thank you, a special thank you, to you, Ambassador Friedman. Thank you, David, for everything you do to bring our countries and our peoples closer together.

Today, you have a special privilege. You are privileged to become the first American ambassador to serve your country in Jerusalem, and this is a distinct honor that will be yours forever. Nobody can be first again.

My friends, this is a great day for Israel. It's a great day for America. It's a great day for our fantastic partnership. But I believe it's also a great day for peace.[3]

Days before the embassy dedication, the Friends of Zion Heritage Center in Jerusalem (which this author founded) raised a billboard at the site of the ceremony and had many more congratulatory messages erected across the city. It was also my distinct honor to be chosen to host an official black-tie US Embassy Gala in Jerusalem following the dedication. More than 375 prominent leaders from the United States were in attendance. Among them were Senator Lindsey Graham (South Carolina), Senator Ted Cruz (Texas), former senator Joe Lieberman (Connecticut), Governor Rick Scott (Florida), Secretary of the Treasury Steven Mnuchin, Ambassador David Friedman, and Jared and Ivanka Trump Kushner. During the event I thanked President Trump and Prime Minister Netanyahu, the two men whose legacy might very well prove to be that of having orchestrated peace between Israel and five or six of the Sunni Gulf States. Saudi Arabia and the other Middle East states that lie on the Persian Gulf and Gulf of Oman share Israel's concerns regarding Iranian ambitions to dominate the region.

Those countries have also been uneasy about close ties between Iran and the Palestinian Authority. (This alliance dates back to the late Yasser Arafat and Ayatollah Ruhollah Khomeini. Arafat was the first foreign leader to visit Iran after the overthrow of the shah. Khomeini had closed the Israeli Embassy in Tehran and bequeathed it to Arafat and the Palestine Liberation Organization.)

Although not located on either of two major waterways, Egypt's leaders are concerned about the radicalism that governs Iran and its incursion into Turkey. Egyptian president Abdel Fattah el-Sisi is also leery of Turkey's support of the Muslim Brotherhood, a radical group with a jihadist approach to Islam.

Israel is the only freely democratic nation among those in the region. She is a staunch US ally and has the military dynamism and capable leadership to help keep Iran in check.

The decision to move the embassy was a prophetic *coup d'état* for President Trump who months earlier was compared by Netanyahu to King Cyrus, a long-ago Persian king. Let me stop here a moment and point out that under the leadership of Cyrus, the Persians exhibited great compassion in allowing the Jews taken captive by Nebuchadnezzar to return to Judah, and to Jerusalem. What prompted the conqueror to allow the conquered to make their way home? None other than Jehovah God! God can move the heart of a king just as surely as He can move the heart of a pauper. As Proverbs 21:1 says: "The king's heart is a stream of water in the hand of the LORD; he turns it wherever he will" (ESV).

"Cyrus was upright, a great leader of men, generous and benevolent. The Hellenes, whom he conquered regarded him as 'Law-giver' and the Jews as 'the annointed (sic) of the Lord.'"[4] In biblical history, Cyrus is first mentioned in 2 Chronicles 36:22–23, and again in Ezra 1:1–3. Both passages record that God moved the heart of Cyrus king of Persia in order to fulfill the word of the LORD spoken by Jeremiah:

> In the first year of Cyrus king of Persia, in order to fulfill the word of the LORD spoken by Jeremiah, the LORD moved the heart of Cyrus king of Persia to make a proclamation throughout his realm and to put it in writing:
>
> "This is what Cyrus king of Persia says:
>
> "'The LORD, the God of heaven, has given me all the kingdoms of the earth and he has appointed me to build a temple for him at Jerusalem in Judah. Any of his people among you may go up to Jerusalem in Judah and build the temple of the LORD, the God of Israel, the God who is in Jerusalem, and may their God be with them.'"
>
> (Ezra 1:1–3 NIV)

So, Cyrus was appointed by Jehovah to free the children of Israel from Babylonian captivity and allow them to go back to Jerusalem. There, they would be permitted to rebuild the City of David. Two heathen rulers: one—Nebuchadnezzar—was raised up by God to dispense judgment on His people, while the other—Cyrus—was tasked with providing freedom and restoration.

On November 8, 2016, just hours before the final vote count in the presidential race between Donald Trump and Hillary Clinton, this writer was having dinner with the Chief Rabbi of Moscow in the business lounge of the David Citadel Hotel in Jerusalem. Nearby sat Dan Shapiro, who was then the US Ambassador to Israel. He revealed to friends at his table that he would soon be traveling to Ramallah to celebrate Hillary Clinton's victory. The Chief Rabbi asked me, "Do you know what all Jews worldwide are reading this week in the *Haftorah* [a short selection from the Prophets]? It is the story of Abraham and the blessing and curses." The Chief Rabbi added, "Donald Trump has chosen to bless Israel and also support life [referring to Trump's stand against abortion]. For that, God will bless him with the presidency; he will be a modern-day Cyrus."

The Chief Rabbi's statement would be repeated by Netanyahu soon after the embassy move:

> I want to tell you that the Jewish people have a long memory, so we remember the proclamation of the great king, Cyrus the Great, the Persian king 2,500 years ago. He proclaimed that the Jewish exiles in Babylon could come back and rebuild our Temple in Jerusalem. We remember a hundred years ago, Lord Balfour, who issued the Balfour Proclamation that recognized the rights of the Jewish people in our ancestral homeland. We remember 70 years ago, President Harry S Truman

was the first leader to recognize the Jewish state. And
we remember how a few weeks ago, President Donald
J. Trump recognized Jerusalem as Israel's capital.
Mr. President, this will be remembered by our people
through the ages.[5]

In 2018, I had the honor of presenting President Trump with the
Friends of Zion award in the Oval Office. I too repeated the words of
Prime Minister Netanyahu when I said to him, "You are a modern-
day Cyrus."

Looking back, I thought of a headline that graced the cover of
Time magazine on April 8, 1966. The question had been posed: "Is
God dead?" It was certainly feasible to think the answer just might be
"Yes," especially after the assassination of President John Fitzgerald
Kennedy. The United States would all too soon be faced with two
other murders that would roil the country: civil rights activist the
Reverend Dr. Martin Luther King on April 4, 1968; and Attorney
General Robert Francis Kennedy (brother of JFK) on June 6, 1968.

These events were precursors to the hippie culture of free love.
While this may initially sound innocuous, the ensuing chaos fomented
by that movement introduced rebellion, the Roe v. Wade court battle
legalizing abortion, the drug-abuse lifestyle, and the Engel v. Vitale
suit that culminated in the removal of prayer from public schools
across the nation. The revolution took over arts, the media, universities, even the White House. The Rev. Dr. Billy Graham's wife, Ruth,

was quoted as saying that if God failed to judge America, he would have to repent for raining judgment down on Sodom and Gomorrah.

Rather than supporting Israel's enemies—those who are determined to drive the Jews into the sea—Donald Trump has taken up the banner of support for the United States' closest ally in the Middle East. As we will see in these pages, he has done much to support Israel.

Vice President Mike Pence spoke to a pro-Israel group in July 2019 of the president's policies toward Israel and Iran, and his pledge to keep his campaign promises:

> As President Trump has said, this administration will always stand in solidarity with our Jewish brothers and sisters, and we will always stand strong for the State of Israel.. . . He's a man of action, and he's a man of his word. He says what he means, and he means what he says, and from the very first day of this administration, President Donald Trump has been keeping the promises that he made to the American people.[6]

The vice president reinforced the president's determination to stand with Israel:

> Ladies and gentlemen, Israel and the United States will always stand together, because America and Israel are more than friends. We are more than allies. The United States and Israel are family.[7]

CHAPTER 2

In the Eye of the Prophetic Storm

You will arise and have mercy on Jerusalem—
and now is the time to pity her, now is the time you
promised to help. For your people love every stone
in her walls and cherish even the dust in her streets.

(PSALM 102:13–14 NLT)

On January 20, 2017, Donald J. Trump stood on the west front of the United States Capitol Building and was sworn in as the 45th president of the United States. His right hand was raised; his left hand rested atop two Bibles—the historic Lincoln Bible, and one that had been given to him by his mother. He was following a tradition established on April 30, 1789, by George Washington, who had placed his hand on a Masonic Bible, randomly opened to Genesis 49, and took the oath of office to become the first president of the American republic. (It is interesting to note that two presidents in recent history also opted to use a Masonic Bible as they took the oath of office: the late George H. W. Bush (41), and George

W. Bush (43). George Herbert Walker took the oath with his hand resting on the very same Masonic Bible used by George Washington in 1789. His son George Walker wanted to use that same Bible, but due to inclement weather and rather than expose the artifact to the elements, a family Bible was substituted.)

Not every president since Washington has followed the same pattern of placing his hand on a Bible as they swore to preserve, protect, and defend the Constitution of the United States. Some opted to simply raise their right hand; John Quincy Adams purportedly chose to use a law volume for the ceremony. Others have selected a specific scripture verse to which the Bible was opened. Some were sworn in with the Bible closed. Often, the choices have proved to be prophetic of that president's term of office, and on occasion the chosen verses have uncannily reflected America's role in the plan of Bible prophecy.

On January 20, 1981, the warmest inaugural day on record—a balmy 55 degrees—Ronald Reagan stepped to the podium to take the oath of office. Notably, as Chief Justice Warren Burger prepared to administer the oath, Reagan's left hand rested on a Bible prophecy that would decide the fate of the nation of which he was taking leadership, as well as the fate of the world. That day the Bible was opened to 2 Chronicles 7:14, a prophecy given in the historic city of Jerusalem to King Solomon. God declared these words:

> If my people, which are called by my name, shall humble themselves, and pray, and seek my face, and turn from

their wicked ways; then will I hear from heaven, and will forgive their sin, and will heal their land. (KJV)

In the 1980s I was invited to the White House during Ronald Reagan's presidency. As we stood in the Oval Office, he pointed out his mother's Bible, which was open to the scripture in 2 Chronicles 7:14.

The president noted where his mother had written in the margin, "Son, this scripture is for the healing of the nations." We walked to his magnificent desk that had been a gift to President Rutherford B. Hayes from Queen Victoria. The heavily carved treasure had been built with timbers from the *Resolute*, a vessel used in British Arctic exploration. This same beautifully ornate desk is used today by Donald Trump.

There are Bible scholars who are convinced that by moving the US Embassy to Jerusalem, President Trump has fulfilled prophecy. Could that be true? Is the United States in prophecy? The answer to that is an unequivocal yes, it is!

In a nutshell, here is how the United States fits into Bible prophecy: America has joined herself to Ishmael and Isaac, half brothers and both descendants of ancient Abraham, who was told by God to get out of Ur of the Chaldees, modern-day Iraq. Recorded in Genesis 12:1–3 are the following verses:

The LORD had said to Abram, "Go from your country, your people and your father's household to the land I will show you. I will make you into a great nation and I will bless you; I will make your name great, and you will be a blessing. I will bless those who bless you, and whoever curses you I will curse; and all peoples on earth will be blessed through you." (NIV)

A covenant between the US and the descendants of Isaac was based on appeasement policies as a result of the deaths of millions of Jews during the Holocaust. Israel, the tiny democratic state in the midst of a sea of instability in the Middle East, and the promised offspring of Abraham, has been of invaluable assistance in deterring Communism, Fascism, and terrorism.

The agreement with the other brother, Ishmael, was one of convenience. A mortal enemy of the younger brother Isaac, Ishmael, the son of Sarah's handmaid, brought a dowry of black gold (oil) to the marriage, and has since employed that commodity to blackmail America. While Middle Eastern oil flows to the West, arms are, in turn, shipped in the opposite direction. In fact, the Middle East region is currently the number one global client of the US for weapons of war. Since the 1980s, Saudi Arabia alone has purchased more than $200 billion in weapons.

Even after September 11, 2001, petrodollars earned by countries such as Iran were used to sponsor terrorism, produce weapons of mass destruction, and finance a gospel of hatred that has been employed in the brainwashing of millions of Islamic youth. Yet America has been unwilling to draw a line in the sand against these actions. Many

Islamic regimes are aware that while they have the oil, as late Israeli Prime Minister Ariel Sharon once said, ". . . we have the matches."[8] It's time for the US to stand up to these bullies and quit capitulating to blackmail. Our future depends on it!

The Organization of the Petroleum Exporting Countries (OPEC) was founded in September 1960 during a conference in Baghdad, Iraq. Its original five members were Iran, Saudi Arabia, Iraq, Kuwait, and Venezuela. Currently, twelve member countries are active in the global cartel. Their major concern is that of controlling the flow of oil and its cost per barrel. In the early 2000s hydraulic fracturing, or "fracking," became a relative newcomer to the oil market. This burgeoning technology has literally thrown the proverbial monkey wrench into the Russian and Saudi Arabian markets. Those two countries had been functioning in a global marketplace boasting few feasible competitors. Suddenly, the US had again risen to the top of oil production with the renewed interest and investment in fracking.

Initially, it was thought that a market led by frackers would falter as soon as oil prices dropped below a certain price point. That has proved to be false, as barrel upon barrel of oil continues to find its way into today's marketplace. According to market analysts, fracking efforts of

> . . . U.S. shale and non-OPEC countries [were] expected to capture all the growth in global demand in 2018. The lower 48-states are expected to grow production by

340,000 barrels per day in 2017 and by 500,000 barrels per day in 2018.[9]

Additionally, America's other ally and partner in the Middle East, Isaac (Israel), has developed the fourth largest nuclear arsenal in the world. Knowing that Islamic fundamentalists are determined to annihilate her, Israel's leaders are determined that what happened in the Holocaust, while the world kept silent, will never be allowed to happen again. So determined was Prime Minister Golda Meir that on the fourth day of the Six-Day War, in an act of desperation, she reportedly opened up three silos and pointed nuclear-tipped missiles toward Egyptian and Syrian military headquarters near Cairo and Damascus.

While we know that Israel has produced nuclear weapons since at least the late 1960s, today Islamic nations are dangerously close to having their proverbial finger poised over the red button as well. It is well-known that Pakistan has nuclear bombs and that the Iranians are in hot pursuit of nuclear capability. As always, the sons of Ishmael seem determined to wreak havoc on the children of Israel.

Through these two political—and spiritual—alliances, the US has stepped into the center of this prophetic storm. America now finds herself trying to accommodate an ancient Jew-hating older brother (Ishmael) who has refused to make peace with the younger (Isaac). In order to live with both, America has attempted to appease each with weapons and inducements.

During the 1991 Persian Gulf War, I had lunch one afternoon with Saudi Arabia's Crown Prince Mohammed Khalid, the then governor of Dhahran. He was also the commander-in-chief of the Saudi Royal Air Force and the Arab multinational forces. During the war, he was over the Syrian high command and the Egyptian Third Army commanders. The US had paid Syria one billion dollars to support the Persian Gulf War with the knowledge that Syria's then president Hafez al-Assad led a terror state. Syria spent that money to buy missiles from North Korea.

As we ate, Khalid and I talked about Islamic fundamentalists and the threat they and their fanatical religion could be to the West. My words antagonized Khalid, and he said, "Listen, your country is a lot more dangerous than ours. You can walk our streets at two in the morning and nobody will bother you. You can't do that in L.A., New York, Chicago, or most of the big US cities."

"You're right," I agreed. "But that's because you cut off people's hands and heads in public squares."

"Well, it works," he retorted. "What do you do? Put color televisions in your prisons and serve them holiday dinners! And besides, don't insult our religion by exaggerating. Islam is a peaceful religion."

"Are you telling me Islamic fundamentalists are peaceful?" I asked.

He shook his head. "No, they're not. But they represent no more than ten percent of Islam."

"Excuse me," I retorted. "That really comforts me to know that only a hundred million or so people want to kill me in the name of their religion."

I've heard this same argument about the impact of Islamic fundamentalism over and over. Liberal politicians and special interest groups continue to propagate the myth that Islam is a peaceful religion. But think about this for a moment: Islam has around one billion adherents worldwide. The actual number is probably higher, but one billion is a nice, round number for the sake of argument. Now, if even ninety percent of the Islamic world is peaceful, as Prince Khalid assured me, it still places the planet on the brink of the greatest crisis in history. Even if 99.9 percent of the Islamic world were completely nonviolent, we still remain in grave danger. If only one-tenth of one percent of all Muslims have been radicalized, that's still a staggering number. It would mean that *only* one million people are intent on killing us! It took nineteen hijackers to wreak massive destruction on New York City and the Pentagon on September 11, 2001. Each one of those men believed he was on an assignment from Allah.

The terrorists' war against America and Israel is rooted in the radical religious doctrine called Islamic fundamentalism. This distorted Islamic belief is very difficult for Americans to comprehend. One reason is that our modern secular world is still getting past the interminable conflict between science and religion—which most assume was won long ago by science and secularism. Suddenly, a religious adversary is attacking mighty, secular America. It's no longer just the streets of Jerusalem that are threatened.

True hope for peace lies in discerning the truth and acting on it, not in believing myths and ignoring bigotry. Yet too many people in America view the real enemy as the "narrow-minded, right-wing, Bible-thumping Christians" who believe in a literal interpretation of right and wrong. The same people who perceive Conservative Christians to be the enemy often attempt to legitimize the acts of cold-blooded murderers as just steps to obtain freedom and peace. These apostles of appeasement have raised the hopes of the Islamic fanatics so high that the national security of America is now at stake.

The question is often asked: "Why do they hate us?" Everyone wants to know that answer. Here it is: Simply because they hate us! The more important question is this: What is fueling that hatred, and how can this engine of hate be derailed? If you don't think bigotry is at the root of it all, you are dead wrong. It is no coincidence that the World Conference on Racism in Durban, South Africa, turned into a "World Conference on Jew-hatred" that ended a mere, and telling, three days before September 11, 2001.

America *is* in prophecy and was, I believe, attacked on 9/11 because of her unholy covenant with the descendants of the eldest son of Abraham, Ishmael—specifically the nations led by or heavily influenced by Islamic fundamentalist populations. These regimes are intolerant and barbaric, still living in the Dark Ages. They remain completely dedicated to the destruction of Israel, America's ally.

Many believe the ongoing Palestinian crisis has much to do with the issue of Jew-hatred. They are correct; it does. The entire Palestinian problem comes down to two things: refugees and terrorism. Has there ever been a refugee crisis anywhere on earth that has drawn the world into such a mess? The answer is, clearly, no. Civilized countries resolve refugee crises on their own. The truth is, the Arab world has fueled and fed the Palestinian refugee crisis, using it to exploit Jew-hatred.

What was the advent of this predicament? From the official journal of the PLO a quote can be found by the current president of the Palestinian Authority (PA), Mahmoud Abbas, aka Abu Mazen:

> The Arab armies entered Palestine to protect the Palestinians from the Zionist tyranny but, instead they abandoned them, forced them to emigrate and to leave their homeland, imposed upon them a political and ideological blockade and threw them into prisons similar to the ghettos in which the Jews used to live in eastern Europe, as if we were condemned to change places with them. The Arab states succeeded in scattering the Palestinians and in destroying their unity.[10]

How was the Jewish refugee crisis in Europe at the end of the Holocaust resolved? Or the crisis in Arab countries where Jewish citizens were being killed simply because they were Jews? Why did the Arab League tell the Arabs to leave Palestine and fight Israel, then turn their backs on the very refugee disaster they created? Why did they make up the myth that Israeli Arabs must have a state inside Israel, even though they have never had such a thing in three thousand years of history? Or that an Egyptian-born billionaire terrorist by the name of Yasser Arafat was their "George Washington"?

Israel has always taken care of her own people. After placing his signature on the Camp David Accords in 1979, Israeli prime minister Menachem Begin approved a massive airlift of Ethiopian Jews. Those refugees had crossed the border from Ethiopia into the Sudan where some ten thousand were stranded in refugee camps. The death toll of those who did not make it to the relative safety of a camp totaled more than two thousand. Wishing to spare further death, the Israelis utilized two massive airlifts that were dubbed Operation Moses and Operation Joshua. Chartered planes from Belgium transported some 6,500 Jews to Israel. The remaining approximately two hundred Jews in the Sudan were aided in their escape by the US Central Intelligence Agency in an airlift named Operation Sheba. Between 1972 and 1985, thousands of Ethiopian Jews were resettled in Israel.

CHAPTER 3

PANDORA'S BOX

Let mine adversaries be clothed with shame,
and let them cover themselves with their own
confusion, as with a mantle.

(PSALM 109:29 KJV)

As a Middle East analyst for over four decades, I strongly believe there is a direct correlation between current events and prophecy. I am firmly convinced that during his presidency, Jimmy Carter unlocked another Pandora's box in the Middle East, complicating matters through unwise interference. Presidents Bill Clinton and Barack Obama later bought in to this mistake.

If America had maintained moral clarity, Iran might still be a pro-Western country. Iraq might never have gone to war against Iran, a war which took the lives of 1.2 million Arabs. The US certainly would not have assisted them in doing so. The USSR might not have invaded Afghanistan, and America would not have mistakenly armed and trained thousands of budding terrorists throughout the Middle East to fight the Soviets.

These same US-trained and armed terrorists, Osama bin Laden's al-Qaeda being the most infamous example, quickly and resolutely turned on America. The truth is: We might never have had to experience the terrorist catastrophe of 9/11 had this country continued its Conservative policies of never negotiating with terrorists.

Barely a month into his first term of office, President Bill Clinton received a wake-up call from Bin Laden's organization: the February 26, 1993, truck bombing of the World Trade Center. While this first attack went relatively unnoticed, and today has been all but forgotten, in it were seeds of the eventual September 11 attacks, and in the very same location. The actual aim of that 1993 bombing had been to topple the towers and kill as many as 250,000 people.[11] If these madmen had succeeded in slaughtering even one percent instead of killing only seven (one of the victims was pregnant), we would today be remembering February 26, 1993, not September 11, 2001.

Instead, however, because Bill Clinton, our president at the time, was more occupied in implementing his economic programs than in keeping the US safe, no one else paid much attention to the bombing, either. In his regular radio address the day after the bombing, Clinton mentioned the "tragedy" but never once used the words *bomber* or *terrorist* in his address. Neither did he ever mention the incident again in public or visit the site of the blast. As the author of *Losing Bin*

Laden, Richard Miniter said about Clinton's inability to deal with Bin Laden throughout his presidency:

> In 1993, bin Laden was a small-time funder of militant Muslim terrorists in Sudan, Yemen, and Afghanistan. By the end of 2000, Clinton's last year in office, bin Laden's network was operating in more than fifty-five countries and already responsible for the deaths of thousands (including fifty-nine Americans). . . .
>
> Clinton was tested by a historic, global conflict, the first phase of America's war on terror. He was president when bin Laden declared war on America. He had many chances to defeat bin Laden; he simply did not take them. If, in the wake of the 1998 embassy bombings, Clinton had rallied the public and the Congress to fight bin Laden and smash terrorism, he might have been the Winston Churchill of his generation. But, instead, he chose the role of Neville Chamberlain [whose appeasements of Hitler in Munich in 1938 are credited with paving the way to the Nazi invasion of Poland that began World War II the next year].[12]

After the British prime minister infamously signed the Munich Pact with Adolf Hitler—a pacification move—Churchill said to Chamberlain, "You were given the choice between war and dishonor. You chose dishonor and you will have war."[13] Churchill continued:

"You ask, what is our aim? I can answer in one word.
It is victory. Victory at all costs. Victory in spite of all
terrors. Victory, however long and hard the road may be,
for without victory there is no survival."[14]

Bill Clinton chose dishonor by ignoring that initial attack on New York's Trade Center, which ultimately led to the war on terror that continues to be fought since 9/11.

It was later discovered that the 1993 WTC bombing had been planned and organized in part by the blind Sheikh Omar Abdel Rahman and Sayyid Nosair, who said:

"The obligation of Allah is upon us to wage Jihad for
the sake of Allah" (Rahman. . . . "We have to thoroughly
demoralize the enemies of God b. . . . blowing up the
towers that constitute the pillars of their civilizatio. . . .
the high buildings they are proud of" (Nosair).[15]

The New York police eventually found forty-seven boxes of Rahman's terrorist literature. Unbelievably, the boxes were marked as "Irrelevant religious stuff," dismissing the very reason for the attacks and failing to connect the literature to the worldwide Islamic fundamentalist movement that had fueled it. Rahman was later sentenced to life imprisonment for his role in the conspiracy.

In October of the same year as the first World Trade Center attack, US troops had been sent on a humanitarian mission to Mogadishu,

Somalia. I was there on October 3 when two Blackhawk helicopters were shot down and a roughly twenty-hour firefight ensued in which eighteen American soldiers and over a thousand Somalis were killed. Shortly after this, Mr. Clinton made the decision to withdraw troops from Somalia.

Evidence was later found that the Somalis who shot down the helicopters had received training from Bin Laden's forces that had become adept at bringing down advance Soviet helicopters in their fighting in Afghanistan with rocket-propelled grenades. Bin Laden eventually even bragged of his culpability in Somalia as reported on CNN:

> In October 1993, 18 U.S. servicemen involved in the U.S. humanitarian relief effort in Somalia were killed during an operation in Mogadishu. One soldier's body was dragged through the streets.
>
> Bin Laden was indicted in 1996 on charges of training the people involved in the attack and in a 1997 interview with CNN, bin Laden said his followers, together with local Muslims, killed those troops.[16]

Osama bin Laden met his demise at the hands of a US Navy SEAL team on May 2, 2011, almost ten years after the attacks on 9/11 and with countless billions of dollars having been spent in his pursuit. The much-sought-after terrorist had incredibly been openly living in a compound with members of his family in Abbottabad, Pakistan.

On May 21, 2017, President Trump addressed members of the Saudi Arabian government during his initial visit abroad as the leader of the United States. His trip bolstered his ongoing relationship with the House of Saud, and was a clear indication that the US stood with them in their efforts to halt Iran's Middle East aggression.

The Obama administration had pandered to the Iranian regime, withdrawing from Iraq and leaving Ayatollah Khamenei and his proxies to further tighten their hold on that country. The refusal to aid Bashar al-Assad's countrymen in their fight for autonomy led to Iran's Revolutionary Guard troops taking up residence in Syria, as well as opening the door for Russia to regain its foothold in the region.

Obama's nuclear pact with the Iranian government did little to stifle the pursuit of nuclear autonomy, and much to further Iran's terrorist activities and the rise of proxy wars in the Middle East. According to Stanford University's Hoover Institution:

> Iran now has a dominant influence in four regional states: Iraq, Lebanon, Yemen, and Syria. Like China, Russia, and Cuba, Iran is also a supporter of [the Nicolás Maduro Moros] dictatorship in Venezuela. Finally, Iran is dedicated to the destruction of Israel, to which end it is a key supporter of Hamas and Hezbollah.[17]

Journalist Elliott Abrams wrote of Trump's visit in Saudi Arabia in a report in the *National Review:*

The president's speech, replete with respect for Islam, added to the sense that far from being a hater of Islam, he was a Westerner approaching it with dignity and common sense. One possible effect: How might federal judges henceforth hold that his executive orders limiting access to the United States for certain Muslims are motivated by nothing more than pure hatred? . . .

Trump was tough as nails on Iran, which will gratify his Saudi hosts and the many Americans who found the Obama approach unconscionable. Obama saw Iran as a potential partner in the Middle East and subordinated every American interest to getting his nuclear deal done. Trump made it clear that he has entirely jettisoned this approach.

Trump's analysis of the terrorists was also powerful: They are nihilists, he suggested, not Muslims. Thus, he said: "Every time a terrorist murders an innocent person and falsely invokes the name of God, it should be an insult to every person of faith. Terrorists do not worship God. They worship death."[18]

Candidate Trump named a number of political objectives in his initial campaign for the White House. One of his goals was to reverse the Obama nuclear deal with Iran. From his first day on the job, President Trump was determined to ascertain that Iran was in total conformity with all Joint Comprehensive Plan of Action (JCPOA) terms. In hindsight, perhaps he should have immediately demanded transparency and accountability regarding any and all agreements made between Iran and the Obama administration. Mr. Trump aimed to be certain that all ambiguities regarding site inspections, enrichment levels, and other issues were addressed and rectified.

Nixing the deal with Iran meant restoring massive pressure, including enacting crippling sanctions aimed at forcing Iran to fully dismantle its nuclear weapons capabilities. There is no doubt that Trump had listened to Israeli prime minister Benjamin Netanyahu's concerns. From the beginning, the president had called the Iran deal the worst deal ever.

Former White House press secretary Sarah Huckabee Sanders explained:

> "The president isn't looking at one piece of this. He's looking at all of the bad behavior of Iran. . . . Not just the nuclear deal as bad behavior, but the ballistic missile testing, destabilization of the region, Number One state sponsor of terrorism, cyber attacks, illicit nuclear program."[19]

According to Trump, Iran had violated the very spirit of the agreement. In July 2019 it was reported that Iran had gone further and breached the key limitation on the amount of nuclear fuel it could stockpile.

One need only look at Iran's funding of Hezbollah, Hamas, and its Shia Crescent, as well as various proxies across the Middle East and its support of Syria's president Bashar al-Assad to see how correct President Trump was.

President Trump has declared that the Iranian regime supports terrorism and exports violence, bloodshed, and chaos. Few question that he is correct in this assessment. The chaotic mix is a toxic poison combining apocalyptic fanaticism with terrorism.

Iran's leaders have not been shy in declaring that sanctions would not deter them from continuing with their goals for developing nuclear fusion. Ali Akbar Salehi, head of the country's atomic energy department, was succinct in his response to queries regarding sanctions:

> "What have we been doing so far? Have the sanctions stopped us? We have enough expertise inside (the country) to move the [fusion] program forward." He said that cooperation with other countries would accelerate the pace.[20]

It is this possibly devastating resource that must be averted by the US for the benefit of local as well as worldwide strength. Even as the JCPOA was being concluded in mid-2015, Salehi brazenly acknowledged that plans were afoot to market nuclear products such as enriched uranium and heavy water to countries, including North Korea. It is horrifying to consider that after October 20, 2025, Iran will again be unrestrained in legally offering both proficiency and products to enemies of the West.

Prime Minister Benjamin Netanyahu addressed this possibility in an interview as far back as 2008:

> Up until now, nuclear weapons have been in the hands of responsible regimes. You have one regime, one bizarre regime that apparently has them now in North Korea. [However,] there aren't a billion North Koreans that people seek to inspire into a religious war. That's what Iran could do. It could inspire the 200 million Shi'ites. That's what they intend to do, inspire them into a religious war, first against other Muslims, then against the West. . . . It is important to understand that they could impose a direct threat to Europe and to the United States and to Israel, obviously. They don't hide it. They don't even hide the fact that they intend to take on the West.[21]

Eleven years later, those words are still true. Missiles launched by Iran with a range of only 1,200 miles could still wreak havoc in Saudi Arabia, Israel, and US bases in Eastern Europe. The Worldwide Threat Assessment released in February 2017 is appalling:

> The Islamic Republic of Iran remains an enduring threat to US national interests because of Iranian support to anti-US terrorist groups and militants, the [Assad]

regime, [Houthi] rebels in Yemen, and because of Iran's development of advanced military capabilities. Despite Supreme Leader Khamenei's conditional support for the JCPOA nuclear deal implemented in January 2016, he is highly distrustful of US intentions. Iran's leaders remain focused on thwarting US and Israeli influence and countering what they perceive as a Saudi-led effort to fuel Sunni extremism and terrorism against Iran and Shia communities throughout the region. . . .

Iran continues to develop a range of new military capabilities to monitor and target US and allied military assets in the region, including armed UAVs [Unmanned Aerial Vehicles or drones], ballistic missiles, advanced naval mines, unmanned explosive boats, submarines and advanced torpedoes, and anti-ship and land-attack cruise missiles. Iran has the largest ballistic missile force in the Middle East and can strike targets up to 2,000 kilometers from Iran's borders. Russia's delivery of the SA-20c surface-to-air missile system in 2016 provides Iran with its most advanced long-range air defense system.[22]

The 2018 report did not show significant improvement:

✧ Iran will seek to expand its influence in Iraq, Syria, and Yemen, where it sees conflicts generally trending in Tehran's favor, and it will exploit the fight against ISIS to solidify partnerships and translate its battlefield gains into political, security, and economic agreements. . . .

✧ In Syria, Iran is working to consolidate its influence while trying to prevent US forces from gaining a foothold. . . . Iran is pursuing permanent military bases in Syria and probably wants to maintain a network of Shia foreign fighters in Syria to counter future threats to Iran. . . .

✧ In Yemen, Iran's support to the Houthis [an armed Islamic movement] further escalates the conflict and poses a serious threat to US partners and interests in the region. . ..

Iran will develop military capabilities that threaten US forces and US allies in the region, and its unsafe and unprofessional interactions will pose a risk to US Navy operations in the Persian Gulf.. . .

Centrists led by President Hasan Ruhani will continue to advocate greater social progress, privatization, and more global integration, while hardliners will view this agenda as a threat to their political and economic interests and to Iran's revolutionary and Islamic character. . ..

✧ Supreme Leader Ali Khamenei's views are closer to those of the hardliners, but he has supported some of Ruhani's efforts to engage Western countries and to promote economic growth.. ..[23]

It is incumbent upon President Trump, and his successors in that office, to devise and follow a plan to drastically reduce Iran's missile timetable before the year 2031, and certainly before the close of the JCPOA initiative. Meanwhile, the president and Israel's prime minister should continue to be determined in restraining Iran's plans of developing nuclear weapons. That could be accomplished by establishing penalties and enticements beyond the ones previously inaugurated. Again in July 2019, Vice President Pence addressed the president's determination regarding Iran:

"Iran should not confuse American restraint with a lack of American resolve. We hope for the best, but the United States of America and our military are prepared to protect our interests and protect our personnel and our citizens in the region. We will continue to oppose Iran's malign influence. We will continue to bring pressure on their economy. . .America will never allow Iran to obtain a nuclear weapon."[24]

Speaking at the same conference, National Security Adviser John Bolton reiterated President Trump's determination:

"We will continue to increase the pressure until it [Iran] abandons its nuclear weapons program and ends its violent activities across the Middle East including conducting and supporting terrorism around the world. . . . I am here to tell you today President Trump's pressure campaign against Iran is working."[25]

According to Bolton, the president's detractors had predicted that new sanctions implemented by the administration would be ineffective, but that "the United States has levied the toughest ever sanctions on the Iranian regime and the Iranian economy is - to quote the Financial Times - collapsing under their weight."[26]

Prime Minister Netanyahu also joined the conference via satellite and addressed the gathering regarding Iran:

"The deal was always based on a lie: that Iran was not seeking nuclear weapons. And we exposed that lie when we sent our brave operatives to the heart of Tehran and brought back the secret atomic archive of Iran. And it just showed that they've been working on developing atomic bombs as early as 20 years ago.

So, the deal is not only based on a lie, it's a terrible deal because it gave Iran a path to getting a nuclear arsenal when the restrictions on Iran's nuclear programs were removed. It didn't block Iran's path to the bomb; it paved it. In fact, it failed to solve the one problem it was supposed to solve. Now, it made other problems worse by removing sanctions on Iran, thereby helping Iran fuel its war machine in the region. See, when you removed the sanctions, Iran got billions and billions—tens of billions of dollars, potentially hundreds of billions of dollars—to fund its aggression.

So it's so important that President Trump decided boldly to leave this bad deal, and he decided to restore sanctions. And Israel is deeply grateful for that, because this is vital for Israel's security, for the security of the region, for the security of the United States, for the security of the world.

Now Iran is trying to lash out to reduce the pressure. They attack tankers, they down American drones, they're firing missiles at their neighbors. It's important to respond to these actions not by reducing the pressure, but by increasing the pressure."[27]

America is the mightiest nation on earth, and has long enjoyed God's blessing of prosperity. Although the US comprises only seven percent of the world's population, she possesses over half of the world's wealth. Yet during the past few decades, we have seen her culture polluted, attempts to dethrone God, and her heroes defiled. Bible-believing Americans have oftentimes been demonized as bigots and extremists. God has been taken out of our schools, courts, and town squares, and even a line of our Pledge of Allegiance—"one nation, under God"—has been challenged several times, both in the federal and state governments. Thus far, these challenges have been overturned.

The same moral compromise that infects our domestic policy has also influenced our foreign policy. In the '90s, terrorists could easily clear customs and freely set up shop inside our borders. In my view, there is absolutely no question that God's hedge of protection has been lifted from America. September 11 was a curse on our beloved nation, but worse is the fact that many God-fearing Americans don't understand why it happened or that it might easily happen again.

CHAPTER 4

PEACE: BOOSTING PALESTINIAN ECONOMY

I search for peace; but when
I speak of peace, they want war!

(PSALM 120:7 NLT)

On June 25–26, 2019, the US hosted an economic seminar in the Middle Eastern city of Manama, Bahrain. The focus of that meeting was to release the Trump administration's first phase of a peace initiative[28], and to encourage international participants to invest in Palestine. Business leaders from Asia, Europe, and the Middle East were invited to attend.

The plan presented the potential for economic opportunities to be offered to the Palestinian people, but it was rejected out of hand. This first step pointedly offered no political resolution to the question of a state with Jerusalem as its capital.

Jared Kushner, President Trump's son-in-law and senior adviser, and Jason Greenblatt, the administration's regional envoy, were firm in their determination to present the economic benefits of peace. The first issue needing to be addressed is money. If there were such a thing as a Palestinian state devoid of an economic plan, it would be catastrophic. One only needs to look at Gaza and the current events there to realize this truth.

This Palestinian generation deserves an opportunity to acquire autonomy and dignity. A proper economic plan would provide both, if the funds provided are not placed in the hands of the Palestinian Authority leadership. Many of those leaders planning to attend the summit were not happy with how the PA has spent its funds in past years. I've heard personal statements from some of these men such as, "They have wasted our money." Or, "Instead of fighting Israel, the Palestinians should be emulating Israel."

Those same men abhor PA president Abbas's obsession with picking a fight with President Trump and his "deal of the century." What could possibly be his motivation? It certainly can't be his concern for the prosperity of the Palestinian people. Perhaps it is the thought that he would lose some of the billions with which he has already lined his pockets, or see an end to his destructive leadership.

The burning political question, of course, is this: What form would a Palestinian state take? There are three things that such an entity could never possess: (1) Israel could never allow the PA to have air space, as it would be an existential threat to Israel's survival, (2) a PA state could never be permitted to raise an army, as a military threat that near Jerusalem would be deadly to the Israelis, and (3) a

PA state could never be allowed to establish treaties. For example, a treaty with Iran would be a devastating threat to Israel.

Truthfully, this would not be a Palestinian state. What the Palestinians deserve are homes, jobs, governance, and security. Israel, and indeed the world, could assist the Palestinians in securing better lives. The dilemma that must be resolved is the rabid racism that is rampant among the Palestinian people.

Gaza has become the new al-Qaeda. Not only do Israelis suffer from post-traumatic stress in the South because of the rockets fired from Gaza; now the terrorists there are using every trick imaginable to try to burn Israel down. There is absolutely no possibility that a rational person should reward such conduct.

According to an unnamed senior Trump administration official: "This [Bahrain summit] will give hopefully the people in the region the potential to see what the economic opportunities could be if we can work out political issues that have held back the region for a long, long time."[29]

Front and center in the rejection of the Trump economic plan to aid the Palestinian people was PA legislator and activist Hanan Ashwari. This is no surprise; we have met before and I was treated to her particular brand of misinterpretation. I dealt with that head- on at the Madrid Peace Conference in 1991 when I debated Dr. Ashwari, a professed Christian Palestinian, on the topic of Bethlehem. She declared, "Bethlehem is a Muslim town where the first Palestinian Christian,

Jesus Christ, was born." My response to her was, "Bethlehem is the Jewish town where the Jewish Messiah, Jesus Christ, was born."

In her latest misperception Ashwari wrote:

> The "ultimate deal" suffers from multiple fatal flaws and misconceptions that several successive US administrations have repeatedly failed to recognise. The spirit of the Palestinian people cannot be broken or brought into submission; nor will we ever succumb to external pressure and blackmail. To expect us to surrender our rights and freedom in exchange for a mythical "economic peace" is nothing short of a flight of fancy.[30]

According to the Foreword of the Peace to Prosperity plan of the Trump administration:

> Generations of Palestinians have lived without knowing peace, and the West Bank and Gaza have fallen into a protracted crisis. Yet the Palestinian story will not end here. The Palestinian people continue their historic endeavor to realize their aspirations and build a better future for their children.
>
> *Peace to Prosperity* is a vision to empower the Palestinian people to build a prosperous and vibrant Palestinian society. It consists of three initiatives that will support distinct pillars of the Palestinian society:

the economy, the people, and the government. With the potential to facilitate more than $50 billion in new investment over ten years, *Peace to Prosperity* represents the most ambitious and comprehensive international effort for the Palestinian people to date. It has the ability to fundamentally transform the West Bank and Gaza and to open a new chapter in Palestinian history—one defined, not by adversity and loss, but by freedom and dignity.

The first initiative will **UNLEASH THE ECONOMIC POTENTIAL** of the Palestinians. By developing property and contract rights, the rule of law, anti-corruption measures, capital markets, a pro-growth tax structure, and a low-tariff scheme with reduced trade barriers, this initiative envisions policy reforms coupled with strategic infrastructure investments that will improve the business environment and stimulate private-sector growth. Hospitals, schools, homes, and businesses will secure reliable access to affordable electricity, clean water, and digital services. Billions of dollars of new investment will flow into various sectors of the Palestinian economy; businesses will have access to capital; and the markets of the West Bank and Gaza will be connected with key trading partners, including Egypt, Israel, Jordan, and Lebanon. The resulting economic growth has the potential to end the current unemployment crisis and transform the West Bank and Gaza into a center of opportunity.

The second initiative will **EMPOWER THE PALESTINIAN PEOPLE** to realize their ambitions. Through new data-driven, outcomes-based education options at home, expanded online education platforms, increased vocational and technical training, and the prospect of international exchanges, this initiative will enhance and expand a variety of programs that directly improve the well-being of the Palestinian people. It will strengthen the Palestinian educational system and ensure that students can fulfill their academic goals and be prepared for the workforce. Equally important, access to quality healthcare will be dramatically improved, as Palestinian hospitals and clinics will be outfitted with the latest healthcare technology and equipment. In addition, new opportunities for cultural and recreational activities will improve the quality of life of the Palestinian people. From parks and cultural institutions, to athletic facilities and libraries, this initiative's projects will enrich public life throughout the West Bank and Gaza.

The third initiative will **ENHANCE PALESTINIAN GOVERNANCE**, improving the public sector's ability to serve its citizens and enable private-sector growth. This initiative will support the public sector in undertaking the improvements and reforms necessary to achieve long-term economic success. A commitment to upholding property rights, improving the legal and regulatory framework for businesses, adopting a growth-oriented, enforceable tax structure, and developing robust capital markets will increase exports and foreign direct investment. A fair and independent judicial branch will ensure this pro-growth environment is protected and that civil society flourishes. New systems and policies will help bolster government transparency and accountability. International partners will work to eliminate the Palestinian public sector's donor dependency and put the Palestinians on a trajectory to achieve long-term fiscal sustainability. Institutions will be modernized and made more efficient to facilitate the most effective delivery of essential services for the citizens. With the support of the Palestinian leadership, this initiative can usher in a new era of freedom and opportunity for the Palestinian people and institutionalize the policies required for successful economic transformation.

These three initiatives are more than just a vision of a promising future for the Palestinian people; they are also the foundation for an implementable plan.

Capital raised through this international effort will be placed into a new fund administered by an established multilateral development bank. Accountability, transparency, anti-corruption, and conditionality safeguards will protect investments and ensure that capital is allocated efficiently and effectively. The fund's leadership will work with beneficiary countries to outline annual investment guidelines, development goals, and governance reforms that will support project implementation in the areas identified within *Peace to Prosperity*. Grants, concessional loans, and other support will be distributed to projects that meet the defined criteria through a streamlined process that will enable both flexibility and accountability.

If implemented, *Peace to Prosperity* will empower the Palestinian people to build the society that they have aspired to establish for generations. This vision will allow the Palestinians to see a better future and realize an opportunity to pursue their dreams.

With the support of the international community, this vision is within reach. Ultimately, however, the power to unlock it lies in the hands of the Palestinian people. Only through peace can the Palestinians achieve prosperity.[31]

The plan calls for the investment of billions of dollars in substantive aid for the Palestinians. The hurdle will be to prevail upon PA leaders to accept help for the people who need it most, rather than using the funds to aid and abet the terrorist factions it supports. As has been the problem in the past, the Palestinian people continue to suffer under the heavy hand of radical leadership.

Despite the disparaging comments from the Liberal Left regarding the Trump Peace Plan, Vice President Pence made one thing abundantly clear in his address to the pro-Israel group in July 2019, when he said:

> "We will keep dreaming and keep working for peace. And let me assure you, while any peace will undoubtedly require compromise, you can be confident of this: The United States of America will never compromise the safety and security of the Jewish State of Israel."[32]

CHAPTER 5

SECULAR VS. SPIRITUAL QUESTS

*So God created man in His **own** image; in the image of*
God He created him; male and female He created them.

(GENESIS 1:27 NKJV)

Donald Trump has not shied away from his support of America as a nation founded by God-fearing settlers. At the National Prayer Breakfast on February 7, 2019, the president assured his audience:

> "As president, I will always cherish, honor and protect the believers who uplift our communities and sustain our nation to ensure that people of faith can always contribute to our society." He added, "All children, born and unborn, are made in the holy image of God."[33]

Today, America's secular political engine is on a collision course with prophecy. Many believe there is nothing we can do about it;

that if foretold, then it must just come to pass. However, if this is our attitude, then we are missing the true point of prophecy. The Bible doesn't tell us what the future holds so that we can sit back and let disaster strike; it helps us to prepare and take the actions necessary to make sure that the future is one of hope for as many as possible. It is up to God-fearing Americans who are willing to step up and make a difference to keep our country headed in the right direction, whether that is through our domestic or foreign policy.

Sooner or later everyone on the planet—rich and poor, skeptic and religious, presidents and paupers—turns to thinking about only one thing: eternity. Can we really plan for the future of our nation—of our world—without considering this, as well? While our nation's form of government may have been conceived in Greece, it was not until Bible-quoting, God-fearing people joined together to form the United States of America that democracy rose to the ideal we know it to be today. Our system may not be perfect, but it is the best our world has ever seen. That is because it is a system that was determined with the underlying moral clarity and wisdom of the Bible.

Dr. Martin Luther King Jr. said, "Nothing in the world is more dangerous than sincere ignorance and conscientious stupidity."[34] Sadly, America moved into the twenty-first century with a terminal case of both!

America is in this position primarily because we are the only nation today in an untenable alliance with both of those historical brothers of prophecy—Ishmael and Isaac. The ancient scriptures of the Bible have a great deal to say about the two spirits behind these brothers that today are fighting it out through the nations of the world. Ishmael was not the son of promise, but the son of a man trying to turn the will of God to that of his own.

God had promised Abraham a son, but his wife Sarah was barren. At Sarah's suggestion, Abraham took Hagar, her maidservant, and impregnated her. The result was Ishmael. Though a man of faith, Abraham acted in his own wisdom and impatience, not God's direction; he justified a foolish deed through moral relativism, tradition, and human reasoning. He tried to obtain God's blessing on his own terms. It was not until some years later when the son of promise, Isaac, was miraculously born that Abraham fully realized the gravity of his mistake. Yet, Jehovah reassured Abraham regarding his "son of human reasoning," a patriarch of the Arabs:

> As for Ishmael, I will bless him also, just as you have asked. I will make him extremely fruitful and multiply his descendants. He will become the father of twelve princes, and I will make him a great nation. (Genesis 17:20 NLT)

Abraham was assured that God had made a special covenant with the "son of faith," a patriarch of the Hebrews:

> Sarah thy wife shall bear thee a son indeed; and thou shalt call his name Isaac: and I will establish my covenant

with him for an everlasting covenant, *and* with his seed after him. (Genesis 17:19 KJV)

Today, America is caught in the same battle. Some want to move forward without God, making our halls of government secular, amoral, and profane. Instead, we are making them immoral and blind. Rather than seeking God for blessings and prosperity, we are looking to our own reasoning and logic. For this reason we are willing to trade almost anything for the commodity that keeps our economy lubricated and running smoothly.

Most Americans are aware that many of the descendants of Ishmael believed the lies Hitler used to twist the minds of the German people—that the Jews are responsible for the ills of the world. The entire world would sleep easier, they reiterated, when the Jews had been annihilated. Yet, what is being done in America to counteract this vile doctrine that is still in evidence today? We reward those who preach these same things by calling them "diplomats," men such as the late Yasser Arafat. Terrorist organizations like the PA, Hamas, Islamic Jihad, and others have forced the Jews to make ever more concessions to the implacably angry descendants of Ishmael, the Muslims.

It seems that radical Muslims will never be appeased with a Palestinian state. We cannot be so naïve as to believe that they will suddenly start to love us if Palestine should become a state.

Dr. Yossef Bodansky and I spent considerable time in Jerusalem discussing this matter. In his book *The High Cost of Peace*, he states that the Palestinians' "step-by-step" plan to retake Palestine actually came from the experience of the Vietnamese in dealing with the US:

> Abu-Iyad [a senior Palestinian field commander] detailed how he brought up the question of why the Palestinian armed struggle was considered terrorism whereas the Vietnamese struggle was lauded and supported throughout the West [to the Khmer Rouge]. His host attributed this phenomenon to the different ways the two liberation movements had packaged their goals. The Vietnamese team agreed to sit with the PA delegation and help them develop a program that would appear flexible and moderate, especially in dealing with the United States, the Vietnamese explained, one must "sacrifice the unimportant if only in order to preserve the essential."[35]

The Vietnamese group emphasized that the PLO must remain committed to its ultimate objective: "the establishment of a unified democratic state in the entire Palestine."

We can never win the war on terrorism by appeasing terrorists on the one hand and trying to root them out on the other. This is a sure guarantee of another September 11—or worse. This tide will never be turned without getting to the root of their hatred for Israel and for us, and then exposing its source.

The teaching of *jihad* must be outlawed in America. Islamic fundamentalists employ religion to recruit *shahids*—martyrs who are willing to kill themselves for the "cause." When the late Yasser Arafat delivered his speeches calling for one million shahids to liberate Jerusalem, he was not simply humoring the crowds. When Islamic fundamentalist clerics call for shahids in the mosques, it is not just religious jargon. Islamic fundamentalism is a religion that kills.

It's not only critical that we understand why we are hated; it is absolutely vital that we understand why these fundamentalists act on that hatred. Simply put, shahids believe they are performing a holy ritual for Allah. From childhood, Muslims are taught that to be a shahid, a martyr, one must be chosen by Allah. They learn that this is the greatest honor in life. Shahids are taught that a martyr does not have a funeral, but rather a wedding. This is the reason Islamic families do not hold funerals when a child commits an act of martyrdom. Instead, a wedding celebration is held.

The prospective shahid is told that when the holy and religious act is performed:

- ✦ He will not feel pain or fear. In essence, the sting of death is removed.

- ✦ He will not die. All souls go into the ground awaiting resurrection except the souls of the shahid. They go directly to paradise; his own personal and immediate resurrection.

✧ He will be honored when he arrives in paradise with a crown of glory with a jewel of the wealth of the world in the center of it. (In Christianity, the crown is placed on the head of Jesus, and the saints lay their crowns at His feet.)

✧ He will attend his own wedding with seventy-two black-eyed virgins. The word *black-eyed* does not denote eye color; it denotes that they are incorruptible—an interesting word. (It is the same word in the scripture used by Bill Clinton when he was sworn into office.) This belief is so strong that before the act of martyrdom, the shahid shaves all pubic hair and tapes his private parts. This is symbolic of what is to come.

✧ He will pave the way for seventy relatives to go to paradise and be exempt from the horrors of hell. In essence, the blood of the shahid atones for sin. It certainly would make for a horrible childhood when all your relatives are lobbying for a spot on your "paradise list." The insane aspect of this is that this diabolical battle for the minds of the children begins in kindergarten. Cartoon characters similar to our Mickey Mouse or Donald Duck are drawn with a message incorporated to seduce and recruit these small children as shahids. Kindergarten camps are taught the principles of jihad. Bridges, roads, parks, and buildings are named after the martyrs. Posters with photos of the martyrs are everywhere. (Thousands upon thousands of children were used to clear the minefields during the Iran–Iraq War. "Keys to heaven" were placed around their necks, and a martyr's badge was pinned to their clothing.)

The war on terrorism that we have today is fueled by Stone Age hatred—that same hatred Cain had for Abel, Ishmael for Isaac, and Satan for Jesus. Terrorists wage a spiritual battle of fear and bigotry beyond anything we understand, and such a war cannot be won with tactical weaponry alone.

Radical Islamic fundamentalists were the reason for the cataclysmic 9/11 attacks and the terrorism war that America is fighting today. Their ideology is as lethal as Fascism or Nazism. So long as godless liberals attempt to dumb down God-fearing Americans with a "don't ask, don't tell" policy on bigotry, the war on terrorism will not only survive, it will thrive. In order to win this war, Americans must speak out on bigotry the same way Abraham Lincoln and then Martin Luther King did. Bigotry is an equal-opportunity employer; bigots kill Christians with the same justifications they use to kill Jews.

There has never been a more urgent time than today for Americans to act with moral clarity, yet there has also never been a time in which we have seemed more complacent. The future of our nation, as well as our world, hangs in the balance between our actions and our apathy.

President Trump made his thoughts on terrorists known in his May 21, 2017, speech in Saudi Arabia:

> The nations of the Middle East will have to decide what kind of future they want for themselves for their country and, frankly, for their families and for their children. It's a choice between two futures, and it is a choice America cannot make for you. A better future is only possible if your nations drive out the terrorists and drive out the extremists. Drive them out. Drive them out of your places of worship. Drive them out of your communities. Drive them out of your Holy Land. And drive them out of this earth.[36]

We have lost the center of our culture that has traditionally held us together—God and the Holy Scriptures—and as our culture spirals away from that center, we no longer hear His voice. As a nation, our innocence is being ravaged. In our halls of justice and our political arenas, those who would speak for God not only lack the conviction to be effective, they are being systematically silenced because of a perverted interpretation of "separation of Church and State."

First Amendment rights are denied to those who would speak for God, while those who fight for self, special interests, and immoralities are passionately intense as the spirit of the world takes over. We have witnessed this spirit being more active in our world than ever before through the "isms": Fascism, Nazism, Communism, and terrorism—the greatest threats to human liberty we have ever faced.

The world's final and prophetic battle will take place in Israel, and it will be over Jerusalem. Could it be that battle lines are even now being drawn, with the nations aligning themselves for the events to come? It is a battle line drawn through the heart of the city of Jerusalem, where time and again peace efforts in the Middle East have been thwarted. Palestinians have repeatedly been offered their own state—first in 1947 by the United Nations, then in 1991 at the Madrid Conference after the Gulf War, next at the Wye River Memorandum of 1998, and once again by a desperate Bill Clinton during his final days in office.

The major stumbling block to peace has always been the control of East Jerusalem—the historic city of David, where the Temple Mount rests. It is the very spot where Heaven and Earth met, and will meet again, where the most dangerous prophecies concerning the nations of the world were written in the stones. It all began with, "But now I have chosen Jerusalem for my Name to be there, and I have chosen David to rule my people Israel" (2 Chronicles 6:6 NIV).

Perhaps one of Donald Trump's most controversial campaign promises was: "We will move the American embassy to the eternal capital of the Jewish people, Jerusalem."[37]

Listed below are a few basic tenets of the Jerusalem Embassy Relocation Act:

✧ The United States maintains its embassy in the functioning capital of every country except in the case of our democratic friend and strategic ally, the State of Israel;

✧ The United States conducts official meetings and other business in the city of Jerusalem in de facto recognition of its status as the capital of Israel;

✧ Jerusalem should remain an undivided city in which the rights of every ethnic and religious group are protected;

✧ Jerusalem should be recognized as the capital of the State of Israel; and

✧ The United States Embassy in Israel should be established in Jerusalem no later than May 31, 1999.[38]

CHAPTER 6

A CAPITAL
REESTABLISHED

For the LORD will rebuild Jerusalem.
He will appear in his glory.

(PSALM 102:16 NLT)

A month after he signed the initial waiver of US policy on Jerusalem on June 17, 1999, president Bill Clinton held a press conference in conjunction with the Israeli prime minister at that time, Ehud Barak. During the gathering, Clinton explained why he signed the waiver:

> That's part of the final status talks. The United States, as a sponsor of the peace process, has asked the parties to do nothing to prejudge final status issues. We certainly should be doing nothing to prejudge the final status issues.[39]

In violation of the overwhelmingly bipartisan determination of Congress, Clinton decided that, unlike any other country in the world, Israel could not be allowed to choose her own capital. What an arrogant and anti-democratic determination for an American president to make!

In the language of the Jerusalem Embassy Act:

> (Section 15) The United States maintains its embassy in the functioning capital of every country except in the case of our democratic friend and strategic ally, the State of Israel. (16) The United States conducts official meetings and other business in the city of Jerusalem in de facto recognition of its status as the capital of Israel. (17) In 1996, the State of Israel will celebrate the 3,000th anniversary of the Jewish presence in Jerusalem since King David's entry.[40]

How does recognizing one of the oldest capitals in the world endanger US security? Conversely, how does *not* recognizing it protect America from terrorists? Did denying recognition of Israel's eternal capital keep Osama bin Laden from attacking the World Trade Center? Has continuing to do so until now appeased Arab rage over Iraq?

This invocation of national security was nothing but a smokescreen to cover America's unwillingness to do the right thing. It was a mistaken belief that giving in to what some lawmakers imagined would be the response of the Arab countries, somehow placating them and encouraging the so-called "peace process." But this ignored the simple truth that Arab bigots have not wanted the US to recognize Jerusalem as Israel's capital, simply because they do not recognize Israel's right to exist.

With the election of George W. Bush, long considered to be a friend of Israel, many were certain he would soon have two outstanding opportunities to apply the ideals of American democracy to the Middle East. In one, he could tell the heirs of Yasser Arafat's murderous organization that crime did not pay. In the other, he could show the world that the United States recognized the capital of its ally Israel.

During the 2000 election campaign, Mr. Bush pledged he would "begin the process" of moving the embassy on his "first day in office." Such are many campaign promises. The failure to recognize Jerusalem was both a violation of US law and a craven surrender to Arab terrorist threats. In the midst of America's war on worldwide terrorism, President Trump has said that it is vital to send a message that the US will not surrender to terrorist blackmail. Indeed, it was the very refusal to move the embassy that undermined America's national security, by encouraging terrorists to believe that the threat of violence would force the US to change its policy on Jerusalem as determined by Congress.

History records that it would not be the moving of the US Embassy to Jerusalem that would rock the American people; it was purely and simply hatred that spurred the terrorist attacks on September 11, 2001.

Zionist Organization of America national president Morton A. Klein has said of the refusal to recognize Jerusalem as Israel's capital:

> "The failure to recognize Jerusalem is a violation of U.S. law and a blatant surrender to Arab terrorist threats. At a time when America is engaged in a life-or-death struggle with terrorists worldwide, it is especially important to implement U.S. law on Jerusalem and thereby send a message to terrorists everywhere that America will not capitulate to their blackmail. It is President Bush's refusal to move the embassy which could undermine national security because it encourages terrorists to believe that threats and violence will force the U.S. to change its policies."[41]

In a 2008 speech, presidential candidate Barak Obama asserted that Jerusalem would be the capital of Israel, but then never followed through on his rhetoric. His administration failed to do anything that would support moving the embassy. Neither did Mr. Obama formally declare that it would be done. In fact, he went so far as to call on the US Supreme Court to prevent American citizens born in the Holy City from listing Israel as their place of birth.

On May 14, 2018, strikingly seventy years to the day after the rebirth of Israel, a ceremony of celebration was held in Jerusalem to recognize that the US Embassy had indeed finally been moved from Tel Aviv to Jerusalem. Rabbi Aryeh Spero wrote in an article for *American Thinker*:

> Seventy years is a completed lifetime, as the Psalmist states: "The years of our life are seventy years". [Psalm 90:10] Seventy years in [the] Jewish outlook is an historical time unit, representing a significant chapter in human history. Seventy years after the first Temple was burned by the Babylonian Nebuchadnezzar and the Jews were driven into Exile, the exile ended and many returned to Israel and rebuilt Jerusalem. Seventy years signifies completion and full circle.[42]

In May 2017, approximately a year before the moving of the embassy, President Trump made history when he became the first US president to pray at the Western Wall in ancient Jerusalem. He said after placing the traditional prayer request in a crevice of the stones forming the wall that his visit had made a lasting impression on him.

In a speech delivered on December 6, 2017, Mr. Trump stated:

> "Through all of these years, presidents representing the United States have declined to officially recognize Jerusalem as Israel's capital. In fact, we have declined

to acknowledge any Israeli capital at all. But today, we finally acknowledge the obvious: that Jerusalem is Israel's capital. This is nothing more or less than a recognition of reality. It is also the right thing to do. It's something that has to be done."[43]

As with President Harry S. Truman defying his State Department heads and making history by recognizing Israel as a nation in 1948, Donald Trump made history seventy years later by fulfilling a campaign promise he made in 2016.

Unlike many of his counterparts, Secretary of State Mike Pompeo strongly supports the nation of Israel. Speaking to a large crowd of pro-Israel Christians in July 2019, Pompeo reminded them of the importance of Truman's decision:

> It fills me with unending pride to know that American hands helped build the modern house of Israel. Our welcoming, the American welcoming, of the new Jewish state into the family of nations was one of the most consequential diplomatic decisions of the 20th century—not just in terms of the world map, but as a statement to the world of who we are as Americans. It proved, as we continue to prove, that we stand for human dignity, that we stand for justice, that we stand for independence.[44]

Since Israel's declaration of statehood on May 14, 1948, when the

US was the first nation to recognize her existence, to Israel's defense in the Yom Kippur war of 1973, and the defense aid the US has given ever since, no nation has stood by Israel as this nation has. On the other hand, since 1945, when President Franklin Delano Roosevelt met with King Ibn Saud of Saudi Arabia and promised that no US decision regarding the Middle East would be made without first consulting the Arabs, no nation has been more closely linked to Muslim nations in that region, either.

In fact, America's influence on both sides goes much farther back. What these relationships have done is to place the United States in the position as the only nation trusted by both Ishmael and Isaac to barter peace between them. And this has placed America squarely in the eye of the storm of biblical prophecy.

For years, the US has been caught in a tug-of-war between these two brothers—between oil, political expedience, and conscience in many cases. It will be this nation's decisions and policies concerning these two figurative brothers that will determine whether the United States will survive future events outlined in the book of Revelation or go the way of the Roman Empire. Only the "People of the Book"—the Bible, and not the Qur'an—can tip the scales in the right direction.

Though we have already had many warnings, America remains much too complacent about such issues. In the last century, we have seen three dress rehearsals for Armageddon. The issues surrounding this biblically predicted event are rapidly delineating the sides of battle just as those earlier "isms" delineated the sides of World

Wars I and II, and the Cold War. Yet we have totally missed the point that the spirit which drove Hitler and Stalin is the same spirit driving terrorism today. It is the spirit of hatred that always begins in the same way: it starts by hating the Jews (anti-Semitism), and then moves on to hating Christians.

Today, we see the same hatred in the extreme Islamic fundamentalists who carry out horrific acts of terror. In fact, if you read some of today's Islamic papers, they are eerily reminiscent of newspapers from the early years of Nazi Germany. It started with killing Jews, then spread to the killing of Christians (between the Nazis and the Soviets, roughly six million Christians were martyred during WWII, though not in the death camps where millions of Jews were murdered[45]). Regrettably, Hitler's gospel has resurfaced in all of its vitriol.

America can ill afford to continue to ignore the signs that another world war could soon be upon us. The increase of rabid anti-Semitism in the Arab world is now revisiting Europe, while daily gaining strength in America. Do you believe there is no way America can be destroyed by terrorists because this is too mighty a nation? Then let me ask you a simple question: If America were to undergo the equivalent number of suicide attacks in our malls, restaurants, and even places of worship that Israel has experienced, would it not be better to declare all-out war on bigotry now, before bigotry declares all-out war on our cities?

Today's Arab leaders are at the tip of a pyramid whose base rests on the blood lust of millions of fanatics, sympathizers, and potential terrorists who lionize the Bin Ladens of the world. As Yale Professor David Gelernter wrote in the *Wall Street Journal*:

> "Terrorists evidently control large segments of Arab opinion the way the Nazis once controlled Germany— by swagger and lies, by dispensing a dangerous hallucinogenic ideology for losers, and by murdering opponents."[46]

Why is the US turning a blind eye to, and even funding, anti-Semitic, terrorist-harboring regimes? Have we learned nothing from past experiences? Have we forgotten the mobs, the voices screaming, "Death to Israel" and "Death to America"? The goal of Arab conquest of Israel is another Holocaust. Islamic extremists hate everything about America—the emancipation of women, freedom, wealth, power, and culture. They want to kill Americans because of all we represent in their oppressed and twisted minds.

After much research both in America and the Middle East, I have experienced some eye-opening revelations about America's role in prophecy—past, present, and future. Below are some of the questions I have sought answers to while researching and writing this book:

- ✧ Why does America continue to offer monetary support to Islamic regimes that are more racist than the KKK, and whose population is taught terrorist-breeding ideologies?

✧ Why does America sell billions of dollars' worth of arms to anti-Semitic Arab states that support radical Islamic ideology?

✧ Why has America not allowed Israel to fight a real war against terrorism?

✧ Why is Hitler's *Mein Kampf* still a bestselling book throughout the Muslim world over fifty years after Hitler's death?

I believe that we can never win against such apocalyptic hatred without first dealing with, and changing for the better, four key issues:

1. America is willfully ignoring the virus that is growing the plague of the Middle East—Jew-hatred (anti-Semitism such as the world saw in the 1930s). Because of this, the US pours billions of dollars' worth of weapons into Jew-hating Arab regimes that are using myths about the Jews to recruit a new generation of suicide terrorists to strike their greatest enemies—Israel and the United States.

2. Millions of Jews would be living today had anti-Semitism been taken seriously and dealt with in the 1920s and '30s. The Great Depression, as well as other American tragedies, occurred because of America's pride and challenge to God Almighty's plan. The events of September 11, 2001, might

never have happened had America fought the same bigotry in the 1990s rather than trying to appease it.

3. The war on terrorism has been fueled by support for Islamic terrorists in Israel. The Arab world also feeds it to save their "thug-ocracies." They never planned to take care of their own like the rest of the world has done concerning refugees. It infected Osama bin Laden, and in fact the entire world as evidenced by the 2001 Durban World Conference Against Racism, which blamed all the world's problems on Israel alone. If that support continues, the war on terror cannot be won.

It seems to me that God's hedge of protection was lifted from America on September 11, 2001. America was weighed in the balance and found wanting. The graveyard of history testifies that God rejects nations that reject Him and His Word. Is God nearing the point of rejecting us once and for all? America's fate will be determined in a final test. It is time to REPENT!

Everyone speaking on the subject of what we face today gives us the sense that events are accelerating toward some fearful outcome. However, if we read the signs of the times and the ancient scriptures correctly, the course America takes relative to the book of Revelation may not be such a mystery after all. Let's turn now to some specific prophecies and see how they apply to America.

CHAPTER 7

AMERICA AND THE FIG TREE

After a period of glory, the LORD of Heaven's Armies
sent me against the nations who plundered you.
For he said, "Anyone who harms you harms my most
precious possession."

(ZECHARIAH 2:8 NLT)

The river of prophecy is filled with rapids, obstacles, eddies, and undercurrents. This often has more to do with the milestones we will see along the way than it does in the details of bringing about something that was foretold. Events tend to collide and conflict in the currents as prophecy moves toward fulfillment. The flotsam and jetsam of experience sometimes seems to move ahead briskly, but at other times it comes to a stagnant halt. It might, perhaps, even disappear from sight only to reemerge farther downstream. This often makes finding ourselves at any one point in the river in a state of confusion; it is easy to get lost if we look only at the currents, gauging our progress in relation to the bank. This is why God gave us mile markers along this river to let us know what to watch for next. Thus, if we look back from where we have come, it can be easier to see how to handle the rapids and undertows on the way to the sea. By understanding the flow of prophecy over the last few centuries, we begin to clearly see what Bible prophecy holds for America.

The US is here today in full strength and regarded as a world leader, and as such is present in the events that will shape the world during the final days of life on this earth. The keys to America's future are not buried in some elusive Bible code, but in understanding the will of God, and specifically as He prepares for the final battle that will put evil away for a thousand years.

Many look at prophecy and think that because certain things have been ordained, this mind-set gives them reason to sit back and wait. As in the days of Noah, however, too many continue to eat and drink, marry and give in marriage, and yet disaster—or deliverance— is at the door. What will be on the other side of the door for us will clearly come from our choices.

While many may think that the fulfillment of biblical prophecy is a sovereign act of God, the scriptures themselves indicate something quite different. When God was about to destroy Sodom and Gomorrah, He said to himself, "Shall I hide from Abraham that thing which I do?" (see Genesis 18:17 KJV). God felt He should take no action of judgment without giving His friend Abraham the right to intercede on behalf of the inhabitants of both cities.

As Daniel was reading in the book of Jeremiah, he came across a scripture that reads, "After seventy years be accomplished at Babylon I will visit you, and perform my good word toward you, in causing you to return to this place" (Jeremiah 29:10 KJV). Daniel did some quick counting—over seventy years had already passed and Israel was still in captivity to Babylon. So Daniel began to remind God of His promises. Thus was the heart of Babylonian King Cyrus turned, and Nehemiah given permission to rebuild Jerusalem and the temple.

As Jesus himself said:

> You are my friends if you do what I command. I no longer call you servants, because a servant *does not know* his master's business. Instead, I have called you friends, *for everything that I learned from my Father I have made known to you.* (John 15:14-15 NIV, emphasis added)

As Jesus' followers, we should know what He is planning concerning the events for our nation. We should be involved with praying about them. As it was with Daniel, God needs those who read His Word, pray His promises into reality, and carry out His plan on this earth.

In the parable of the fig tree (Matthew 24:32–44), Jesus told His disciples that when we begin to see the events He foretold earlier in Matthew 24, they would be indications of the end of this age—just as new leaves on the fig tree indicate that summer is coming. He taught that the generation that saw these things would also see end-time prophecy fulfilled. Look for a moment at what Jesus said would mark the final age and His return:

✧ Many would come in His name setting themselves up as Christ and establishing their own religions (Matthew 24:5, 11). Too many denominations have, for the most part, abandoned biblical truth. One example is the ordination of an openly gay bishop in the Episcopal Church, a controversial move that has threatened the unity of that entire denomination. I have no doubt the late Rev. Gene Robinson of New Hampshire was sincerely committed to his faith and wanted to help the people of his parish. The problem was that he was living a lifestyle that directly contradicts the clear teaching of Scripture. God does not hate gays, far from it; but He does not want His followers misled.

This is not a new problem, by the way. The church at Corinth claimed homosexuals, adulterers, and drunkards among its members. The difference was that they had all given up their former lifestyles when they accepted Christ as their Savior:

Do you not know that the unrighteous will not inherit the kingdom of God? Do not be deceived. Neither fornicators, nor idolaters, nor adulterers, nor homosexuals, nor sodomites, nor thieves, nor covetous, nor drunkards, nor revilers, nor extortioners will inherit the kingdom of God. *And such were some of you.* But you were washed, but you were sanctified, but you were justified in the name of the Lord Jesus and by the Spirit of our God. (1 Corinthians 6:9–11 NKJV, italics added)

✧ There will be wars and rumors of wars; and nations will rise up against nations (Matthew 24:6–7).

All we need do is turn on any news channel to hear of these wars and their rumors. How long have 24-hour news channels been around? The first, CNN, began broadcasting in 1981. Now terrorist strikes and the ongoing battle on terrorism are reported seemingly hourly.

✧ There will be famines, epidemic diseases, and earthquakes all over the world (Matthew 24:7).

While food abounds in our world, drought,

war, and poverty have always brought instances of famine.

Despite longer life expectancy, AIDS and other sexually transmitted diseases are today devastating nations. Viruses such as West Nile, Ebola, and SARS have thrown many into panic. We have acquired more knowledge than ever before about diseases and the latest technology and techniques; yet at the same time we also face epidemic increases in cardiovascular disease, diabetes, and Alzheimer's. Diseases such as measles, tuberculosis, and scarlet fever, all of which were thought to have been nearly eradicated, have recently been on the rise.

Since 1900, the world has experienced more than a hundred different earthquakes where a thousand or more were killed, and of the twenty-one earthquakes in the history of the world where more than 50,000 were killed, over half have taken place in the last century. Since the turn of the century, earthquakes with massive fatalities have struck India (20,085), Iran (31,000), Sumatra (227,898), Pakistan (86,000), China (87,587), and Haiti (222,521). The globe has been ringed with other quakes with a high death count.[47]

✧ Persecution shall increase (Matthew 24:8–10).

Over 65 percent of the nearly 69.5 million Christians who have died for their faith, died in the twentieth century. Today, an average of 435 Christians die for their faith *every day*.[48]

✧ Sin shall flourish and Christian love will grow cold (Matthew 24:12).

I have seen this prophesied "falling away" in my lifetime, and it is rapidly increasing. An article in *Christianity Today* reported on a Pew Research Center poll regarding beliefs of people in America:

> "We believe in God," Amy Grant famously sang in the '90s. Today, 4 out of 5 Americans still say the same. But . . . what they mean by God varies a lot. Pastors and theologians often warn Christians against ascribing to a "God of their own making," knowing that not all who say they believe understand God as described in Scripture or in the traditional creeds of the church.[49]

✧ Liberals have used "freedom of speech" to legalize every form of perversity. What used to be hidden and spurned is taking to the streets and steadily growing. At the same time, Christians in the US seem less and less sure of themselves as much of our culture has turned against God. Christian expression is being increasingly limited in our schools and society in general.

Meanwhile, our pews are occupied by people who are biblically illiterate. Why? Because churches have abandoned Christian education in favor of a feel-good faith! We pay more attention to the music we sing than the gospel that is preached. We hold "seeker-sensitive" services to gently introduce sinners into the church environment. Don't get me wrong: I'm all for reaching out to those who don't know the Lord; after all, it's our Great Commission. There is, however, a fine line between making churches more seeker-friendly and compromising biblical truth. Our marching orders are to go into the world and "make disciples. . .baptizing them. . .teaching them to observe all things" (see Matthew 28:19–20) that God commanded. The goal is not for converts; it is for disciples. And making disciples requires more than a "don't-worry, be-happy" gospel. It requires faithful preaching of *all* of

Scripture, including the parts that are difficult to hear and convict our hearts.

✧ There shall also be an honored remnant of believers who will not grow cold, but will become more diligent. They will see that the gospel of God's kingdom will be preached in every nation. (See Matthew 24:13–14)

While there are other signs of the end times foretold in the Bible, I think these are sufficient to reveal that the season Jesus spoke of is upon us. While we don't know the day or the hour, the leaves of the fig tree have definitely sprouted and the tree is flourishing.

CHAPTER 8

A PRECARIOUS PRECIPICE

Look! The LORD is coming! He leaves his throne in
heaven and tramples the heights of the earth.
The mountains melt beneath his feet and flow into the
valleys like wax in a fire, like water pouring down a hill.

(MICAH 1:3-4 NLT)

t is time that we understood the significance of today's events and our nation's precarious position, so that we will know what to do in the days to come. In order to do this, we must first identify the milestones for which to watch. According to Bible prophecy as it has been interpreted by those who have dedicated much of their lives to studying and understanding it, here are the most significant biblical milestones, past and present, with respect to the salvation of God's people:

✣ Jesus' birth, His first coming (Isaiah 53; Psalm 41:9 55:12–14; Zechariah 9:9; 13:7)

✧ Jesus' death on the cross and His resurrection (Jeremiah 31:15; Psalm 22)

✧ Jesus' ascension to the right hand of the Father and the gift of the Holy Spirit to the church (John 20:17)

✧ The destruction of the temple and Jerusalem (Matthew 24:1–2)

✧ The scattering of the Jews to the nations of the earth (the Diaspora) (Genesis 49:7; Leviticus 26:33; Nehemiah 1:8)

✧ The reunification of the nation of Israel on May 14, 1948 (Isaiah 11:1; 35:10; Jeremiah 31:10)

✧ The rapture of the church (1 Corinthians 15:51–52; 1 Thessalonians 4:16; Luke 17:34)

✧ The Antichrist's seven-year peace pact with Israel (marking the beginning of the tribulation) (Daniel 9:27)

✧ The rebuilding of the temple (Ezekiel 43:2–5; 44:4; Acts 15:13–17)

✧ Gog and Magog (most commonly seen as representing Russia or a coalition of forces led by Russia, or perhaps some of its former Soviet Republics) attack Israel, but are thwarted by the supernatural intervention of God (Revelation 20:8)

✧ The temple's desecration by the Antichrist (marking the beginning of three and a half years of great tribulation) (Daniel 9:27)

✧ The battle of Armageddon (Revelation 18)

✧ Jesus' second coming (1 Thessalonians 4:16–17; Acts 1:11; Matthew 24:30; 1 Peter 1:7; 4:13)

✧ The millennium (Revelation 20:1–5)

✧ Satan again loosed for a season (Revelation 20:6–10)

✧ The great white throne judgment (Revelation 20:11–15)

✧ Eternity

In looking at these prophetic mile markers, there are a couple of keys to notice; namely, where we are in this series of events today, and when and how they have occurred. One is that, since the destruction of the temple and Jerusalem by the Romans in AD 70, the single most significant event of prophecy has been the reunification of the nation of Israel.

A second thing to notice is that this puts us on the doorstep of one of the next three events: (1) the rapture, (2) the seven-year peace treaty between the Antichrist and the nation of Israel that marks the beginning of the tribulation, or (3) the rebuilding of the temple in Jerusalem. While Bible scholars disagree on which of these will happen next (though many think it will be in the exact order given here), it is clear that they will probably all occur within a short period of time from one another (a span of only a few years). If we are reading the signs of the time correctly, they are likely to happen soon, possibly within our generation. Though we have been told this to the point where its urgency has been lost for many of us, it is nevertheless true if we are reading these scriptures correctly. Since Jesus said, "When you see all these things, know that it is near—at the doors. . . . this generation will by no means pass away till all these things take place," (Matthew 24:33–34 NJKV), it seems very likely that the events we are currently observing in the Middle East are setting the stage for what will happen in the world during the tribulation.

Another thing to notice is there are two currents of salvation flowing in the river of prophecy: one according to the Old Testament and one according to the New, because there are two currents that represent God's people—Jews and Christians; Israel and the Church. As these two currents often flow together and intermingle, many have made the mistake of thinking that there is only one. With respect to the prophecies of final events, the differences between them become enormous. Certainly they are one in the end and in heaven, but until that point God still has an obligation to deal uniquely and differently with the people of Isaac because of His covenant with Abraham. Though the New Covenant supersedes and fulfills the Old, it has not voided it.

This is why there are so many things on this list that apply uniquely to Israel. This makes sense. Once the church has gone in the rapture, the rest of salvation for the world's population centers around the Jews. This is also visible in the fact that the spirit of Antichrist that has been so active in the last century is, not surprisingly, rabidly anti-Semitic. While the twentieth century was the worst period of Christian persecution in the history of the world, it was also the time of the Holocaust and Soviet pogroms designed to rid Russia of the Jews. Today, the greatest persecution of Christians occurs in fundamentalist Muslim countries under *Sharia* law (the religious criminal code set forth by the Qur'an), whose news media are also rife with open disdain for the Jews. These are the white-hot embers that keep the fire of anti-Semitism and terrorism ablaze. This evil spirit that will one day burst fully grown into what John called the Antichrist has also been behind the greatest threats to freedom we have seen in the last century: Fascism, Nazism, Communism, and now Wahhabism—the form of fundamentalist Islam that today is fueling worldwide terrorist rage. If we read trends correctly, it is also the spirit behind much of liberalism's secular relativism that is attempting to silence God's voice in America. Though this spirit has also infected the church from time to time, and turned it toward apostasy (as it seems to again be doing today) and anti-Semitism (as it has done often in the past), we should not be confused by this seeming conundrum. The true church will always be the one following the Spirit of Christ, exhibiting His true fruit and gifts, not those who have turned to political correctness rather than the love of God to rule them.

While America is clearly in this river of prophecy, it is evident that nations such as Jordan (represented by the ancient lands of Ammon, Moab, and Edom), Egypt, Iran (biblical Persia), Iraq (biblical Babylonia), the European Union (the ten toes of the book of Daniel), Russia (Rosh), and Saudi Arabia (Sheba and Dedan), among others, are *specifically* mentioned in the Bible. Some have also proposed that America is written in prophecy disguised as the "tall and smooth-skinned" people who are "feared far and wide, an aggressive nation of strange speech, whose land is divided by rivers" (see Isaiah 18:1) or as a young lion of Tarshish (see Ezekiel 38:13), the "two wings of the great eagle" (see Revelation 12:13–17), or even the spiritual Babylon of the end times. In fact, some highly respected evangelical leaders such as the late Rev. David Wilkerson believe that America is the Babylonia of Revelation 18, with New York City as the spiritual Babylon. Look for a moment at how the Bible describes the nation that will one day coordinate the world's final attack on Israel:

✧   It is a city/nation of immigrants—Revelation 18:15

✧   It is a cultural city/nation—Revelation 18:22

✧ It has a deep water port—Revelation 18:17–19

✧ It has the wealth of the world in its grasp—
   Revelation 18:15–19; Jeremiah 51:13

✧ It is the last super power on the earth (Babylon the
   Great)—Revelation 17:5

✧ The world's leaders will assemble there. (The
   United Nations is headquartered in New York
   City.)—Jeremiah 51:44

✧ It will be a world policeman—Jeremiah 50:23

✧ It will also be a land of military and air power, and
   of widespread air travel—Isaiah 18:1

✧ It would seem to be connected to outer space.
   (NASA is headquartered in Texas.)—Jeremiah 51:53

✧ It would have some amazing stealth-type technology—Isaiah 47:10–13[50]

With things going as they are today, becoming spiritual Babylon
may not seem unlikely from contemporary evidence, either. Should
the US cut her ties with Jerusalem and continue down the road of
moral relativism that seems to have drugged the State Department
and most liberals in the US, it is easy to discern how we could certainly be this nation.

However, while this may be a remote possibility, I believe America has another course. As the Bible says, "Blessed is the nation whose God is the LORD" (see Psalm 33:12 NKJV) and "Righteousness exalts a nation, but sin is a reproach to any people" (Proverbs 14:34 NKJV). Our politics and the course of our nation is a *result* of what is in our hearts; they do not *determine* what is found there. If God is to truly heal our land, it is not just a question of proper foreign and domestic policy. The churches in the United States must eradicate relativism and earnestly seek God above all else.

Our battle is not a conflict between Christian and secular *culture*, but between good and evil, between the Spirit of Christ and the spirit of Antichrist, between revealing Jesus to today's world and being satisfied with complacency and lukewarm spirituality. America's roots were firmly established under the moral clarity of the Bible and prayer. If we call on God to heal our land, America might well be aligned with Israel in the end times, not swallowed up in the spirit of the world that would put us on the losing side of the battle of Armageddon.

Whether the rapture is tomorrow, or not for a few years, there are things we can do to secure peace in our time, win the war on terrorism, and continue those reforms that have kept us from abandoning the Middle East as other nations have done. With the help of God we can accomplish what no other nation on earth can even hope to do, but we can't do that without a major course correction. It is time to realign our moral compass to its proper heading. The church needs to be an eternal, purpose-driven body of Believers, determined to preach the truth from the pulpits in America, determined to be salt and light to a dark and hopeless world.

We stand as Nineveh did when Jonah delivered the message Jehovah had given him: We have the choice to either continue as we have and leave God behind, or we can repent and experience revival. We are at a crossroads, and more significantly, we are sometimes in the literal crosshairs of those who hate Christians and Jews, and all things for which the United States and Israel stand. To these, we must respond with Christian love and compassion and political wisdom based on clarity of vision and moral integrity. It is a worthy calling far more powerful than the Islamic call to the martyrdom of its suicide bombers. Yet until *we* live with greater conviction than that for which *they* die, our generation will see nothing of what God wants to do with and for us.

Had the church obeyed the Great Commission to be witnesses unto Him in Jerusalem, Judea, and Samaria, Islamic fundamentalists such as ISIS, Hamas, and Hezbollah could not have been able to corrupt the minds of Muslim children with hatred for all Jews and Christians. Instead, they would be filled with Jehovah God's love. The truth is: Revival might now be spreading across the Middle East, and the events of 9/11 might never have happened. Christians from every nation of the world do not blow up Jews!

Did the church fail this nation and our Lord? Is it too late? No, it's not! But if ever the church of Jesus Christ needs to repent and obey the Great Commission, rather than continuing to pursue the "Great Omission," it is now!

I pray that pastors will begin to preach on the second coming of the Lord. There never was a time in history when God dwelt in a church with an earthly perspective. It is time to proclaim this message. Why? The world has taken over the church, as recent headlines have revealed. Regrettably, abortion, divorce, pornography, drugs, alcohol, and even homosexuality are alive and well in many of today's churches. Often, pastors allow fear of retaliation to keep them from preaching against these matters.

The Bible says, "I know your deeds, that you are neither cold nor hot. I wish you were either one or the other! So, because you are lukewarm—neither hot nor cold—I am about to spit you out of my mouth" (Revelation 3:15–16 NIV). We must understand the currents of American prophecy so that we know how to navigate the waters that lie ahead.

CHAPTER 9

A CHRISTIAN NATION

Where the Spirit of the Lord is, there is liberty.

(2 CORINTHIANS 3:17 KJV)

From the charters drafted by the Pilgrims who colonized what would one day become the United States of America, our forefathers purposed to be a force for good on the earth as defined by the Bible and its prophecies. As stated in the Declaration of Independence, they believed these truths to be "self-evident, that all men are created equal, that they are endowed by their Creator with certain unalienable Rights, that among these are Life, Liberty and the pursuit of Happiness."

Thomas Jefferson, one of the framers of the Declaration, further asked: "Can the liberties of a nation be thought secure when we have removed their only firm basis, a conviction in the minds of the people that these liberties are of the gift of God? That they are not to be violated but with his wrath?"[51] From this first declaration, and by invoking the blessings of God in its foundations, the framers of its Constitution placed the United States into the hands of God both for its existence and its future.

Donald Trump has declared that America is a nation founded on Judeo-Christian principles. He went one step further at his inauguration when he invited a Jewish rabbi and five Christian pastors to pray during the ceremony. He seemed to be trying to erase the statement made by former president Barack Obama, who so infamously said, "Whatever we once were, we are no longer just a Christian nation; we are also a Jewish nation, a Muslim nation, a Buddhist nation, a Hindu nation, and a nation of nonbelievers."[52]

Bible prophecy begins and ends with Israel. When our founding fathers established this nation, endowing it with the same values and scriptures as those handed down by biblical patriarchs, America stepped into an alliance with God's chosen people. This decision would eventually lead her to be a key player in the most significant prophetic event in nearly two millennia: the rebirth of the nation of Israel.

Though some scholars may debate whether the United States was founded as a Christian nation, it is difficult to peruse the writings of our founding fathers and not detect their faith. There are many books that do a better job of proving this than I can in this limited space, but suffice it to say that up until the latter half of the twentieth century this debate would never have been broached. In fact, in 1892, in the case of *Church of the Holy Trinity vs. United States*, the Supreme

Court ruled that the church has precedent over state and federal law, because "This is a Christian nation." In the opinion written by Mr. Justice Brewer, the court felt that:

> . . .no purpose of action against religion can be imputed to any legislation, state or national, because this is a religious people. This is historically true. From the discovery of this continent to the present hour, there is a single voice making this affirmation.. . .[53]

Continuing, Justice Brewer gave various examples of America's connection to Christianity with documents ranging from the foundational principles set forth for the colonies to the constitutions of several of the states. He also cited myriad court cases supporting biblical principles, all of which reinforced Christianity as the basis for our laws and government. One argument from the state of Pennsylvania even went so far as to say that the defense of Christianity is a necessity, while the defense of the religions of the "imposters," Muhammad and the Dalai Lama, were not. From these precedents, Mr. Justice Brewer had this to say in his concluding remarks:

> These and many other matters which might be noticed, add a volume of unofficial declarations to the mass of organic utterances that this is a Christian nation.[54]

If the Supreme Court of our nation found this to be "a Christian nation" even 116 years after the Declaration of Independence was written, it is odd that some feel otherwise today. Somewhere along the way we have lost contact with our roots; our moral compass has been replaced by moral relativism and the ship of our great nation has begun to drift off course.

Considering these roots, it is not surprising that the Christian men who set the very foundations of our nation felt in their day an ingrained bond with the displaced nation of Israel. They were the other people of the Bible, and we seemed to feel a kinship with the people of Isaac from the very beginning, and with good reason.

For instance, at the beginning of the American Revolution, when the Colonial soldiers were poorly armed, starving, and on the brink of defeat, Hyman Solomon, a Jewish banker from Philadelphia, approached Jews in America and Europe and amassed a gift of one million dollars for the support of American troops. He presented this money to General George Washington, who used it to purchase clothing and arms to outfit the American soldiers. This was an incredible amount of money at that time, calculated to be over 3 billion, 31 million dollars in today's currency.

To show his appreciation, Washington directed the engravers of this nation's one-dollar bill to include a memorial to the Jewish people over the head of the American eagle. If you look closely at a one-dollar bill, you will see thirteen stars over the eagle's head, which form the six-pointed Star of David. Around this is a cloudburst representing the glory in the tabernacle in Jerusalem. President Washington specified that this was to be a lasting memorial to the Jewish people for their help in winning the war.

Textbooks of American history at one time carried a story that illustrated where Washington's heart was concerning God and how God's hand was upon him. On July 9, 1755, in a battle during the French and Indian War near Fort Duquesne in Pennsylvania, General Washington was the sole mounted officer to survive uninjured. This, despite the fact that he had four bullet holes in his coat and two horses had been shot from under him.

That day, over half of the nearly 1,300 American and British troops with him were killed or wounded, including their commanding officer, the British major general Edward Braddock. History eventually dubbed Washington "bulletproof" for this incident and the fact that he was never wounded in battle.[55] The Ruler of the Universe required a godly man to be the first president of the godly nation of the United States, and it appears that His hand of protection was upon Washington through-out his life.

While America was founded as a Christian nation, and remained such throughout the Civil War, can that be said of her today? If we are not, what does that portend for us as Americans? Has the hand of God that protected George Washington and the United States through World Wars I and II been removed?

Washington was not alone in his faith or feelings of brotherhood for the Jews. At the Continental Congress of 1776, Benjamin Franklin suggested that the Great Seal of the United States should bear the

likeness of a triumphant Moses raising his staff to divide the Red Sea
with the waters crashing in on the armies of Pharaoh in the background. Thomas Jefferson, on the other hand, preferred an image that
showed more perseverance: that of the children of Israel marching
through the desert following the cloud and pillar of fire.[56]

As President, Washington welcomed the Jews as partners in
building our new nation. In a letter to the Jews of Newport, Rhode
Island, in 1790, he wrote:

> "For happily the Government of the United States, which
> gives bigotry no sanction, to persecution no assistance,
> requires only that they who live under its protection
> should demean themselves as good citizen. . . . May the
> Children of the stock of Abraham, who dwell in this land,
> continue to merit and enjoy the good will of the other
> Inhabitants; while every one shall sit under his own
> vine and fig tree, and there shall be none to make him
> afraid."[57]

As we have seen, the United States was built on Christian principles with the Ten Commandments and biblical law as the basis for
its own bylaws. The newly born nation refused tyranny, creating a
constitution of checks and balances to control governmental power,
and also refused to embrace Old World struggles as part of its culture.
The fledgling government took literally the scripture, "old things are
passed away; behold, all things are become new" (see 2 Corinthians

5:17). This admonition was a true source of the "separation between Church and State." It assures that all faiths have the right to freedom of religion and that the State (nation) shall not dictate what church you attend. Neither will it silence any from expressing their faith while in public office nor in the halls of government.

Today, this seems not to apply to Christians. Dr. Franklin Graham, son of the late Rev. Dr. Billy Graham, has recalled the story from the book of Daniel about King Belshazzar. He was the ruler who infamously saw handwriting on the wall of his palace. Daniel properly interpreted the message as one from God, one that declared Jehovah's judgment on Belshazzar. The handwriting warned that the king had fallen short and his kingdom would soon fall into the hands of another. Graham has said:

> I wonder if the handwriting is now on the wall for America. Has God decided that our idolatry, immorality and godlessness has become such a stench in His nostrils that we as a people will experience a harsh form of divine judgment? Have our iniquities grown so foul and vast that we will reap the bitter harvest of our wickedness and rebellion against Almighty God?
>
> I don't know the answer to that, but I do believe that God is able to restore and heal us if we repent of our sins— personal and corporate— and turn to Him in humility and reverence. The Bible tells us that the Lord

is patient toward us, "not willing that any should perish, but that all should reach repentance," (2 Peter 3:9).[58]

America's founding fathers saw no conflict between national freedoms and wearing their religious beliefs on their sleeves as they went about their daily business as citizens and civic leaders. They had chosen not to silence any religion, nor the voice of those who choose not to believe in God at all. The government was not to be anti-religious, amoral, or secular as the courts seem to rule today, but rather full of the Judeo-Christian virtues of love and a dedication to pray for others rather than to try to force them to change.

As the second president of this young nation, John Adams had an equal admiration for the people of Israel. He wrote to Jefferson: "I will insist that the Hebrews have done more to civilize man than any other nation." He also once expressed to a Jewish petitioner his wish that

> . . . "your Nation may be admitted to all Privileges of Citizens in every Country of the World. This Country has done much. I wish it may do more, and annul every narrow idea in Religion, Government and Commerce."[59]

Near the end of his life, Adams even expressed, "For I really wish the Jews again in Judea an independent nation." This later became a slogan among the early Jewish nationalists, though they did not add the rest of his desire in this letter, that this gathering of Jews might also be an opportunity for them to find peace and be more open to taking steps towards Christianity.[60]

This feeling of kinship of spirit with the Jews by early American founders would be taken to even more prophetic fidelity just a few decades later. In 1814, at a dire point during the War of 1812, Americans caught a glimpse of what their nation would grow to become just over a century later: a nation integral to the rebirth of Israel.

This came about when John McDonald, a Presbyterian pastor in Albany, New York, made a startling discovery while lecturing on Old Testament prophecy to his congregation. He had been teaching on the subject for some time, with special focus on prophecies in the book of Isaiah. These spoke of the restoration of the nation of Israel and the subsequent redemption of humankind.

One day, while pouring over Isaiah 18, he read a challenge to "the land shadowing with wings, which is beyond the rivers of Ethiopia: That sendeth ambassadors by the sea" (see Isaiah 18:1–2). In this he saw that "beyond Ethiopia" meant a nation far to the west of Israel. It was a nation shadowed by wings. Could it be a nation whose symbol was a great bird, perhaps the bald eagle? Was it one that sent its ambassadors by sea? What other nations were forced to send their ambassadors across the sea besides those on the then-unknown continent of America?

In McDonald's eyes this prophetic nation took shape; it had to be the United States! And what was the challenge to this nation? According to Isaiah 18:2, 7, it was:

Go, ye swift messengers, to a nation scattered and
peeled, to a people terrible from their beginning hith-
erto; a nation meted out and trodden down, whose land
the rivers have spoiled. . . . In that time shall the present
be brought unto the LORD of host. . . . to the place of the
name of the LORD of hosts, the mount Zion. (KJV)

In that chapter, McDonald felt he had heard a clarion call from
God for this great nation to send ambassadors to help reestablish a
kingdom for the Jewish people upon Mt. Zion, the city of Jerusalem![61]

While Washington and other founding fathers had called the
Jews friends and allies of our nation and had deemed the establishing
of the United States of America as a parallel to the Jews possessing
their promised land of Canaan, McDonald had seen in the scriptures
a divine call to champion the Jews in regaining their own nation.

That nation was not to be just anywhere in the world, as was
initially projected by early Zionists, but in the original Holy Lands
with Jerusalem as its capital. In his eyes, America was the nation of
prophecy that would "send their sons and employ their substance in
his heaven-planned expedition"[62] to reestablish the nation of Israel.

Soon thereafter, a flamboyant New York City Jew by the name
of Mordecai Manuel Noah stepped into the pulpit of the synagogue
Shearith Israel in New York on April 17, 1818, and struck a similar note
that would resonate for over a century and a quarter. In his address
that day, he stated that the Jews

... will march in triumphant numbers, and possess them-selves once more of Syria, and take their ranks among the governments of the worl. . . . This is not fanc. . . . [Jews] hold the purse strings, and can wield the sword; they can bring 100,000 men into the field. Let us then hope that the day is not far distant when, from the operation of liberal and enlightened measures, we may look towards that country where our people have established a mild, just, and honorable government, accredited by the world, and admired by all good men.[63]

This image of 100,000 Jews marching to Palestine was *this exact number* of possible European Jewish refugees that had been displaced by the Holocaust, and that diplomats had discussed returning to Palestine.

Retired president John Adams even picked up this figure in writing to support Noah in his efforts:

If I were to let my imagination loose, I could find it in my heart to wish that you had been at the head of a hundred thousand Israelites and marching with them into Judea and making a conquest of that country and restoring your nation.[64]

Noah's efforts, however, didn't peak until 1844, only seven years before his death. During that year, he seized upon the same passage that McDonald had, though with a somewhat different emphasis. He continued to call for American Jews to work for the restoration of a state for their people in Palestine, but added to this a rallying cry from Isaiah 18 for American Christians to join them in this quest.

Noah declared in an address at the Broadway Tabernacle in New York to an overflow audience:

> Christians can thus give impetus to this important movement, and lay the foundation for the elements of government and the triumph of restoration. This, my friends, may be the glorious result of [our. . . . promoting the final destiny of the chosen people.[65]

The 1830s and '40s saw a great influx of Jews into the United States from Central Europe. The unrest that inspired these families to seek new hope in America was also a herald of what would unfold over the next century. "The Jewish Problem"—i.e., the displaced peoples of Israel scattered among the nations without a land to call their own—would be an issue of debate that would fuel the Zionist movement and eventually lead to Hitler's attempted "final solution to the Jewish problem" in the death camps during World War II.

Thus, roughly a century before Israel's rebirth, the groundwork had been laid in the American conscience for its support of, and relationship with, the nation of Isaac. The call had begun for America to be an international ambassador to help the Jews reestablish a land and a state for themselves. Over the next century, every American president would be faced with the issue of being part of, or ignoring, the prophecies stating that the people of Isaac would again have their own land and government.

CHAPTER 10

ISRAEL REBORN

Like birds hovering, so the LORD of hosts will protect
Jerusalem; he will protect and deliver it; he will spare
and rescue it."

(ISAIAH 31:5 ESV)

As the idea of a reborn State of Israel gained traction, some in the United States were against providing arms and munitions to the Israelis. As we will see in a later chapter, that changed most notably with Richard Nixon.

President Trump, however, made his own inroads in providing materiel to the Jewish state. On Monday, August 13, 2018, Trump made a bold move to aid the nation of Israel. He authorized passage of the National Defense Authorization Act. The NDAA contains $550 million in support for Israel. At the same time, it provisionally halted the sale of F-35 fighter jets to President Recep Tayyip Erdoğan of Turkey, while supplying the same jets to Israel.

Why was this move important for the safety and security of the Jewish state? The F-35, or Lightning II, is described as

> . . . a single-seat, single-engine fighter aircraft designed for many missions with advanced, integrated sensors built into every aircraft. Missions that were traditionally performed by small numbers of specialized aircraft, such as intelligence, surveillance and reconnaissance and electronic attack missions can now be executed by a squadron of F-35s, bringing new capabilities to many allied forces.[66]

Aerospace giant Lockheed Martin, along with a group of similar global firms, including Northrop Grumman and Britain's BAE Systems, implemented the stealth technology that would make the F-35 an extraordinary aircraft. Pratt & Whitney was charged with developing the system that would boost the power of this formidable jet fighter. The aircraft is capable of outstanding responsiveness and provides its pilots with more effective equipment that promotes greater survival probabilities. This exceptional craft is now a part of Israel's defense corps.

The act signed by President Trump was named the "John S. McCain National Defense Authorization Act for Fiscal Year 2019." It also contains monetary resources for exploration and creation of the Iron Dome, Arrow 2, Arrow 3, and David's Sling systems that all aid Israel in detecting and combating rocket and missile attacks.

An additional $50 million was included to assist with development of systems to deter the digging and construction of tunnels used by terrorists to gain entry into Israel.

Trump's refusal to sell the aircraft to Turkey was followed by tariffs placed on Turkish aluminum and steel. The result was the crash of that country's currency, the lira. Diliman Abdulkader, director of the Kurdish Project at the Endowment for Middle East Truth, assisted US lawmakers with the plan regarding Turkey. He said:

"The F-35 is a big step in basically telling Turkey you're not too big to fail. Yes, they are a NATO ally, but the United States is also concerned for its own national security interests, and based on the rhetoric coming from Erdoğan , he seems to be threatening not only NATO interests but the United States as well. The United States must adapt to the reality that we are not dealing with the same Turkey as in the past. Turkey under Erdoğan is aggressive and contradicts American interests both in Europe and in the Middle East. Therefore, we have to change our foreign policy accordingly that will further isolate and pressure Turkey. We have to keep in mind all of Turkey's internal and external problems are the doing of the Turkish government themselves not the United States. . . . There are countless of human-rights violations by Turkey that must be considered part of the equation, including Turkish threats against Americans in Syria, the Kurds and, most recently, an attempt to raid and arrest American officials in Incirlik Air Base."[67]

At one time, the United States looked upon Turkey as a major ally. Why? Turkey sits as a sentinel between the East and West in one of the most unstable areas of the world. That relationship became tense because of President Erdoğan's crumbling democratic principles and practices.

Senator James Lankford of Oklahoma said regarding Turkey's leader:

"President Erdoğan has continued down a path of reckless governance and disregard for the rule of law. Individual freedoms have been increasingly diminished as Erdoğan consolidates power for himself, and Turkey's strategic decisions regrettably fall more and more out of line with, and at times in contrast to, U.S. interests."[68]

The relationship was anything but reinforced when Washington refused to provide F-35 aircraft to Turkey. Unfortunately, the move may well have signaled Russia's readiness to cultivate a relationship with any country showing even the slightest fracture in its East/West ties.

Sarah Stern, founder and head of the Endowment for Middle East Truth reported:

"Both the United States Senate and the House had the good wisdom to cancel the proposed sale of 100 of the highly sophisticated and powerful F-35 stealth jet fighters to Turkey. Turkey under Erdoğan is not the same secular, democratic Turkey it had been in the past. Erdoğan has called for a Muslim army to invade Palestine and has compared Israelis to Nazis."[69]

Contention over the sale of F-35s is a reflection of the growing lack of cooperation between the two countries. Détente is at an all-time low, and is especially problematic with the ongoing rise of anti-Americanism. Added to that issue is Turkey's purchase of S-400 surface-to-air missiles from Russia. It was determined by US officials that the coupling of F-35s with the Russian missile would provide President Vladimir Putin with a way to appropriate classified information about the new fighter jet.

With the dustup over the F-35s, did Turkey become an enemy or, as such countries are currently called, a "frenemy"? Whereas Saudi Arabia was once an enemy and Turkey an ally, times have certainly changed. Saudi has moved up on the "allies" ladder, while Turkey has slipped several rungs. Unfortunately for the Saud Kingdom, the murder of Saudi journalist Jamal Khashoggi in October 2018 provided a circus that delivered a bull's-eye for the media.

Malicious crusades organized during the Arab Spring failed to target the Muslim Brotherhood, and those who questioned the organization's integrity were labeled "Islamophobes". The same malevolent line is being engaged in anti-Saudi Arabia publicity. Erdoğan, who seemed to have taken the lead in the promotion, faced no such movement when he expunged and sometimes incarcerated roughly 100,500 Turkish government officials and journalists, and reportedly discreetly engineered an attack against peaceful protesters outside a venue in Washington, D.C. The US State Department quickly condemned the assault:

> "We are concerned by the violent incidents involving protestors and Turkish security personnel Tuesday evening. Violence is never an appropriate response to free speech, and we support the rights of people everywhere to free expression and peaceful protest. We are communicating our concern to the Turkish government in the strongest possible terms."[70]

Did the Turkish leader endure the same bad press that the Saudi Arabian government faced over the death of Khashoggi? Doesn't that speak of discriminatory outrage? Why was there such rapid-fire finger-pointing by Erdoğan and Turkish intelligence? Saudis were well aware that cameras were trained on consulate corridors. The main issues were the resultant video and the quote from the Turkish paper, the government-run mouthpiece for Erdoğan.

Turkish officials immediately leaked the Khashoggi affair to Al Jazeera, the official television channel of Qatar—a country at odds with Saudi Arabia. Following the death of the journalist, the station offered a 24/7 discourse on the matter, using any and all means to implicate the Saudi crown prince. It produced information that Khashoggi had asked his fiancée, Hatice Cengiz, to personally contact Erdoğan's chief aide, Yasin Aktay, should he not return from the consulate. That direct link to Turkey's president was deemed undesirable and prompted an order that Aktay should halt appearances on Al Jazeera, and to stop making references to Erdoğan.

Leaks from Turkish intelligence (MIT) regarding events inside the consulate were so detailed that one has to wonder how, when, and, of course, why clandestine devices were planted inside the building, as well as in the home of the Saudi consul. MIT must have known that an attempt to kidnap Khashoggi was imminent. Not surprisingly, Erdoğan initially refused to present taped recordings of conversations inside the Saudi consulate that were made days before the death of the journalist. Any speculation on the *why* of Khashoggi's disappearance must include the theory that the Turkish president knew of the plan to return the journalist to Saudi Arabia. In November 2018, he relented and made the tapes available to the US and other select countries.

Turkey under Erdoğan seems to be headed in the same direction as Iran—an oppressive, tyrannical, Islamic leadership with only a so-called democracy. Such a happenstance would make it as difficult for the United States to have a working relationship as does that of Iran. Rather than fostering a rapport with the West, Turkey's leader seems determined to destroy the association by the choices he makes.

When given the opportunity, Erdoğan chooses to side with Iran and Qatar rather than with the United States and the Saudis. He seems determined to drive an impenetrable wedge between himself and the House of Saud.

The Turkish leader has also directed harsh words against Israel. After normalizing relations between the two countries in 1949, various conflicts have caused the rift between Turkey and Israel. In 2013, Erdoğan and Benjamin Netanyahu once again restored friendly contact between their nations. Pointedly, though, the relationship has sharply deteriorated since that time.

With the announcement that the US Embassy would be moved to Jerusalem and the resulting deaths of more than fifty Palestinians due to rioting and Israel's response, Erdoğan denounced Israel for what he called "genocide" and for having become a terrorist state. The Turkish leader declared three days of mourning for his country, recalled its ambassador from Tel Aviv, and ejected Israel's ambassador to Turkey.

Prime Minister Netanyahu tweeted:

> "Erdoğan is among Hamas's biggest supporters and there is no doubt that he well understands terrorism and slaughter. I suggest that he not preach morality to us."[71]

The Turkish leader's definition of a terrorist is much like that of the Liberal Left in the US. According to him, Hamas is not a terrorist organization, but rather a "resistance movement." Netanyahu responded with, "A man whose hands are stained with the blood of countless Kurdish citizens in Turkey and Syria is the last one who can preach to us about combat ethics."[72]

Was the death of Jamal Khashoggi on Turkish soil an opportunity for Erdoğan to retaliate against the Saudis on the world stage? How will the Trump administration work with both Turkey and Israel to reestablish détente in that region? Might that possibly happen were Erdoğan to be replaced by a less repressive leader?

The Liberal Left employs a language of hypocrisy that is familiar to its own intellectuals, but offers little to US Conservatives who are constantly placed in the position of having to avoid the "slings and arrows" of the nation's media. Former president Barack Obama entered office with a determination to lessen America's footprint in Middle East politics. That aim was achieved, leaving the US less a power broker and nothing more than a toothless tiger in the region. President Trump possesses the will and fortitude to rebuild America's role as world leader in the practice of practical concepts, especially where Israel is concerned.

CHAPTER 11

PRESIDENTS IN PROPHECY

"Who has heard such a thing?
Who has seen such things? Can a land be born in one day?
Can a nation be brought forth all at once?
As soon as Zion travailed, she also brought forth her sons."

(ISAIAH 66:8 NASB)

Virtually every American president has in some way been impacted by prophecy. From George Washington's divine protection during the Revolutionary War to every other president's decisions concerning the direction of our nation in its relationship to Israel and Arab nations in the Middle East. Our leaders have navigated the often-murky waters of foreign policy and what America's role would be in world affairs. The US constituency has elected these men and also directed how America will account for its stewardship of the power entrusted to them. It seems that though each of us may have been called upon to be used of God in this world,

we will ultimately have much to answer for because of our sluggish-
ness in responding to that call and taking our appointed place of
leadership.

As President Harry S Truman defied his State Department heads
and made history by recognizing Israel as a nation in 1948, Donald
Trump has made history seventy years later by fulfilling the campaign promise made in 2016—to move the US Embassy from Tel Aviv
to Jerusalem.

Truman, the successor of President Franklin D. Roosevelt,
assumed the mantle of chief executive upon FDR's death on April
12, 1945.

A mere three years later, Truman would be faced with a monu-
mental decision regarding Palestine. Nagging questions regarding the
Middle East would plague this succeeding president. Had Roosevelt
not succumbed to ill health, and had Truman not become president,
would the events of May 14, 1948, have taken place with the blessing
of the United States? Might FDR, with his desperate longing to be
liked by everyone and his concern that Jews in Palestine would be
massacred by the Arabs, have capitulated to the pressure from King
Ibn Saud of Saudi Arabia and his ilk and denied Israel recognition as
a nation?

It was a momentous moment when President Truman boldly
recognized the State of Israel. At midnight on May 14, 1948, the British Mandate expired, and sixty seconds following the end of that
era, David Ben-Gurion, Israel's primary founder and initial prime

minister, stepped to the radio microphone and declared the rebirth of a Jewish homeland in Palestine. Just eleven minutes later, Truman moved to legitimize that declaration with America's support of the new nation.

At 6:11 that evening, White House Press Secretary Charlie Ross read the following statement dated May 14, 1948, approved and signed by President Harry Truman:

> "This government has been informed that a Jewish state has been proclaimed in Palestine, and recognition has been requested by the [provisional] government thereof. The United States recognized the provisional government as the de facto authority of the new [State of Israel]."[73]

The United States of America, in the year of its 172nd anniversary as a nation independent of British rule, was the first foreign nation to recognize the sovereign State of Israel; the USSR would follow three days later.

The new State of Israel would soon face the first of countless attacks by her enemies. With the declaration of Israeli statehood by Ben-Gurion, Arab nations surrounding the tiny spot on earth that had been allotted the Jews pounced on the new entity, determined to totally destroy all who had taken refuge there.

Truman chose not to run for a third term in the White House. He felt it was time to revert to the traditional two-term policy, which had been temporarily shelved by Roosevelt during the World War II years. Truman retired from public affairs in 1953, on the day General Dwight D. Eisenhower was inaugurated.

The eight years of Eisenhower's presidency were perhaps the iciest of US–Israeli relations. Eisenhower steadfastly refused to meet with Jewish leaders, keeping Israel at arm's length for the most part. One might think that having witnessed firsthand the aftermath of brutality in the liberation of Nazi death camps, the former five-star general and the first supreme commander of the allied forces in Europe would have more readily supported Israel in her fledgling years.

Truman's successor would be faced with a Middle East region in the throes of a coup in Iran that had been backed by the Soviets, as well as a crisis encompassing the Suez Canal, and forced intervention in Lebanon, on Israel's northern border.

Once in office, Eisenhower's secretary of state, John Foster Dulles quickly attempted to sway the new chief executive in favor of the Arabs, and principally Egypt's president Gamal Abdel Nasser.

Unfortunately for Egypt, on July 26, 1956, the Eisenhower administration withdrew funds designated for erection of the Aswan Dam in Egypt, and Nasser became incensed. He proceeded to nationalize the canal—which connects the Mediterranean and Red Seas and offers a needed trade route for Israeli shipping interests, as well as other Middle Eastern enterprises.

Nasser's actions took the entire world by surprise, especially British and French stockholders of the Universal Maritime Suez

Canal Company. Leaders in Britain and France immediately began to make plans to forcibly wrest the canal from Nasser. Joining with Britain and France in what became known as the "tripartite collusion," Israel attacked the Egyptians across the Suez on October 26, which was followed by the other two countries joining the battle on Israel's side.

When the Russians became involved in support of Egypt and issued threats to Britain, France, and Israel, President Eisenhower forthrightly responded with, "If those fellows start something, we may have to hit 'em—and, if necessary, with everything in the bucket."[74]

Canadian Minister of External Affairs Lester Pearson suggested the formation of a UN Emergency Peacekeeping Force to be sent to Egypt to form a buffer zone between the Egyptians and the tripartite group. The presence of the peacekeeping force slowly eased the threat, and units were withdrawn in December 1956. The canal was then returned to Egypt's oversight. Israel, however, remained at Sharm El Sheik and in Gaza.

Eisenhower had been spared the move for military intervention, but having taken Dulles's advice, the president proceeded to alienate the pro-Israel lobby in Washington with his attempts to placate the Arabs, who had been soundly defeated by the Israelis during the Sinai Campaign. Ike took to the airwaves in February 1957 to demand Israel's immediate and unconditional withdrawal from Sharm El Sheikh and Gaza. Eisenhower threatened sanctions if his demands were not met. Obviously, that action did not endear him to the Jewish community. However, senators and representatives alike were convinced that a tough and robust Jewish state would be a safeguard against Arab expansion in the Middle East.

Both the president and Secretary of State Dulles were infuriated when Ike received a letter from congressional members outlining their disagreement with Ike's plan to implement sanctions. So upset were the two, a plan was developed to disallow private contributions to Israel through Jewish organizations and the purchase of Israeli bonds. Jewish representatives in the US went straight to Congress with this ploy and were rewarded when Eisenhower was forced to dispense with his proposal.

The president was then placed in the awkward position of having to soothe the rightfully ruffled feathers of Israeli prime minister David Ben-Gurion. Eisenhower asked the prime minister to consider withdrawal and assured Ben-Gurion he would be amply rewarded for his statesmanship in the matter. Sadly, neither Truman nor Eisenhower ever visited Israel during their presidency.

John F. Kennedy, as the freshman senator from Massachusetts, was invited to address the Zionist Organization of America convention in June 1947. He articulated his undeniable support for a Jewish homeland:

"It is my conviction that a just solution requires the establishment of a free and democratic Jewish commonwealth in Palestine, the opening of the doors of Palestine to Jewish immigration and the removal of land restrictions. Then those members of the people of Israel who desire to do so may work out their destiny under their chosen leaders in the land of Israel. If the USA is to be true to its own democratic traditions, it will actively and dynamically support this policy."[75]

With his 1960 election to the office of president, the young and charismatic Kennedy held sway in the "Camelot" of his time in office of exactly 1,036 days. It would be the warm personality of JFK that would take US–Israeli relations out of Eisenhower's deep freeze and into a new position of prominence in the eyes of Americans. Kennedy had announced in his inaugural address:

"Let every nation know, whether it wishes us well or ill, that we shall pay any price, bear any burden, meet any hardship, support any friend, oppose any foe to assure the survival and success of liberty."[76]

It was Kennedy's aim to find out just who did wish the US well or ill in the Middle East; who *would* support democratic liberty there, and solidify our friendships with those nations to promote further freedom and peace in the world.

In his book *John F. Kennedy and Israel*, Herbert Druks wrote:

The Arab leaders used Israel as their scapegoat and a means to gather popular support from their people.

They claimed that all their troubles came from the fact that Israel existed. Instead of improving the life of their people in such countries as Egypt, Syria, Jordan, Lebanon, Arabia, Iraq, the Sudan and Libya they bought weapons with which to dominate and control other countries and to control their own people.

For Israel, it was a basic question of survival and not a desire to dominate or rule the world. It was not a question of an arms race. Israel needed weapons in order to protect itself from such countries as Egypt, Syria and Iraq that sought its annihilation.[77]

In the words of Abraham Lincoln on Gettysburg's battlefield: "The world will little note, nor long remember what we say here, but it can never forget what they did here." So, too, the world will never know how John F. Kennedy might have aided the Israelis. His life was cut woefully short by gunfire on the streets of Dallas, Texas, on November 22, 1963. Because of that cowardly action, the entire world *will* long remember what was done there.

Kennedy's successor, Lyndon Baines Johnson, a Democrat from Texas, demonstrated throughout his presidency that he too was a friend of the nation of Israel. He began as a young lawmaker who worked intensely to see that as many Jews as possible were rescued from Europe. During Israel's formational years, Johnson backed pro-Israel legislation in Congress, and then, as president, granted

DONALD TRUMP AND ISRAEL

theretofore unparalleled financial and military assistance to the Jewish state. Unlike Eisenhower, who had forced Israel to make one-sided compromises following the Suez debacle in 1956, Johnson stood resolutely with the Jewish nation when the times got tough.

It would, however, be Richard Nixon who next resolutely stepped up to champion Israel. In the annals of support for Israel, Nixon is perhaps best noted among previous American presidents for having literally saved that nation during the 1973 Yom Kippur War. Accounts of the activities that took place in the White House and Pentagon on that defining day in 1973 are as varied as the two men who were the main rivals in that action: Secretary of State Henry Kissinger and Secretary of Defense James Schlesinger. What *is* known from the differing accounts is that President Nixon was the catalyst. Journalist Walter Z. Laqueur wrote in an article for *Commentary Magazine* in September 1974:

> The most widely publicized of these accounts [of the disagreement between Kissinger and Schlesinger] is what might fairly be called the Dinitz-Kissinger version, after Israel's Ambassador to the United States, Simcha Dinitz, and Secretary of State Henry Kissinger. . . . The Dinitz-Kissinger version is straightforward. Almost from the very beginning, and well before the full gravity of the conflict could be appreciated in either Washington or Tel Aviv, the Secretary of State had decided that Israel

141

should be allowed to obtain military supplies in the United States. But the Pentagon disagreed. Seemingly more concerned with oil interests and oil supply than with the survival of Israel, Secretary of Defense James R. Schlesinger and his senior aides rejected an Israeli request for selected items of ammunition and spare parts on the morning of Monday, October 8. They also refused to authorize the accelerated delivery of the Phantom fighter-bombers, forty-eight of which had been promised long before the war broke out. Told of the flat refusal of the Pentagon, Kissinger said he would help.[78]

On October 6, Yom Kippur, the Day of Atonement and holiest day of the Jewish year, the Arab Coalition, comprised of Egypt, Syria, and Jordan, struck Israel with a sneak attack in the hope of finally realizing their unshakeable desire to drive the Jews into the Mediterranean. Israel was tragically caught off guard. Most of her citizenry were in synagogues, and the country's national radio was off the air. Because people were enjoying a restful day of reflection and prayer, Israel could make no immediate response to the coordinated attacks. Tragically, Israeli intelligence had not seen the assault coming, and the military was ill prepared for war.

At the outset of hostilities, Egypt attacked across the Suez Canal. The battle raged for three days with Egyptian forces advancing nearly unopposed into the Sinai Peninsula. But by the third day, Israel had mobilized her forces and halted the Egyptian army, resulting in a stalemate. On the northern border, Syria launched an offensive on the Golan Heights. The initial assault was successful but quickly lost momentum. By the third day of fighting, several thousand Israeli soldiers had been killed. More Israeli soldiers fell on that first day than in the entire Six-Day War of 1967. Forty-nine planes, one-third (more than five hundred) of her tank force, and a good portion of the buffer lands gained in the Six-Day War were also lost. The Israelis seemed to be on the brink of another holocaust.

On the fourth day of the war, Prime Minister Golda Meir reportedly opened several silos and pointed the nuclear-tipped missiles toward Egyptian and Syrian military headquarters near Cairo and Damascus.[79] Army chief of staff Moshe Dayan was reported to have said, "This is the end of the Third Temple," in one of the crucial meetings. Later he told the press, "The situation is desperate. Everything is lost. We must withdraw."[80]

In Washington, Nixon intervened in the inter-cabinet squabbles between Kissinger and Schlesinger and lit a fire under those who were inundated by legislative lethargy. As preoccupied as he was with the Watergate scandal, Nixon came straight to the point, insisting that Israel must not lose the war. He ordered that the deliveries of supplies, including aircraft, be sped up and that Israel be assured it could freely expend all of its consumables—ammunition, spare parts, fuel, and so forth—in the certain knowledge that these would be completely replenished by the United States without delay. Author and investigative journalist Seymour M. Hersh noted that earlier in his presidency:

> Nixon made it clear he believed warfare was inevitable in the Middle East, a war that could spread and precipitate World War III, with the United States and the Soviet Union squaring off against each other.[81]

Nixon was now staring down the barrel of that war. His insistence that armaments be airlifted to Israel to ensure her victory was because the president had assigned a great sense of exigency to the task. He once shouted, "You get the stuff to Israel. Now. Now!"[82] White House aide Alexander Haig said of Nixon's focus on Israel:

> As soon as the scope and pattern of Israeli battle losses emerged, Nixon ordered that all destroyed equipment be made up out of U.S. stockpiles, using the very best weapons America possessed. . . . Whatever it takes, he told Kissinge. . . . save Israel. The president asked Kissinger for a precise accounting of Israel's military needs, and Kissinger proceeded to read aloud from an itemized list. "Double it," Nixon ordered. "Now get the hell out of here and get the job done."[83]

In a *Jerusalem Post* editorial, Nixon insider Leonard Garment was quoted as saying:

"It was Nixon who did it. I was there. As [bureaucratic bickering between the State and Defense departments] was going back and forth, Nixon said, this is insane.... He just ordered Kissinger, 'Get your [behind] out of here and tell those people to move.'"[84]

Secretary of Defense Schlesinger suggested that the United States dispatch three transports loaded with war materiel in what became known as Operation Nickel Grass. When he presented the proposal to the president, Nixon quickly sent the secretary to do his bidding. When Kissinger returned later to explain yet another delay in the president's orders being carried out, Nixon snapped that the delayed planes were to get off the runway immediately.

Every available American military plane transported conventional arms to Israel. The resulting supply to defend Israel was larger than the Berlin airlift following World War II, and it literally turned the tide of the war. Nixon's rapid response saved Israel from almost certain extermination and the world from a possible nuclear conflict. He had carried Kennedy's agreement to militarily support Israel to the next logical level: a full military alliance.

The Israel Defense Forces (IDF) launched a counteroffensive within the week and drove the Syrians to within twenty-five miles of Damascus. Trying to aid the Syrians, the Egyptian Army went on the offensive, all to no avail. Israeli troops crossed the Suez Canal and surrounded the Egyptian Third Army. When the Soviets realized what was happening, they scrambled to further assist Egypt and Syria. The Soviet threat was so real that Nixon feared direct conflict with the USSR and elevated all military personnel worldwide to DefCon III, meaning increased readiness; that war was likely, and that US forces should be ready to deploy within six hours. However, a cease-fire was hurriedly negotiated between the United States and the USSR, adopted by all parties involved, and the Yom Kippur War—called the Ramadan War by Muslims—was ended.

There are those who ascertain that Nixon acted only because of the threatened use of nuclear weapons by the original "Iron Lady," Golda Meir. That is rebutted by Mordechai Gazit, who opined that Israel's relationship with the United States was not solidified sufficiently for Nixon to have been so manipulated by Meir. It was J. J. Goldberg in his book *Jewish Power*, who wrote:

> [John F.] Kennedy initiated the first U.S. arms sales to Israe. . . . Johnson continued and intensified Kennedy's policy of warmth toward Israel. . . . In 1966, Johnson approved the first sale of American warplanes to Israel.
>
> Nonetheless, it remained for Richard Nixon, a Republican elected with little Jewish support, to create a now familiar U.S.-Israel alliance of more recent decades. It was Nixon who made Israel the largest recipient of U.S. foreign aid; Nixon who initiated the policy of virtually limitless U.S. weapons sales to Israel. The notion of

Israel as a strategic asset to the United States, not just a moral commitment, was Nixon's innovation.[85]

Israeli president Chaim Herzog, when asked about Nixon's anti-Semitism, responded:

"He supplied arms and unflinching support when our very existence would have been in danger without them. Let his comments be set against his actions. And I'll choose actions over words any day of the week."[86]

Wily as he was, Richard Nixon had no misconceptions regarding how his role in the Israel airlift would be regarded by historians. It was teacher and evangelist Oswald Chambers who wrote:

God has a long track record of calling people the world thinks are lightweights, cowards, or no good and making them great in his service. Who else but God called Gideon to lead the fight against the Philistines? God called Gideon even though Gideon had all the excuses in the world for not heeding the call to fight. He rattled off all excuses in the book. Still, God's angel called him a 'mighty man of valor.' Gideon might have laughed since this description hardly squared with his own perception of himself.[87]

On July 16, 1974, Richard Nixon became this nation's the first sitting president to visit the reborn Jewish state.

Later, James Earl "Jimmy" Carter rose through the ranks of Georgia's local and state politics to become the 39th president of the United States. What is perhaps astounding about the former president is that Carter still today is said to feel that his short and arguably failed attempts at governing the United States somehow endowed him with great influence in the world arena. This is the same man who, in his early days of campaigning for the White House, elicited the response, "Jimmy who?" Perhaps the better question might have been: "Jimmy? Why?" Even then, Carter's duplicitous approach was evident. The ever-grinning Carter was an enigma. Journalist Bill Moyers observed: "In a ruthless business, Mr. Carter is a ruthless operator, even if he wears his broad smile and displays his Southern charm."[88]

It is incomprehensible to think of Jimmy Carter, the lay preacher from Plains, Georgia, as being anti-Semitic. After all, he had read the same Scriptures that confirmed Christian Zionists have read; when and where did he make the leap from Bible-believer to enemy of the Jewish people? Was it during the Camp David talks, when he was ensconced with Menachem Begin and Anwar Sadat? Was it the Israeli prime minister's intractability when it came to giving away Israel for Mr. Carter to achieve his ultimate goal of a two-state solution between Israel and the Palestinians?

Despite Yasser Arafat's record of murderous terroristic activities, Carter chose to embrace the petty despot. In fact, he is said to have gone so far as to assist Arafat with writing a generic speech to be delivered to Western audiences. Carter's advice to Arafat was to try to drum up as much sympathy as possible from world leaders and to depict Israel in as bad a light as possible, as often as possible. He was said to have given the PLO leader specific examples; sympathetic illustrations that could be changed or embellished to suit the audience in question.[89] This reported aid from Carter came regardless of the fact that in 1980 Arafat cried out, "Peace for us means the destruction of Israel. We are preparing for an all-out war, a war which will last for generations."[90]

Carter's presidency was followed by that of Ronald Wilson "Dutch" Reagan. The past several decades, especially those surrounding the rebirth of Israel, have produced a number of presidents who were pro-Israel. However, none equaled or surpassed Reagan, the 40th president of the United State; that is, before the election of Donald Trump. Reagan was, until now, perhaps, the best friend of Israel ever to sit behind the desk in the White House.

During the early years of the Reagan administration, I was invited into the Oval Office. There I saw the family Bible that President Reagan had used at his inauguration. It was still opened to 2 Chronicles 7:14:

> If my people, which are called by my name, shall humble themselves, and pray, and seek my face, and turn from their wicked ways; then will I hear from heaven, and will forgive their sin, and will heal their land. (KJV)

Even before he began his quest for the presidency, Reagan had become widely known for his support of Israel. He spoke at pro-Israel rallies during the 1967 Six-Day War. As governor, he persuaded the California State Legislature to permit banks to invest in Israeli bonds. He was greatly influenced by a strong, conservative Jewish think tank, and appointed members of that group to posts in his administration. While stumping for the presidency, Reagan readily condemned the PLO and often told his audiences that he considered Israel to be a vital tactical resource in the Middle East. At a reception for a Jewish group in New York, he averred that Israel was "the only stable democracy we can rely on as a spot where Armageddon could come."[91]

Reagan, wanting to cement friendly and interdependent relations between the US and Israel, set about to reestablish defensive and financial ties. Perhaps more importantly, the president enjoyed a spiritual intimacy with the Israeli people. Reagan understood that Israel is important not only because of her tactical location but also because of her biblical history.

Israel's prime minister Shamir said of the Reagan White House:

> "This is the most friendly administration we have ever worked with. They are determined that the strong friendship and cooperation will continue and even be strengthened despite the differences that crop up from time to time."[92]

Like that of Donald Trump, Reagan's empathy with leaders in

Israel and with American Jews was based on his belief in the biblical concept of a Jewish homeland for the People of the Book. He also understood the necessity of a strong, democratic Israel in the Middle East. He admired the courage of the people whose state had been forged by the fires of adversity, who for centuries had vowed, "Next year, Jerusalem." He proclaimed:

> "In Israel, free men and women are every day demonstrating the power of courage and faith. Back in 1948 when Israel was founded, pundits claimed the new country could never survive. Today, no one questions that Israel is a land of stability and democracy in a region of tyranny and unrest."[93]

Reagan seemed to be at ease in his dealings with Israel partly because, experts believe, he knew and recognized the importance of a strong Jewish state in the region. He strongly believed that Jerusalem should not be divided and that a Palestinian state co-opted by terrorists would mean the end of Israel.

Not all American presidents have been Zionists; certainly neither William Jefferson (Bill) Clinton, nor Barack Hussein Obama could be described as such. If challenged, each might vow their acceptance of Israel as a US ally, but each also had issues with America's number one ally in the Middle East.

One of President Clinton's greatest hopes apparently had been to go down in history as the man who finally resolved the Arab–Israeli conflict in the Middle East. In order to do this, he, too, used his tremendous brush of image transformation to paint the terrorist and murderer Yasser Arafat as a "freedom fighter" and a diplomat. Arafat became the most welcomed foreign leader to the White House during the Clinton administration. It also seems likely that Arafat received some coaching from Clinton and his advisers on what to say, how to speak, and what to do to help in this metamorphosis, much as Arafat had obtained from Jimmy Carter.

Arafat and his entourage proudly marched into the White House on thirteen different occasions during the Clinton era as welcome guests to negotiate the release of what some called "Palestine's occupied territories." Clinton's aim was to proverbially hold the hands of the half-brothers, Isaac and Ishmael, as he walked both the Israelis and the Arabs through the "peace" process. He succeeded only in legitimizing one and applying pressure on the other.

Israel was at the center, and thus the focus of Clinton's pressure to force agreements. According to the Oslo Accords, Israel would negotiate separate peace agreements with Jordan, Syria, and the Palestinians, yet only Jordan signed the document on October 26, 1974. For Syria, Israel's deportation of 415 Hamas members in December 1992 precipitated a crisis in continuing negotiations. Syria demanded the PLO be a part of their discussions and be given the power of veto.

The fate of the Golan Heights was also a major issue. These mountains near the border of eastern Israel provide a natural protective barrier from which to launch attacks against the country, as

Ambassador David Friedman, Jared Kushner, and Jason Greenblatt
with Dr. Mike Evans

Ambassador David and Tammy Friedman, Dr. Mike Evans,
with Jared Kushner and Ivanka Trump-Kushner at banquet.

Dr. Mike Evans, Ivanka Trump-Kushner, Jared Kushner,
and the Chief Rabbi of Jerusalem.

Chief Rabbi of Jerusalem

Dr. Mike Evans, Sarah Huckabee Sanders, Mike Huckabee

President Donald Trump at the Western Wall in Jerusalem

Trump Campaign in Jerusalem

Ambassador David Friedman and Dr. Mike Evans

President Donald Trump holding up the signed proclamation recognizing Israel's sovereignty over the Golan Heights with Jared Kushner, Prime Minister Benjamin Netanyahu, Jason Greenblat, and Ambassador David Friedman.

Prime Minister Benjamin Netanyahu and Sarah Netanyahu with Dr. Mike Evans at the opening of the U.S. Embassy in Jerusalem

Benjamin & Sarah Netanyahu, Ivanka Trump-Kushner and
Jared Kushner, Ambassador David and Tammy Friedman at the
opening of the U.S. Embassy in Jerusalem

Ivanka Trump Kushner at the opening of the U.S. Embassy in Jerusalem

Dr. Mike Evans, Ambassador David Friedman,
and Prime Minister Benjamin Netanyahu

Prime Minister Benjamin Netanyahu

Dr. Mike Evans at the Annual Night of Heroes

Dr. Mike Evans, Ambassador David and Sally Friedman,
Prime Minister Benjamin and Sarah Netanyahu

Former Mayor of Jerusalem Nir Barkat, Sheldon and Miriam Adelson,
and Dr. Mike Evans.

Ambassador David Friedman and Jared Kushner

The late President Shimon Peres, Pope Francis,
and Dr. Mike Evans at the Vatican

Former President Shimon Peres visiting the Friends of Zion Museum

Dr. Mike Evans, former President George W. Bush,
and former President Shimon Peres

Mike Evans hosting Prime Minister Menachem Begin
at the Waldorf Astoria in New York

Dr. Mike Evans and Benjamin Netanyahu at their first meeting

President Donald Trump and Prime Minister Benjamin Netanyahu
show members of the media the proclamation recognizing Israel's
sovereignty over Golan Heights

Jared Kushner speaking at the White House
Hannukah reception

President Trump and First Lady host Hannukah reception
at the White House

President Trump signs executive order opposing anti-Semitism

President Donald Trump and Dr. Mike Evans

Pen used to sign the Executive Order
against anti-Semitism

Robert K. Kraft, owner of the New England
Patriots with Dr. Mike Evans (holding one of the
team's six Super Bowl rings)

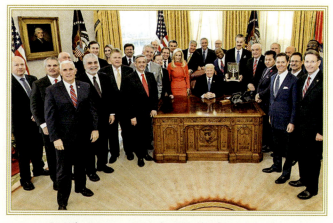

Dr. Mike Evans presents the Friends of Zion Award to
President Donald Trump with the Evangelical Advisory Board

did those coming from Syria during the Six-Day War. Prime Minister Yitzhak Rabin had stated during his election campaign in 1992: "He who considers withdrawing from the Golan Heights forsakes the security of Israel."[94] At least for that time, Rabin saw no mutual basis upon which Jerusalem could negotiate with Damascus.

During the negotiations, Rabin gave President Clinton a document that became known as the "deposit." It stated that if all Israel's security needs were addressed and her demands regarding normalization and a timetable were met, the country's leaders would be willing to carry out a full withdrawal from the Golan Heights. Clinton betrayed Rabin and showed the Syrians the "deposit" that had been intended for his eyes only. It was Rabin, however, who was viewed by many as a traitor and as a result was assassinated by an Israeli extremist on November 5, 1995. Standing at Rabin's state funeral, I watched as a tiny bead of sweat rolled down Bill Clinton's face. He appeared sullen and tired but not remorseful. The damage done to negotiations was irreversible, and talks with the Syrians deteriorated until they abruptly ended in late 1998.

As a side note to the Golan Heights debate, President Trump has removed any US negotiations regarding that region. In March 2019, the president placed his signature on a proclamation conferring recognition of the Golan Heights as Israeli territory. Trump handed the pen used to sign the document to Prime Minister Netanyahu, who was standing behind him in the Oval Office. This move by the US actually lessens the stature of Syria's dictator Bashar al-Assad, while underscoring his inability to circumvent the recognition of Golan as Israeli ground.

In June 2019, Netanyahu named a proposed new settlement "Trump Heights" in thanks for the president's recognition of that region. Said the prime minister:

> "We are proud that we have the opportunity to establish a new settlement and to give thanks to a great friend. We will continue to grow and develop the Golan for all of our citizens—Jews and non-Jews together."[95]

The relationship between Benjamin Netanyahu and Donald Trump is vastly different from that which Bibi had with Bill Clinton.

With the election of George W. Bush (43), long thought to be a friend of Israel, many were certain he would soon have two outstanding opportunities to apply the ideals of American democracy to the Middle East. In one, he could tell the heirs of Yasser Arafat's organization that crime did not pay. In the other, he could show the world that the United States recognized the capital of its ally Israel.

Continuing failure to officially recognize Jerusalem has been both a violation of US law and a craven surrender to Arab terrorist threats. In the midst of America's war on worldwide terrorism, it was vital to send a message that the US would not surrender to terrorist blackmail. Bush recognized the precarious position in which Israel reposes and vowed to give her his full support as president of the

United States. In an address to the National Commemoration of the Days of Remembrance on April 19, 2001, he observed:

> "Through centuries of struggle, Jews across the world have been witnesses not only against the crimes of men, but for faith in God, and God alone. Theirs is a story of defiance in oppression and patience in tribulation, reaching back to the exodus and their exile into the diaspora. That story continued in the founding of the State of Israel. The story continues in the defense of the State of Israel."[96]

As the sands in the hourglass of his presidential era began to seep slowly to the bottom bulb, it became apparent that Bush's successor would likely be Barack Hussein Obama. And it quickly became clear that the next chief executive would have little regard for Israel. Perhaps Rabbi Steven Pruzansky put it most succinctly in his blog:

> Jews will have to cultivate warmer relations with the new Republican House and friendly Democratic congressmen, and bear in mind that Israel's base of support in America today is not in the White House, but in the Congress and, more importantly, with the American people. They are the ones who will resurrect and strengthen this relationship that reflects so well on both countries and can yet benefit all of mankind.[97]

It is difficult to define what fashioned the 44th president's view of Israel. Would that I could write that Barack Obama is a Christian Zionist and tell of his uncompromising support for the Jewish people, but the opposite has proven to be true. The appalling deterioration of the relationship between the United States and Israel during Obama's presidency created a strain not apparent since the days of Bill Clinton.

Shortly after taking office, Obama seemingly did his best to alienate American Jews and their Israeli counterparts. He made every effort to visit Muslim countries, including making two trips to Indonesia and Afghanistan, and one each to Turkey, Iraq, Saudi Arabia (where America's president was caught on camera infamously bowing to King Abdullah), and Egypt. Less than six months after assuming office, Mr. Obama flew to Cairo to deliver a major speech designed to impress the Muslim world. Secretary of State Mike Pompeo said in his speech at the American University in Cairo on January 10, 2018:

> "These fundamental misunderstandings set forth in this city in 2009 adversely affected the lives of hundreds of millions of people in Egypt and all across the region. Remember, it was here, here in this city that another American stood before you. He told you that radical Islamist terrorism doesn't stem from an ideology. He told you that 9/11 led my country to abandon its ideals—particularly in the Middle East. He told you that the United

---

States and the Muslim world needed 'a new beginning.' The results of these misjudgments have been dire."[98]

Obama's tactics were elementary: He simply became president with his global platform to demand that Israel halt settlement construction as a prerequisite to peace talks. This included barring the building of homes for Jews in their own Jewish Quarter. Reportedly, his first contact after becoming president was a telephone call to Palestinian Authority president Mahmoud Abbas, not to the prime minister of Israel, the chief US ally in the Middle East.

In March 2009 I was in The Hague, Netherlands, attending the International Conference on Afghanistan. It didn't take long to discover just what Hillary Clinton, Obama's secretary of state, would deliver to Iran, whose Islamic Revolutionary flag was flying just a few feet from the US flag on the dais. The only flag not in evidence at that convention was Israel's. But then, why should Israel have been invited when the majority of Arab states continue to refuse to recognize her basic right to exist?

I stood and spoke boldly against Secretary Clinton's assurance to those in attendance that the majority of the Taliban were "moderates" and the US would accept them if they desired to join forces. What? I reminded those present that the Taliban are extremists who decapitate Jews and Christians, and is the forerunner to ISIS. Its adherents throw acid in the faces of young girls or shoot them at point-blank range just for going to school. I stated that there is no such thing as a moderate Taliban, just as a moderate ISIS would be ludicrous.

I was outraged to realize that the terrorist nation whose proxies are killing Jews and that wants to wipe Israel off the map with an atomic bomb would be invited to assist the US in winning the terror war in Afghanistan.

In one of his last ploys as president, Barack Obama took the proverbial knife in hand and added another stab wound to Israel: He declined to veto UN Security Council Resolution 2334, which states that "Israel's settlement activity constitutes a 'flagrant violation' of international law and has 'no legal validity.'"[99] Actually, by his inaction, Mr. Obama *did* vote; he tried to decimate the close relationship that has been fomented between Israel and the United States since the days of Harry Truman. It was one that men such as presidents Ronald Reagan and George W. Bush carefully maintained. It is one that Donald Trump, our 45th president, is working diligently to rebuild following the 44th president's disastrous attempts to single-handedly destroy Israel.

CHAPTER 12

PROMISES KEPT

There has not failed one word of all His good promise,
which He promised through His servant Moses.

(1 KINGS 8:56b NKJV)

Since the ringing of the final bell on the election count and the Electoral College announcement of Donald Trump as the winner, the Liberal Left has employed seemingly every tactic in its repertoire to discredit him. He beat the "anointed one"—Hillary Clinton—and for that crime alone has been under near-constant assault. Rioters have shouted, "Trump is not my president!" Or called for his impeachment. He has battled the claims of Russian involvement, and as one writer opined, "I should think Putin would have been on Team I'm With Her, because her failures as Secretary of State would make her a pushover compared to a dealmaker like Trump."[100]

Of course, no mention is made by these naysayers of both Bill Clinton's and Barack Obama's backroom interference in Israel's elections. Neither man was a fan of Benjamin Netanyahu; neither wanted him in office. According to a *New York Post* column by journalist Benny Avni:

> Obama tried and failed to defeat Bibi [Benjamin Netanyahu] in two Israeli elections, in 2009 and again in 2015—sending to Israel a battery of political consultants, pollsters, funds, you name it. A congressional inquiry over the summer found that the Obama administration spent hundreds of thousands of dollars to boost an anti-Bibi campaign in Israel run by a former Obama campaign staffer.[101]

The Clinton interference is well-known, as was the past president's dislike for Netanyahu. In an interview on Israel's Channel 10, Clinton admitted:

> "I did try to be helpful to him [Peres] because I thought he was more supportive of the peace process. And I tried to do it in a way that was consistent with what I believed to be in Israel's interest, without saying anything about the difference in domestic polices, without anything else."[102]

Given this above information, the Democrats' chest-beating over Trump's victory in 2016 seems more than somewhat self-serving.

Simply put, the Liberal Left lost the election. Their loud-spoken grief over this truth has thrown the nation into political turmoil—not Mr. Trump and his policies. He has been targeted for some of the same issues that were tacitly allowed to slide with Bill Clinton, Barak Obama, and certainly with former secretary of state Hillary Clinton. And, horror of horrors, rather than lie down and let the arrows strike where they may, this scrappy president has fought back—something he was not expected by many to do.

This president has had to counter attacks by disciples of Liberal Left community organizer and writer Saul Alinsky, whose political premise is: Choose the target, immobilize it, and divide it. During the run-up to the election, Mr. Trump often came under personal attack. He has been labeled everything from reprehensible to shameful, and those are the less vile of these accusations. When the name-calling failed to stop his momentum, the naysayers began to target Trump's family and campaign aides. The charges were not only personal but also openly antagonistic. Not even former administration officials with close ties to the brutal attack in Benghazi or other scandals were treated to such vitriolic attacks.

Another Alinsky tactic was to simply continue pressuring individuals until they folded from the stress. Since that day the election results were announced in November 2016, the Trump White House has been under cataclysmic pressure that would have stopped lesser men in their tracks and dropped them to their knees in surrender.

Not only was President Trump bombarded by Alinsky-ites, he has faced the radical anti-Fascist group Antifa, radical Left protesters, and the massive amounts of money invested by billionaire George Soros in anti-Trump campaigns. While Antifa might, at first glance, be labeled "pro-Trump," their antics have cast the president in an overly zealous light. It might certainly be said that this global organization employs Fascist tactics.

Antifa members have repeatedly shown up at demonstrations in attempts to quash supporters of the president. Their arrival has triggered mayhem and even murder. *National Review* writer David French wrote of one event that took place in Berkeley, California:

> What you'll notice (and what you'll experience, if you ever find yourself in the middle of violent left-wing protest) is that the rioters and the "peaceful" protesters have a symbiotic relationship. The rioters break people and destroy things, then melt back into a crowd that often quickly and purposefully closes behind them. They're typically cheered wildly (to be sure, some yell at them to stop) and often treated as heroes by the rest of the mob— almost like they're the SEAL Team Six of left-wing protest.[103]

Antifa hoodlums have employed coarse and uncivilized methods against Trump team members:

- ✧ Homeland Security Secretary Kirstjen Nielsen—forced from a Washington, D.C., eatery by an Antifa group;

- ✧ Press Secretary Sarah Huckabee Sanders—hounded from a Lexington, VA, restaurant;

- ✧ Stephen Miller, a Trump supporter—tossed an $80 order of sushi after being taunted by the chef who prepared it (Miller feared the chef had spat on the food);

- ✧ Trump adviser Kellyanne Conway—ambushed at her local food market;

- ✧ A cocktail waitress at a Chicago bar spat on Eric Trump, the president's son, while he was having dinner;

- ✧ Others accosted in a bookstore, at a movie theater, and various places where they were sure to be embarrassed by the hubbub.

And then there has been the George Soros effect. The billionaire freely contributed in excess of $25 million to Hillary Clinton and other Democratic contenders during the former first lady's losing bid to win the presidential election in 2016. Soros claims to have anticipated someone like Donald Trump making a run for office, but he, like countless others, never dreamed that anyone could displace the anointed Democratic candidate. According to his speech delivered during the World Economic Forum in Davos, Switzerland, in January 2018, Soros was not at all favorable about a Trump presidency:

> In the United States, President Trump would like to establish a mafia state but he can't, because the Constitution, other institutions, and a vibrant civil society won't allow it.[104]

By July 2018, Soros had not wavered from his pronouncement. He reiterated to *New York Times Magazine* writer Michael Steinberger:

> "For every Trump follower who follows Trump through thick and thin, there is more than one Trump enemy who will be more intent, more determined . . ." He is doing his part to shorten the Trump era: In advance of the midterm, Soros has so far contributed at least $15 million to support Democratic candidates and causes.[105]

Apparently, Mr. Soros is a non-practicing Jew, whose outlook is no more positive toward Israel than it is toward President Trump. According to an article in the *Jerusalem Post* by writer Dennis Prager:

"Soros and his wealthy Jewish American friends have now decided to aim their fire directly at Israel...to form a political lobby that will weaken the influence of the pro-Israel lobby AIPAC [American Israel Public Affairs Committee]."[106]

In the book by writer Anna Porter, *Buying a Better World*, she quoted Soros regarding his view of Israel: "I don't deny the Jews to a right to a national existence—but I don't want anything to do with it."[107]

Soros has liberally funded non-governmental organizations (NGOs), including those that have participated in the Boycott, Divestment and Sanctions (BDS) programs against Israel. In an article by Liel Leibovitz for *Tablet*, in 2016 it was revealed that Soros's Open Society Foundations allegedly have "designated annually to organizations highly critical of the Jewish state, some of whom deny its right to exist."[108]

The question arises: Does George Soros hide behind his Jewish roots only when it is convenient? It seems as if the answer to that question is an unequivocal "yes."

Harvard Law professor Alan Dershowitz issued this warning to the Liberal Left:

What you do to Donald Trump today becomes a precedent and can be used against Democrats and independents or anybody in the future. That's why all Americans who care about civil liberties, who care about constitutional rights, ought to be very concerned about the investigation that's being conducted and targeting Donald Trump, whether you like him or not."[109]

If you are a regular viewer of CNN, MSNBC, or a reader of the *New York Times* or *Washington Post,* you may have missed much positive news regarding the Trump presidency. According to the more liberal news outlets: Mr. Trump has sold out to Vladimir Putin; has the US on the brink of a nuclear war with—just choose one—North Korea, Pakistan, Russia, Iran; or scrapped Roe v. Wade; declared war on Mexico or Canada; or sold the free press down the proverbial river of no return. These tactics are designed only to harm Mr. Trump and his presidency.

In rebuttal to the media's "fake news," the president didn't fire special counsel Robert Mueller, nor did he sell subscriptions to the Lincoln bedroom. Actually, the opposite has been true. While Trump has no love affair with prophets of "fake news" or the antics of the Democratic Party, the Union is arguably in a far better state than it was when he took up residence at 1600 Pennsylvania Avenue.

Perhaps we need only to review Genesis 12:3 for some indication as to why that might be:

> "I will bless those who bless you, and whoever curses you I will curse; and all peoples on earth will be blessed through you." (NIV)

CHAPTER 13

Drilling for Dollars

But before he [Abraham] died, he gave gifts
to the sons of his concubines and sent them off
to a land in the east, away from Isaac.

(GENESIS 25:6 NLT)

A s the nation that helped the Jews find a state of refuge in the land that had been theirs two millennia before, but that had raised Ishmael's princes from obscurity with the power of the petrodollar, America stepped out of the eye of the prophetic storm on 9/11 and into the hurricane of a plummeting stock market. It was the day that the beautiful economic house of cards the Clinton administration took credit for began to topple. The nation sank from a time of unprecedented hope and economic confidence into the throes of despair in a matter of but a few hours.

When the stock market reopened on Monday, September 17, following the attacks, it saw record losses in the first hours of trading. Not only did the US economy take a precipitous plunge, but that also occurred in those of countries around the world that depend largely on the US consumer market. In the weeks following, the market rebounded, only to be hit again and again as consumer confidence appeared to have been misplaced. Tech stocks quickly corrected from being grossly overvalued. Corporate accounting scandals hit such companies as Enron, WorldCom, and Tyco. America had been robbed by the inflated economic optimism preached in the '90s and by more than a few corrupt corporate leaders. The airline industry took a hit as a result of the attacks, and United Airlines was forced into filing for Chapter 11 Bankruptcy.

However, one industry *did* boom—the security industry. Americans have spent more trying to stay safe in recent years than ever before. The new Department of Homeland Security (DHS) created by the Bush (43) administration was allotted $37.70 billion for its 2003 budget—almost double its 2002 budget. This is, of course, a department that didn't even exist when Bill Clinton completed his second term, and was just one more expense to be covered by US taxpayers.

Children lost mothers or fathers, men and women lost a spouse, a friend, or a son or daughter—nearly every life was somehow changed on that fateful day, September 11, 2001. For the first time, I and many others deeply felt the real loss and madness of those attacks. Innocent lives were scarred in an instant because of a murderous doctrine of hatred. There has never been a moment in this country's history that better defined the senselessness and horror of terrorism.

Unfortunately, despite the increased awareness brought about by 9/11, our deep ties to the descendants of Ishmael persist in clouding our vision. Warning signs continue to be ignored by many. One example came from a group of Americans serving on the U.S. Commission on National Security chaired by senators Gary Hart and Warren Rudman. They tried to sound a warning twice—in September 1999 and again in January 2001. The commission's initial report predicted: "Americans will likely die on American soil, possibly in large numbers" as the result of terrorist attacks.

This 1999 warning was virtually ignored by top government officials and the news media. The commission continued its work, however, and on January 31, 2001, seven months before the attacks on the World Trade Center and the Pentagon, the commission's final report of 150 pages was presented to newly elected president George W. Bush. It was called the "Road Map for National Security: Imperative for Change." In it, the commissioners reissued their warning, along with a detailed plan of action to make America safer from terrorism. Again, the report was ignored—until after the September 11 attacks.

In the wake of that darkest of days on US soil, the Saudis hired several public-relations firms to polish their tarnished image in the eyes of the US public. According to Justice Department filings, the Saudis spent some $17 million on this. The firms hired included one of Washington's most prominent team of international lawyers, Squire Patton Boggs, which reportedly received some $200,000 a month in fees. Squire Patton Boggs is especially known for its contacts among

Democrats. Thomas Hale Boggs, Jr., a well-connected Democratic lobbyist, founded that firm. His father, Representative Hale Boggs, had been House majority leader, and his sister was the late journalist Cokie Roberts.

The *New York Times* reported that the Saudi government also hired Akin, Gump, Strauss, Hauer & Feld, a firm founded by Robert Strauss, former head of the Democratic National Committee, with the Saudis paying out $161,799 in the first half of 2002. Frederick Dutton, a former special assistant to President John F. Kennedy and a long-time adviser to the Saudis, received $536,000 to help manage that nation's handling of the aftermath of 9/11. The Saudi government's agents purchased hundreds of television and radio commercials in virtually every major American media market and placed advertisements in publications like *People* magazine and *Stars & Stripes*, presumably for the US troops in Iraq.

Ex-Washington officials have also been paid handsomely from the Saudi king's coffers in recent years. That list included such figures as Spiro Agnew, Jimmy Carter, Clark Clifford, John B. Connally, and William E. Simon. The *Washington Post* listed other former officials, including George H. W. Bush, who found the Saudi connection "lucrative." It also quotes a Saudi source as claiming that the Saudis have contributed to every presidential library in recent decades.

Obviously, it was not enough to discover that fifteen of the nineteen September 11 terrorists were Saudis, nor that Saudi Arabia is the largest supporter of al-Qaeda. These considerations were suspiciously overlooked in an attempt to keep the oil that lubricates our national economy flowing. We have accepted the cultural unconsciousness of the last few decades that have assured us again and again, "Everything will be all right. The economy will recover. Go back to sleep."

The ebb and flow of prophecy is beginning to coalesce as the various currents come together and more and more quickly take us toward the rapids ahead. It becomes easier to look at the present world stage and watch the players slipping into position:

1) Israel

Against all odds and vast opposition, the Jews have pulled themselves up from near obscurity as Israel was reborn. Israel now stands on the world stage as a nuclear power and one that has, as we have written, reportedly brandished that power in the wake of a feared invasion and potential defeat (the Yom Kippur War of 1973 is the most prominent example of this). Israel seems prepared to take on the world if need be—and indeed, she may soon be required to do so.

2) The European Union (EU)

Nations occupying the same lands that the Roman Empire did have traditionally been seen by biblical scholars as the "ten toes" of Nebuchadnezzar's dream, revealed in Daniel 2:31–45. However, this mixture of iron and clay representing the alliance of two substances that cannot truly blend together—like oil and water—may more likely be the alliance of two forms of government. These are so different they are not easily combined—such as Middle Eastern monarchies and European democracies—whose leadership is based in the lands of ancient Rome. Whatever this alliance may be, it seems likely the EU will be at the center of it. As a member of the Quartet (the US, EU, UN, and Russia) that tried to force the Road Map down Israel's throat, it can easily be seen as part of the end-time government that will ratify a false seven-year peace agreement with Israel. It has, in recent years, become even more obvious that the Islamic invasion of Europe continues to be achieved through an overwhelming influx of refugees. Gatestone Institute journalist Guy Millière wrote of the growing Islamic population in the EU:

> Those who rebuilt Europe after World War II thought that an enlightened elite (themselves) could make a clean sweep of the past and build a dream society where peace and perpetual harmony would reign. . . . Populations of Western Europe increasingly think that the dream society that had been promised has turned into a nightmare. The sudden and often brutal arrival of hundreds of thousands more Muslims most likely prompts Europeans to think the nightmare will get worse. They see, powerlessly, that their leaders speak and act as if they have no awareness of what is happening.[110]

3) The United Nations

This member of the Quartet has become a major proponent of the Arab League and anti-Semitic thought in the past decades. While the

UN has done everything to emphasize the Palestinian refugees' plight since the War for Independence of 1948, it has also spoken with one voice against Israel. Of all the nations cited for Human Rights violations, Israel remains unique under the UN's twisted scrutiny—not North Korea or China, nor nations ruled by Sharia law, nor any other. This masquerade extends even further when representatives of terrorist-supporting states such as Syria became the head of the Security Council or Libya became the head of the Human Rights Commission. No wonder the UN Human Rights Commission proclaims that the Palestinians can use "all available means, including armed struggle" to regain their "occupied territories"—a not-so-veiled endorsement of suicide bombings. (See UN Resolution 37/43.)

At the previously mentioned World Conference on Racism in Durban, South Africa, in 2001, almost every conference attendee agreed to condemn one nation as blatantly racist—Israel. Incredibly, the only democracy in the Middle East committed to civil rights, the rule of law, and Arab participation in democratic government was accused of genocide, ethnic cleansing, and apartheid.[111] Attendees from Israel and the United States walked out of that conference on September 4, exactly one week before the attacks on the World Trade Center and the Pentagon. These allies were the only two nations willing to acknowledge the lunacy and prejudice of the entire proceedings. It is patently obvious that this organization has changed greatly from its original intent and will be a mere puppet of Islamic fanatics in the latter days of the earth as we know it.

4) Russia

Since the fall of Communism in Russia, we have been encouraged to no longer view this superpower as a threat. The Cold War might have ended, but as the world edges inexorably toward a World War III to be fought over control of global oil supplies, this former superpower will be a key player. This is especially true when one considers that Russia may be sitting atop oil reserves rivaling those of Saudi Arabia, Iraq, Iran, and Kuwait combined. At one time, those countries were believed to control as much as two-thirds of the world's remaining oil reserves. As a member of the Quartet, the leader of the Communist world, and a nuclear power, Russia has become the probable leader of Gog and Magog, the biblical coalition that will sweep down from the north to attack Israel.

5) China and the East

These nations can also be seen easily fitting into an anti-Israel coalition because of their links to the former Soviet Union and their utter dependence on outside sources for oil. We also know from Revelation 16:12–16:

> Then the sixth angel poured out his bowl on the great river Euphrates, and its water was dried up, so that the way of the kings from the east might be prepared. And I saw three unclean spirits like frogs coming out of the mouth of the dragon, out of the mouth of the beast, and out of the mouth of the false prophet. For they are spirits

of demons, performing signs, which go out to the kings
of the earth and of the whole world, to gather them to
the battle of that great day of God Almighty. "Behold,
I am coming as a thief. Blessed is he who watches, and
keeps his garments, lest he walk naked and they see his
shame." And they gathered them together to the place
called in Hebrew, Armageddon. (NKJV)

This event occurs at the close of the period known as the "tribulation." It is from this passage that China is generally identified as
the "kings from the East." Either Chinese forces or a coalition led by
China will cross what was once the great Euphrates River to join with
the Antichrist in the assault against Israel.

In contemporary times, China has gradually changed from an
underdeveloped country to a rising world power. This Eastern giant
has developed immense military clout; regained Hong Kong from the
British; overran Tibet, claiming it as Chinese territory, and thus forcing the essential evacuation of the Dalai Lama; continued to attempt
to intimidate the Taiwanese and other regions; pursued global economic dominance; spouted aggressive rhetoric on the world stage;
and, of course, continued to persecute Chinese Christians. It is no
longer difficult to conceive that the group known as the "kings from
the East" would be China.

6) The Terrorists

The most vocal plea from fanatics in the Middle East has always been for the destruction of Israel and the return of Jerusalem, the third holiest site in Islam, to Arab control. Most experts agree that the war had begun much earlier with the US. But on September 11 this Satanic plot reared its ugly head, and the US and Israel have been consolidated as targets. Blatant Jew-hatred is the glue that will surely unite the anti-Israel coalition at the battle of Armageddon.

7) The United States

An Executive Order signed by President Donald Trump in January 2017 prohibited all citizens of Iraq, Libya, Yemen, Iran, Syria, Somalia, and Sudan from entering the United States with a visa from any category. At this writing, the president is working diligently despite an ongoing, all-out battle from the Liberal Left to fulfill his campaign promise to build a wall along the southern border of the US to provide additional protection from any who would enter the country illegally.

Our position in the last days will be determined by our allegiances: Will the growing liberal tendencies of our nation pull us toward joining the EU, UN, and Russia in a globalization movement that will, in the end, force a false peace on Israel? This seemed to be the intent of former president Barack Obama. Or will we with our moral clarity, large Jewish populace, and Christian consciousness align ourselves so closely with Israel in the final conflict that we become literally indistinguishable in the final chapter of Bible prophesy?

As you should be able to tell from this brief summary of the players, such a decision will be one we make ourselves, not one imposed by foreign nations. While outside forces continue to influence us, either through negotiations or terrorist attacks, the final decision will be up to us. What will we do? Will we trade our freedom away for cheap and plentiful oil, globalization, and moral relativism? Or will we stay the course our forefathers outlined, and hold to the Bible as our guide? Will our nation be on God's side in the final conflict? Will we give in to the lunatics, liberals, and liars in weakness? Or will we stand strong and seek a revival of moral clarity in our land?

It has become easy for many to see that, much like Europe, the United States is already in trouble from within her own borders. In the 2018 election, two female Democratic Muslims, one from Michigan and one from Minnesota, were seated in the nation's House of Representatives. Conservative columnist Michael Reagan wrote:

> But Ilhan Omar. . .is so radical she scares the pants off me. After watching Omar in action, it's pretty clear to me that the Muslim Democrat hates America almost as much as she hates Israel.
>
> Before she got to Washington she had already raised eyebrows for her support of the socialist dictator who's wrecked Venezuela, Nicolas Maduro, and her call to abolish ICE, the Immigration and Customs Enforcement agency.

She's also a big fan of sanctuary cities and opposes President Trump's border wall because it's "racist and sinful."

But last week, Omar got in big trouble for a tweet insinuating that the prime reason U.S. politicians so faithfully support Israel is because they get lots of money from AIPAC, the largest pro-Israel lobbying group in the country.

She apologized profusely, but only after Republicans and the grown-up members of her own party loudly condemned her statements as anti-Semitic and "deeply offensive.". . .

And because the entrenched men and women in Washington refuse to do their jobs and solve important issues like immigration or health care reform, they'll keep the side door to Congress open for more radical socialists and Jew-hating Muslims.[112]

A Pew Research Center estimate reveals:

Political debates over Muslim immigration and related issues have prompted many people to ask how many Muslims actually live in the United States. But coming up with an answer is not easy, in part because the U.S. Census Bureau does not ask questions about religion, meaning there is no official government count of the U.S. Muslim population. . . .

Since our first estimate of the size of the Muslim American population, the number of U.S. Muslims has been growing rapidly, albeit from a relatively low base. When we first conducted a study of Muslim Americans in 2007, we estimated that there were 2.35 million Muslims of all ages (including 1.5 million adults) in the U.S. By 2011, the number of Muslims had grown to 2.75 million (including 1.8 million adults). Since then, the Muslim population has continued to grow at a rate of roughly 100,000 per year, driven both by higher fertility rates among Muslim Americans as well as the continued migration of Muslims to the U.S.[113]

In one of Aesop's fables, a farmer took compassion on a snake nearly frozen from the cold. He took it up and warmed it in his bosom only to be mortally bitten when the serpent recovered. Then there was the story of the frog dropped into a pot of cold water before it was placed on the fire. Will we be cooked, and served up before ever realizing the danger?

CHAPTER 14

THE HEART
OF JERUSALEM

But I have chosen Jerusalem, that my name might be there;
and have chosen David to be over my people Israel.

(2 CHRONICLES 6:6 KJV)

B
oth Israel and the Palestinians declare Jerusalem as their capital, yet most countries still have their embassies in Tel Aviv, not Jerusalem. The reason for this is the hesitancy to back one side or the other. It was a major step when President Trump ordered the US Embassy to be moved to Jerusalem. It meant that no longer were we only *symbolically* recognizing Israel's declaration of the Holy City as rightfully hers. Actually, for the Palestinian Authority to claim Jerusalem as the capital of a state that does not exist is ludicrous.

I once met with New York's mayor Rudolf Giuliani to discuss Jerusalem and asked him about the most important things Jerusalem and New York have in common. He answered:

"The most important thing we share is that we both live in freedom. We are both blessed with freedom and democracy. Much of the world doesn't have freedom and democracy. Because we share the same principles on which government and society are based, then all of the other friendships become even stronger.

The relationship of blood also exists between New York and Jerusalem. There are so many who have family in both places.

We have the relationship of religious significance for Jews, Christians, and Muslims—the historical significance and the reality that we are two of the world's great cities. Jerusalem is older than New York. A good deal of the world passes through both places. We share great bonds.

New York and, indeed, America hold a great bond with Jerusalem—the city that will be the center of the whole earth's attention during the final days."

The lines for the future battle of Armageddon have been drawn by UN resolutions, terrorist demands, and US acquiescence. They follow Israel's June 4, 1967, boundaries declaring the Golan Heights, Gaza Strip, West Bank, East Jerusalem, and the Temple Mount as so-called "Occupied Territories." On three different occasions from 1991 to 2001, the PLO (now the PA) was offered those areas, minus control of East Jerusalem. Each time, they ultimately refused and escalated their violence. The conclusion is only too obvious: Palestinian leaders will not sign any final agreement with Israel; it is all or nothing at all!

The Temple Mount is the holiest site in Judaism, and perhaps to Christians; second only to Golgotha, which is just across from it. Mecca is the first and then Medina the second holiest place in the world to Muslims, while Jerusalem is considered the third. However, neither Palestine (*Filistin* to Arabs) nor Jerusalem (*al-Quds*) are mentioned in the Qur'an. For the Jews, it is the place of which God said, "In this house [the temple], and in Jerusalem, which I have chosen before all the tribes of Israel, will I put my name for ever" (2 Chronicles 33:7 KJV, insert added).

Why has Jerusalem been a bone in the throat of the world? Why is such a tiny city so much in world news? It is because of an ancient prophecy whose fulfillment Jehovah himself guarantees!

Every nation that has come against Jerusalem has been cursed. In 586 BC, the Babylonian army besieged Jerusalem, and the temple was ransacked. In April 2003, the Iraqi National Museum in Baghdad was plundered by a lawless society. More than 170,000 ancient and priceless artifacts were stolen. These relics covered the entire 7,000 years of Babylonian history.

Saddam Hussein, who claimed to be Nebuchadnezzar incarnate, ended up cursed just as the first Nebuchadnezzar was. Saddam should have read the Bible. Who would ever have believed that the man who caused nations to tremble would end up with matted hair, a nasty, unkempt beard, a diet of rotten food, and in a hole in the ground?

I am concerned about Jerusalem because there is no city in the world on which Jehovah pronounces a blessing on those who bless it, and a curse on those who curse it (see Genesis 12:1–3). The nations that divide Jerusalem will be stricken beyond their ability to comprehend. If that happens, no amount of prayer or repentance will reverse the curse on that nation. Jehovah's anger will emerge. The psalmist wrote, "Let God arise, let His enemies be scattered" (Psalm 68:1 NKJV).

Many US presidents have placed their hands on the prophecy God gave to King Solomon in 2 Chronicles 7:14 as they were sworn into office. They trusted that Jehovah would bless America and their term in office. It is uncertain, however, that many might have read another prophecy by the same king found in 2 Chronicles 6:6: "But I have chosen [bachar] Yaruwshalaim that my name [shem] might be there." This amazing prophecy denotes that Jerusalem is the only city in the world on which Jehovah has chosen to place His name.

Is it important that Jerusalem not be touched? Yes! Heaven and earth met in Jerusalem (the coming of Jesus Christ), and will meet again (His return). The prophecies say that Jerusalem will be united—not divided—when the Messiah returns. He is not coming back to a Muslim city!

At the end of the age, Jerusalem will be the center of all prophecy:

I saw the Holy City, the new Jerusalem, coming down out of heaven from God, prepared as a bride beautifully dressed for her husband. (Revelation 21:2 NIV)

As the prophet Amos proclaims,

The LORD also shall roar out of Zion, and utter his voice from Jerusalem. (Joel 3:16 KJV)

The prophet Zechariah declares:

I will return to Zion and dwell in Jerusalem. (Zechariah 8:3 NIV)

It is no coincidence that the first words of the New Testament mention David, the first king of Jerusalem, a forerunner of the true King of Jerusalem, Jesus Christ.

The final battle of the ages will be over Jerusalem. If America chooses to side against Scripture, she will find herself fighting against Jehovah, and will definitely lose!

Satan's challenge to Jehovah can be found in Isaiah 14:12-15:

How you have fallen from heaven, morning star, son of the dawn! You have been cast down to the earth, you who once laid low the nations! You said in your heart, "I will ascend to the heavens; I will raise my throne above

the stars of God; I will sit enthroned on the mount of
assembly, on the utmost heights of [the sacred mountain.]
I will ascend above the tops of the clouds; I will make
myself like the Most High." But you are brought down
to the realm of the dead, to the depths of the pit. (NIV)

Notice that Lucifer says *he* will sit on the Temple Mount in Jerusalem, on the north side. Yet Jehovah says, "You will be cursed and
brought down to the far reaches of the pit."

Most wars have been fought over disputes of ownership concerning land and property. Personal battles have sometimes raged
over someone illegally using the name of another to write a check or
buy goods. This is called "fraud." The person who commits fraud is
severely punished in most societies. America even has laws that grant
a citizen the right to bear arms to protect his property. Jerusalem's
title deed does not belong to anyone; it belongs exclusively to Jehovah.
He placed His Name there!

A brilliant and respected scholar whom I have known for decades
told me:

If you look at a satellite image of the city of Jerusalem,
you will see the Tetragrammaton JHVH. It is clearly
visible in the photo. What does JHVH mean? It is the
Hebrew for Jehovah—the name of God! Yes, mystically
inscribed in the very city of Jerusalem is God's Name.

Biblical prophets also declare:

> Then shall the LORD go forth, and fight against those
> nations, as when he fought in the day of battle. And his
> feet shall stand in that day upon the mount of Olives,
> which is before Jerusalem on the east, and the mount
> of Olives shall cleave in the midst thereof toward the
> east and toward the west, and there shall be a very
> great valley; and half of the mountain shall remove
> toward the north, and half of it toward the south.
> (Zechariah 14:3–4 KJV)

It's amazing that the United States, supposedly a Christian
nation, has attempted to divide Jerusalem and cede East Jerusalem
to a terrorist regime, the PA, to become an Islamic state.

The same scholar who told me about his discovery in the satellite
image of the city of Jerusalem also told me:

> The geological formation created by the Kidron Valley
> between the Mount of Olives and the Treble Mounts,
> the Tyropaean Valley and the Hinnom Valley (Gehenna),
> which lies at the bottom of the Temple Mount and
> sweeps northward, forms the Hebrew letter for *shem*
> that looks like a warped "W." God's name is buried in the
> very geological foundations of Jerusalem—and cannot
> be removed.

If he is, indeed, correct, this is another fascinating and prophetic sign concerning ancient Jerusalem, and man's futile battle over it.

There is, indeed, in ancient prophecy, a curse that Jehovah will place on any nation that divides Jerusalem:

> Behold, I will make Jerusalem a cup of trembling unto all the people round about, when they shall be in the siege both against Judah and against Jerusalem.
>
> And in that day will I make Jerusalem a burdensome stone for all people: all that burden themselves with it shall be cut in pieces, though all the people of the earth be gathered together against it.
>
> In that day will I make the governors of Judah like an hearth of fire among the wood, and like a torch of fire in a sheaf; and they shall devour all the people round about, on the right hand and on the left: and Jerusalem shall be inhabited again in her own place, even in Jerusalem.
>
> In that day shall the LORD defend the inhabitants of Jerusalem; and he that is feeble among them at that day shall be as David; and the house of David shall be as God, as the angel of the LORD before them. (Zechariah 12:2, 3, 6, 8 KJV)

And this shall be the plague wherewith the LORD will smite all the people that have fought against

Jerusalem; Their flesh shall consume away while they stand upon their feet, and their eyes shall consume away in their holes, and their tongue shall consume away in their mouth.

And Judah also shall fight at Jerusalem; and the wealth of all the heathen round about shall be gathered together, gold, and silver, and apparel, in great abundance. (Zechariah 14:12, 14 KJV)

According to Genesis 22, Jerusalem is the location were Isaac was to be offered to God as a sacrifice before the angel stayed Abram's hand. Conversely in Muslim tradition, it was Ishmael, not Isaac, who was offered there. It is also said to be the place from which Muhammad ascended one night into heaven for a special visit. Muslims do not refer to the area as the Temple Mount, but as the Noble Sanctuary.

The Mosque of Omar, more commonly known as the "Dome of the Rock," was built over the place upon which Muslims believe Abraham laid *Ishmael* to sacrifice him. The mosque was built sometime around AD 700. Caliph Omar I, the successor to the prophet Muhammad, overran Jerusalem in AD 637. This is the Golden Dome, which you see in all modern photographs of Jerusalem that include the Temple Mount.

Though it is the more famous of the two mosques of the Noble Sanctuary because of its brilliant dome, it is not considered by Muslims as the holiest. That quality rests with the second mosque on the

Mount, called the *al-Aqsa* Mosque, which means "the farthest place of worship of the One God." This refers to its distance from Mecca when built; it is just to the south of the Dome of the Rock. It is the largest mosque in Jerusalem, built soon after the Dome of the Rock was dedicated to Muhammad's purported "night visit" to heaven, and supposedly rests upon the place from which he took that journey.

It is also this location that became the focal point for the beginning of the Second *Intifada* (rebellion), which is also called the *al-Aqsa Intifada* because it began when Prime Minister Ariel Sharon visited this holy site. Though the violence had already begun in smaller outbreaks some days before, on September 28, 2000, it rose to new heights after Sharon stood at the door of the *al-Aqsa* Mosque. Though Sharon entered none of the mosque buildings on the Temple Mount, his mere presence caused an explosion of shouting and rock throwing that resulted in twenty-eight Israeli policemen being injured, three of whom had to be hospitalized. There were no reported Palestinian injuries on the day of Sharon's visit. The next day, however, significant and orchestrated violence erupted after the Muslims' Friday prayers. This resulted in deaths and injuries on both sides. Thus began the worst period of Palestinian violence in Israeli history. From September 29, 2000, to September 11, 2002, Israel saw 427 civilians and 185 members of Israel's security forces killed, and 3,202 civilians and 1,307 security members injured.

The violence had probably already been planned before Yasser Arafat walked out of the Camp David talks with Israel in July. The fact that Sharon's visit to the Noble Sanctuary was used as the catalyst for the violence to begin in earnest is a testament to how close control of the Temple Mount is to the heart of the conflict. Another outbreak on September 24, 1996, was the result of the Israelis opening a new exit to the Hasmonean Tunnel, an archeological site that runs along the Western Wall and under part of the Old City of Jerusalem.

It has traditionally been believed that the Dome of the Rock will have to be removed before the third temple can be built—a prophecy well-known to the Arabs and a reason for their further distrust of Jewish custody of the Mount. Prophetically, the rebuilding of the temple will be one of the bargaining chips used by the Antichrist to draw Israel into the seven-year peace pact with him. (See Daniel 9.)

CHAPTER 15

THE RISE OF THE ANTICHRIST

For thou hast said in thine heart,
I will ascend into heaven, I will exalt my throne
above the stars of God: I will sit also upon the mount
of the congregation, in the sides of the north:

(ISAIAH 14:13 KJV)

Jerusalem is now often the center of world attention even as it has always been the center of Jewish and Muslim attention. The fate of Jerusalem will eventually become the greatest reason for hope in the world as the prophesied seven-year pact is signed. It will also be the site of the final breakdown of hope when the Antichrist enters the rebuilt temple and desecrates it, marking the beginning of the great tribulation.

If the spirit of antichrist truly is behind the actions of the Palestinian Authority and other terrorist groups, and I firmly believe it is, that adds a spiritual dimension to why Jerusalem is the key to the

Palestinian Authority's acceptance of a treaty with Israel, and why it is a sticking point for anyone proposing peace for the region. It is about much more than how many have died in suicide bombings; it is about who controls the center of the world and the rock upon which God made His initial covenant with humanity.

Not only has the line firmly been drawn, but both sides also know what each is willing to sacrifice to get what it wants: the Palestinians to chase the Jews from the land the Palestinians regard as theirs. Though America and the USSR each desired to avoid an arms race in the Middle East, they could not while at the same time retaining their loyalties. In response, the Soviets armed Nasser's Pan-Arabists.

The United States eventually promised to keep Israel one step ahead of her neighbors following the Yom Kippur War. This proved more difficult when America also agreed to supply weapons to Saudi Arabia, Egypt (after President Anwar Sadat signed a treaty with Israel in 1978), the United Arab Emirates, Kuwait, Bahrain, Jordan, Oman, Lebanon, Qatar, and Yemen. The agreement stipulated that if any one of these were to receive an advanced weapons system, i.e., missiles, planes, ships, tanks, or other materiel, the US would be obliged to offer the same or better to Israel. Thanks to this largess, those on each side of the imaginary line running through Jerusalem are well prepared to wage conventional warfare in order to control the city.

So far, the edge has gone to the Israelis, not only because America has promised to keep them one step ahead in this race to obtain US arms, but because of Israel's nuclear strike potential. Almost from

Israel's rebirth, Prime Minister David Ben-Gurion saw that nuclear power could be useful in making the Negev desert bloom by supplying it with electricity, thus also powering desalinization plants to provide it with drinking water.

Unquestionably, Ben-Gurion had his eyes set on Israel becoming a nuclear power for several reasons. Throughout his contacts with the United States, Ben-Gurion would continue to push for a promise that Israel could find sanctuary under the umbrella of America's nuclear weapons. Because he could never acquire this promise, Israel looked to protection of her own.

By 1953 Israel's Weizmann Institute had developed an improved ion-exchange mechanism for producing heavy water and a more efficient method for mining uranium, which it bartered with the French for a formal agreement to cooperate in nuclear research. By 1958, Israel had begun construction of her own nuclear facility near the Negev desert town of Dimona, which the Israelis patterned after the French nuclear research facility at Marcoule. Perhaps by then Ben-Gurion had realized that, after Eisenhower's reaction to the Suez Crisis, the US was not as interested in Israeli security as he had hoped. Israel would continue her research for a decade before the first nuclear bombs were produced. The facility went into full-scale production at that point, turning out what experts believe were four or five bombs a year. The US was certain of the purpose for the Dimona installation, but simply turned a blind eye knowing that Israel had little choice other than to defend herself.

Some members of Congress even supported Israel's actions. A few days before talks with President Kennedy to further discuss Israel's Hawk missile purchases, Shimon Peres met with Missouri senator Stuart Symington, a Kennedy supporter and ranking member of the Senate Armed Services Committee. Symington is said to have encouraged the production of Israel's atomic bombs.

This struggle didn't come without its political casualties. In the spring of 1962, President Kennedy was pushing hard for Prime Minister Ben-Gurion to supply solid answers about Dimona, or at least genuine promises that its research was not for military purposes. Ben-Gurion stood his ground. As a result, Kennedy shut Ben-Gurion out in the midst of a growing threat of nuclear proliferation. It was in April 1962 that Iraq joined Egypt and Syria in the short-lived Arab Federation, making the threat of another Arab invasion such as that of the War of Independence much more likely.

By 1973 Israel had what was thought to have been about twenty-five nuclear warheads with three or four missile launchers in place and operational at Hirbat Zachariah, a missile site west of Jerusalem. The nation also had a number of mobile Jericho I missile launchers at her disposal. Israel had acquired the capability of launching nuclear weapons and striking targets as far away as Tbilisi and Baku in southern Russia. Damascus and Cairo were within easy range.

As previously noted, when the Yom Kippur War broke out, the United States was slow to act as attacks began. Several sources suggest that President Nixon and Secretary of State Henry Kissinger planned to let Israel suffer a bloody nose before responding. However, it was at this point that Israel developed what became known as the "Samson Option." Once the United States discovered this, it pulled out all stops to help Israel win a conventional war that would reduce the possibility of nuclear proliferation in the Middle East.

The Samson Option emerged from Israel's determination that there would never be another Holocaust at the hands of a foreign power. As the Jews had done at Masada, they believed it was better to die by their own hands rather than be captured by an oppressing force. However, it was not Masada but Samson from whom they took their example. As the Bible relates, in his last hour, a blinded and weakened Samson was marched into the temple of Dagon as an example to the Philistines of their preeminence over the Jews. As mocking catcalls fell upon his ears, Samson prayed, "O Lord God, remember me, I pray thee, and strengthen me, I pray thee, only this once, O God, that I may be at once avenged of the Philistines for my two eyes" (Judges 16:28 KJV). Then, placing his hands firmly on two pillars supporting the roof of the temple, Samson prayed again, "Let me die with the Philistines" (Judges 16:30 KJV) and with all his might pushed the columns over, bringing the roof crashing down upon him and all the Philistines who had ridiculed him. The Bible tells us that in this final act he killed more Philistines than he had ever done previously.

The Samson Option thus illustrates Israel's willingness to bring the world into a nuclear war and destroy much of it, rather than to allow another holocaust at the hands of an anti-Semitic nation. Israel's leaders understood the consequences of attacking Egypt and Syria; the Soviet Union would launch an all-out nuclear attack on Israel, and Armageddon would most assuredly arrive.

Thus, just a few days into the war, Prime Minister Golda Meir is said to have ordered the arming and aiming of Israel's nuclear missiles at Egyptian and Syrian military headquarters near Cairo and Damascus. She didn't know what else to do to boost the confidence of her countrymen. However, to prevent that move the United States significantly came to Israel's aid to keep the war on a footing of fighting with conventional, non-nuclear weapons.

By 1979 Israel was routinely gathering US satellite intelligence to target cities in the Soviet Union. Israelis had learned a key factor that the United States and Soviet Union had comprehended during the Cold War: In a nuclear war, it doesn't matter how many times you can blow up your enemies, only that you *can* blow them up. Thus, Israel joined the list of the world's nuclear-armed superpowers.

In essence, the victory Israel won in the Yom Kippur war was achieved by staring down the barrel of a nuclear missile launcher. Since Israel possessed nuclear weapons and her neighbors did not, this further bolstered her position as a nation that could not be easily defeated in open warfare. If the Arabs developed nuclear weapons, however, that distinct advantage would be lost. So it was that on June 7, 1981, Israel employed US F-15s and F-16s that had been purchased supposedly for defensive purposes and took out Saddam Hussein's Osirak nuclear reactor, which was twelve miles southwest of Baghdad, before it became operational. Then as now, Israel desired to avoid a Samson vs. the Philistines scenario.

Israel knew the seriousness of the strike and was ready for possible retaliation. Before the bombing, the Israelis shut down Dimona in case of a counterstrike, and left it down for roughly a year. While the world fumed, the US merely gave Israel a mild reprimand for this planned preemptive strike. According to Richard V. Allen, Ronald Reagan's national security adviser, when the president was informed of the attack, the conversation went like this:

"Mr. President, the Israelis just took out a nuclear reactor in Iraq with F-16s." . . .

"What do you know about it?"

"Nothing, sir. I'm waiting for a report."

"Why do you suppose they did it?"

The President let his rhetorical question hang for a moment, Allen recalled, and then added: "Well. Boys will be boys."[114]

The White House announced that the next installment of the 1975 sale of seventy-five F-16s would be suspended because of that attack. However, two months later the suspension was lifted with little attention drawn to that fact, and the initial shipment of four new F-16s was delivered to Israel without incident.

It also appears that Israel had found a way to get around restrictions it had been given on the use of America's extremely advanced and secret KH-11 spy satellite system. President Jimmy Carter had agreed the Israelis could receive satellite pictures of areas within one hundred miles of Israel's borders so they could watch for troop movements in neighboring countries that might alert them to a new invasion by Arab forces. Somehow, though, in addition to that information, they received enough images of Osirak—a locale roughly 550 miles from Jerusalem—that they could also launch a surgical strike against Iraq without being detected until Israeli pilots arrived at their targets.

Later in the 1980s, Israel planted nuclear land mines along the Golan Heights. Additionally, she now also has impregnable submarines—each one carrying four nuclear cruise missiles. In June 2000 an Israeli submarine launched a cruise missile that hit a target 600 kilometers or slightly more than 370 miles away, making Israel the third nation after the US and Russia with that capability. However, in the spring of 2002, Iran launched a missile that covered a similar distance. When asked about Iran's nuclear capabilities on May 24 of that same year during the Bush–Putin summit in Moscow, Russian deputy chief of the general staff, General Yuri Baluyevshy huffed:

> "Iran does have nuclear weapons. Of course, these are nonstrategic nuclear weapons. I mean these are not ICBMs with a range of more than 5,500 kilometers and more."[115]

They might not have the range to reach Moscow or Washington, but they could certainly reach Tel Aviv and Jerusalem. Goliath is quickly closing in on Samson's military edge. Again, it doesn't matter how many times you can blow someone up, just that you *can*.

The Samson Option again came into play in the 1991 Gulf War. I had called senior adviser to several of Israel's prime ministers, Reuben Hecht, who lived in Haifa, the target of a SCUD missile attack during the Persian Gulf War. He said to me, "We have picked up intelligence that Saddam has given the order to put chemical and biological weapons aboard SCUDs. I need to get into a sealed room quickly. I can assure you, however, that if they hit our cities, Baghdad will be a radioactive dustbowl. Israel has mobile missile launchers armed with nuclear weapons. They are facing Baghdad even as I speak, and are ready to launch on command. We are on full-scale nuclear alert."

Today, names like Dimona, the Samson Option, Project 700, the Zechariah Project, the Temple Weapons, and Z-Division are all part of one of the most massive nuclear arsenals in the world, and located in Israel. Now, new terms are being heard: Pumped X-ray Lasers, Hydrodynamics, and Radiation Transport—the new Armageddon generation of weapons. Israel has over 300 tactical and strategic weapons that include more than 100 nuclear artillery shells, nuclear land mines, and neutron bombs that can destroy biological life without creating an explosion. They also have lasers for their planes and tanks and electromagnetic weapons that shut down radar.

On November 14, 2003, Israel took her first order of US F-16I fighter jets. She would receive 102 of them by 2008, making it the largest arms deal in Israel's history. The new jets can reach nations as far away as Iran and Libya, and have AMRAAM air-to-air missiles and Northrop Grumman APG-68 radar, giving them the capability of shooting down other jets from over thirty miles away.

At *least* nine nations currently have the capability of attacking an enemy with a thermonuclear bomb: Russia, the United States, China, Israel, France, Great Britain, India, Pakistan, and (it appears) Iran, and quite possibly North Korea. This gives them all the potential to unleash a plague of nuclear or neutron bombs that would be very much like what is described in Zechariah 14:12:

> And this shall be the plague with which the LORD will strike all the people who fought against Jerusalem: Their flesh shall dissolve while they stand on their feet, their eyes shall dissolve in their sockets, and their tongues shall dissolve in their mouths. (NKJV)

In the last great battle described in the book of Revelation, Russia, the European countries (Great Britain and France), and the Eastern countries (Iran, Pakistan, India, China, and North Korea) will be on the other side of the line from tiny Israel. But where will the United States be? If we don't handle the next steps in the war on terrorism correctly, Soviet nukes or weapons of mass destruction will very likely fall into the hands of terrorists.

Since this terrorist network stands poised against the US as well, it would seem to be only a matter of time and money before one of those reportedly missing Soviet suitcase nukes is used to decimate a major American city. Thus far, the war on terrorism has taken us from the attacks of 9/11 to victory in Iraq. But if we are to ultimately win this conflict and prevent these weapons of mass destruction from striking our cities, where do we need to focus now?

CHAPTER 16

WINNING THE WAR
ON TERRORISM

Blessed is the nation whose God is the LORD,
The people He has chosen as His own inheritance.

(PSALM 33:12 NKJV)

T he war on terrorism cannot be won without the desire for total victory, without a conviction to call terrorism evil (whomever the instigator may be) and without the resolve to win the battle first in the spirit realm through prayer. Natural insight is not enough to win this fight; one needs God's guidance. When a nation's resolve and conviction begins to weaken, it develops an ambivalence toward viewing dead children or those with missing extremities, while allowing those who killed or maimed them to walk free. I'm not talking about being hateful or mean-spirited, nor am I preaching a racist hatred of Arabs and Muslims. I'm talking about values. We cannot violate our rules of law and evidence to go after such people, but we can't let terrorists and murderers walk free for political reasons, especially when we hold in our hands the evidence to convict them. What I *am* talking about is God's love that includes justice, but not vengeance.

If we are to win the overall battle against terrorism, we must win it first in Israel. I believe in order to do that, we must also take some clear and concise steps toward that end. Many of the things America needs for this, in fact, are already in place. Wanting to send a clear message to terrorists that their reign of terror is over, President Trump has pushed for the passage of the Taylor Force Act, named after a young American MBA student at Vanderbilt University's Owen Graduate School of Management.

The excitement of a trip to Israel permeated the group strolling along a boardwalk in Jaffa when suddenly Bashar Massalha, a knife-wielding Palestinian, attacked those on the promenade, fatally stabbing Force and wounding ten others, five critically. On a school-sponsored trip to study Israeli start-up companies, Taylor, a US Army veteran, was a graduate of West Point and had served in Iraq and Afghanistan. Having safely navigated the dangerous sands of those two countries, he would now travel home from the Middle East in a flag-draped coffin, the victim of a terrorist.

Elliott Abrams, former deputy national security adviser, wrote of Force's murder:

> In a grotesque example of glorification of terror, official PA television covered the murderer's funeral and

referred to him as a "shahid" (an Arabic word clearly meaning "martyr" in this context) eleven times; the official PA newspaper also said he "died as a martyr. . . . Perhaps Palestinian leaders will find other donors to make up the shortfall [caused by cutting off funds], or perhaps they and a majority of Palestinians would rather forgo the assistance than stop honoring terrorists like Taylor Force's killer as "martyrs." But we will have taken a stand; we will have made it clear that we find such conduct intolerable.[116]

As a result of the murder, Republican senators Lindsey Graham, Dan Coats, Ted Cruz, Bob Corker, and Roy Blunt introduced the Taylor Force Act, a bill designed to stop economic aid to the Palestinian Authority. Funds designated to the PA would no longer be available to a state sponsor of terrorism—the same entity that has for decades ludicrously been called Israel's "partner for peace."

The Palestinian Authority is well-known for its Martyrs Fund that compensates families of terrorists who are killed, incapacitated, or jailed as a result of attacks on Israelis. This onerous fund has sometimes been labeled "pay for slay" when fanatics are summarily rewarded for violence. Money to support the fund has been skimmed from payments to the PA—ostensibly donations by Western nations in support of the Palestinian people.

According to Middle Eastern scholar Bassam Tawil of the Gatestone Institute:

> The Western-funded Palestinian Authority (PA) government, through its various institutions, provides a monthly salary and different financial benefits to jailed Palestinian terrorists and their families. Upon their release, they will continue to receive financial aid, and are given top priority when it comes to employment in the public sector. Their chances of getting a job with the PA government are higher than those who went to university, because by carrying out an attack against Jews they become heroes, entitled to a superior job and salary.[117]

In early 2018, the US Congress voted to penalize the PA for its terrorist-support policy. The Taylor Force Act cut funding to the PA by $200 million until it halted its onerous reward system for terrorists and their families. Australia soon followed suit, but other Western allies have so far resisted such a move.

Itamar Marcus, founder of the Palestinian Media Watch, a group that monitors the PA, responded to the action:

> "The international community, first of all, has to recognize that the Palestinian Authority paying salaries to terrorists is really a symptom of the fundamental

problem and that is that the Palestinian Authority sees killing Israelis, killing Jews as something heroic. . . . So the Palestinian Authority has put these killers on a pedestal. They've turned them into heroes and role models for the Palestinian people. By now, they can't even back off. They can't even backtrack. They are going to keep rewarding these killers with the money that they're getting, to a large extent, from foreign donors. . . . We've got Abdallah Barghouti. . .I would say the most notorious Palestinian mastermind of terror. He built the bombs for suicide bombings of Sbarro restaurant, Zion Square, Hebrew University; killed Americans, killed Europeans, killed altogether 67 people. He's serving 67 life sentences, these are among the 67 people, and he's already also received about $200,000...and he will continue receiving a salary, eventually receiving $3,500 a month."[118]

Mahmoud Abbas, chairman of the PA, vowed to distribute every cent to those who murder Jews:

"By Allah, even if we have only a penny left it will only be spent on the families of the martyrs and prisoners and only afterward will it be spent on the rest of the people."[119]

How much do imprisoned terrorists receive in compensation from the Palestinian Authority? An article in the official PA paper is very informative:

> Government resolution #19 of 2010: . . .
>
> The minimum salary for a prisoner, to be paid to him from the beginning of his detention and for up to 3 years, is 1400 Shekels [$376 USD]. Prisoners who have been imprisoned between 3 and 5 years will receive 2,000 Shekels [$538]. Those imprisoned between 5 and 10 years will receive 4,000 Shekels [$1075]. Those imprisoned between 10 and 15 years will receive 6,000 Shekels [$1613]. Those imprisoned between 15 and 20 years will receive 7,000 Shekels [$1882]. Those imprisoned between 20 and 25 years will receive 8,000 Shekels [$2150]. Those imprisoned between 25 and 30 years will receive 10,000 Shekels [$2688]. Those who have been imprisoned 30 years or more will receive 12,000 Shekels [$3226].

That adds up to quite a tidy sum over the course of a prisoner's lifetime incarceration. It sends a very loud and clear message: It really *does* pay PA terrorists to murder "infidels," and especially Jews.

When the Taylor Force Act was passed in both houses of Congress, House Chairman Ed Royce of California said of the bill:

Too many grieving families go to sleep every night knowing that money is changing hands as a reward for the violence that killed their loved ones.

With this bill, we are using the weight of U.S. law to help see that no more families—American, Israeli, or anyone—join their tragic ranks.

We do this in the name of one brave American, Taylor Force, to honor the memories of all victims and, importantly, help prevent future victims.[120]

President Trump signed the bill into law on March 23, 2018.

It is my belief that areas of Foreign Policy and National Security will continue to dominate the debate for political elections over the next few decades, as will the question of "How do we win the war against terrorism?" As I write this, I see winning the war on terror as one of the most fundamental avenues for securing a peaceful future. For the first time in history we must fight a war against a deadly religious ideal, Wahhabism, rather than only a political ideal or a madman bent on taking over the world. We can no longer tolerate every belief, hoping that will somehow lead to all of us getting along. Some beliefs in the world are, indeed, damningly deadly.

As our nation enters more deeply into the twenty-first century, we citizens truly face the greatest threat ever to America's existence and our way of life. While atheistic Communism once posed the greatest potential of a new imperialistic culture, that threat significantly decreased with the disintegration of the Soviet Union and the end of the Cold War. The current struggle we face in the war on terrorism is no longer just a fight for the supremacy of a political ideology through military might; it is now a battle for hearts and minds through the twisting of truth that turns our enemies into zealous sociopaths willing to give their lives to murder others. This is not a religion such as Christianity that can be practiced within most cultures transforming them to righteousness through love. It is a tyrannical system that brutally overpowers cultures and governments and dictates its own version of truth. The repressive Taliban government is perhaps the best example of what the late Bin Laden and the Wahhabis, a strictly conservative Muslim sect, really want the world to look like. With Islamism becoming the force empowering impoverished nations against their economic superiors, the greatest threat to our country today is a foreign policy that denies truth for the sake of a house-of-cards prosperity coupled with a lack of resolve to win the war on terror.

In this age of moral relativism, political correctness, fear of offending others, self-justification, and liberalism, we sympathize with the murderer and blame the victim; we too often point fingers at the rape victim and make excuses for the rapist; we blame the innocent for the attacks that kill and maim while the attackers incredibly become "freedom fighters."

In a culture where wickedness is condoned, the innocent suffer, frequently victimized by the criminal, the courts, and the media. We rationalize this grotesque game we play to justify our lack of moral virtue and to make ourselves feel better.

Those of Isaiah's time were little different than people today. They, too, called evil good and good evil, and thereby provoked a dire warning from God. Rather than being smart and skillful, they were woefully ignorant. Having had their understanding blinded, they seemed unaware that God is all-knowing and cannot be deceived by feeble attempts to rationalize.

According to His precepts, sin is sin; murder is murder; evil is evil. This will not change no matter how we attempt to minimize it. *We* may change; we may try to bend God's laws to suit our own desires and purposes, but God has stated unequivocally that *He* does not change. Every man will one day stand before God and be judged according to his actions—moral and immoral.

Many seem to believe that the United States needs to return to the more isolationistic stance we took at the beginning of the twentieth century and look after our own, letting the rest of the world take care of itself. I don't believe this isolationism is possible any longer in a world that can send emails, tweets, and television broadcasts around the globe in mere seconds, and where journeys that once took months now require only hours. We have come a long way from Jules Verne's fantastic idea of going *Around the World in Eighty Days* to a time that satellites circle the globe in about ninety minutes. Also, since more and more of our consumer products are manufactured abroad today, Americans are irreversibly tied to the rest of the world as never before.

When Wahhabis call us "polytheists" and "crusaders," that is more than just a demonization of our point of view or a misunderstanding of who we are. When we hear that pamphlets are circulated calling American Christians polytheists because of our belief in the Trinity, we too often just shake our heads and mark their materials as "irrelevant religious stuff." However, when Wahhabis call us "polytheists," they are marking us as targets of jihad, little more than animals for the slaughter. Brutally murdering *mushrikun* ("polytheists") is to them an act of worship and devotion just as it was for the original followers of Muhammad ibn Abd al-Wahhab in the mid-1700s.

We often mistakenly think of the Crusades as having been the horrific blunder by the Church of the Middle Ages or the mascot of the local Christian school's basketball team. Conversely, Wahhabis speak of Crusaders as the evil force that wrested Jerusalem and the Noble Sanctuary from them—a power they see as being gathered to wipe out Islam in the same way that *jihadists* are imbued with the aim of extinguishing Judaism and Christianity. In their minds, it also lowers their adversaries to a status of something less than human, as was exemplified by Sallah al-Din's breaking of his peace treaty with the Crusaders to recapture Jerusalem. Jihadists believe there is no need to keep one's word to "apes and pigs."

Countless wars of the past were launched because of religious differences, but never before had those conflicts aimed at eradicating the foe's ideology from the face of the earth. This brings a spiritual dimension to today's war on terrorism. It is a battle against a group that aspires to become martyrs and will tolerate no cease-fires. Such a war cannot be decided without a tremendous dedication to truth and prayer and actions designed to win this battle for hearts and minds in the spiritual realm. We must support righteousness, not relativity, as the basis for rule of law and our relationships with other nations.

The Bible tells us that the "love of money is the root of all evil" (see 1 Timothy 6:10). This has never been more evident than it is today when we watch much of what is good and holy in our nation being traded away for economic gain. While money is indeed nice to have, we need to realize that it is certainly not more valuable than God's blessings of freedom and security.

The war on terrorism cannot be won by vowing to defeat the jihadists on one hand while trying to appease them on the other. We need to realize that the major front in this war is the line drawn through the heart of Jerusalem.

Though liberals in the United States have painted the struggle of the Palestinians as a political revolution for freedom from oppression, no other nation in the world has strictly targeted civilians in order to overthrow its enemies. The war fought by terrorists is a war on innocents. Fanatics don't care who their victims are as long as it gets them headlines, even if it means killing babies and children, as has happened all too often. The truth must be recognized: Abbas, Arafat before him, and those aligned with them are not "freedom fighters";

they are terrorists. Israel's struggle against the PA, Hamas, Islamic Jihad, ISIS, and other such organizations is her own war on terror.

How can we ignore an ally's fight against terrorism trying to force those allies to appease the terrorists, while expecting to win our own skirmishes? Terrorists are terrorists, and if we hope to win the battle against them, we have to treat them all as criminals, not diplomats. If a man breaks into your home to steal something or harm your family, you don't negotiate with him about which rooms he can occupy; you dispatch him, or at the least, have him arrested! We can no longer afford to legitimize terrorism as a negotiating technique to win more concessions from sovereign governments. As we have seen, there will be no appeasing these thugs with their desire to have it all.

In mid-October 2003, I attended the initial Jerusalem Summit, a forum designed to discuss establishing peace in the Middle East. I had the honor of being the keynote speaker on the first evening of the conference, alongside world leaders and media celebrities who also spoke during those three days. Speakers included such men as Israeli prime minister Benjamin Netanyahu, director of the Middle East Forum Daniel Pipes, Israeli minister of tourism Benny Elon, the Honorable Richard Perle, syndicated columnist Cal Thomas, and Ambassador Dr. Alan Keyes. Interestingly enough, the theme of this introductory summit was "Winning the War on Terrorism through Moral Clarity," with the scripture Zechariah 8:19 on the cover of the program: ". . . so love truth and peace."

As he addressed the conference, Prime Minister Netanyahu had this to say:

> "Conscience is a moral compass. Conscience is absent in some societies and they endorse terrorism. Terrorism is deliberate and systematic action to kill innocent civilians. Israel is fighting terrorism. But the UN doesn't make the distinction between these two kinds of 'violence,' because that would say some of the UN members are perpetuators of war crimes, or terrorism. . . .
>
> The UN will not stop the terrorists; only an alliance of free states led by the US, geared to bring down regimes that fuel and propagate terrorism, can do that. We must implant values and morality in civilizations. Salvation will not come from the UN. . . .
>
> The Israeli Defense Forces must continue to fight terrorism, for Israel's survival as a nation, and to uphold justice and morality."[121]

The minister of Strategic Cooperation between the US and Israel, Uzi Landau, added this:

> "No cause justifies terror. . .Israel is a small target; America is the big one. But we are on the front line. If terror is not defeated here, it will move to the US and to Europe. Our war is a war of free societies against terror."[122]

And as Ambassador Keyes noted:

"In the wake of September 11th we should have taken a stand clearly and unequivocally, that if you practice terrorism you lose your claim to legitimate participation in all and any international processes whatsoever. . . .

The hope and heritage of righteousness and faith. . .says, 'Come what may, do evil what it will, God is God and I shall stand for Him.' This, I believe, is the moral heritage that transcends any struggle for evil. . . . We shall fight the fight as it is necessary in the world but we shall win it first in our own souls and spirit. So that at the end of the day we shall stand—not as people who have defeated evil, but as people who have once again vindicated the truth that—come what may—you cannot crush out that faith which holds on forever to the righteous will of God."[123]

CHAPTER 17

WOLVES IN SHEEP'S CLOTHING

Do not let me fall into their hands.
For they accuse me of things I've never done;
with every breath they threaten me with violence.

(PSALM 27:12 NLT)

f the United States would resolutely step forward to declare the Palestinian Authority a terrorist organization and remove it once and for all from being a valid representative to negotiate for the Palestinians, this would send a clear message that terrorism no longer pays. Second, it would clear the way for a legitimate group to arise from the indigenous Palestinians. This would come through municipal and rural council elections as Israel and Jordan had first planned in the late 1980s. Such a move would be a tremendously positive one toward bringing peace to the region. The Palestinian people can never have peace, nor can Israel, so long as a terrorist organization presides over their destinies.

Furthermore, once the PA is placed back on the list as a terrorist organization, the US government should freeze its billions of dollars in assets and imprison, or at least allow Israel to imprison, its leaders. Such actions would be the next step in winning the war on terrorism and putting the PA on trial for its crimes. Then the billions of dollars that Mahmoud Abbas has tucked away to support his schemes could be released and used to build schools and establish a Palestinian economy and democracy. This is something that neither Yasser Arafat nor Abbas has ever done since Israel has turned lands over to PA jurisdiction.

First, Arabs need to be required to end the Palestinian Refugee problem by welcoming refugees into their countries just as Israel, Germany, the United States, Jordan, and other nations have done with other refugee groups.

Palestinian refugee camps are the world's longest-standing facilities of their kind, and the *only* ones where children and grandchildren of those in the camps have ever been considered refugees as well. Jordan has been the only Middle Eastern nation willing to grant citizenship to those within its borders. Neither Lebanon nor Syria, or any other Arab nation has offered to do so. Those in the camps have not been allowed to settle elsewhere.

The blame for their predicament has been erroneously laid squarely on Israel and the war fought in 1949. After seventy years, the Palestinians continue to be little more than pawns in the game played by the Arab States to de-legitimize the state of Israel in any way they can.[124]

Perhaps in light of the violence they breed, the refugee camps are Israel's problem, but they cannot truly be considered her responsibility. The refugees have grown from 700,000 to over 4 million under the watchful eyes of the UN and the Arab League—a vast disgraced and disgruntled horde with no hopes of a home or a homeland. No wonder they become suicide bombers!

According to Dr. Alex Safian, head of the Committee for Accuracy in Middle East Reporting in America:

> Palestinians still live in refugee camps, even when the camps are in Palestinian Authority controlled areas, because the PLO opposes and prevents refugee resettlement. As the PLO slogan goes, A Palestinian refugee never moves out of his camp except to return home (ie, to Israel). While the PLO has done its best to keep Palestinians in refugee camps, Israel has done its best to move Palestinians out of the camps and into new homes.[125]

While other nations have dealt with refugees often not even of their own making, Arab States have always refused to take in those they call "brothers." The refugee status came not because the Israelis forced them out, but because the Arab nations ordered them to "Get out so that we can get in."[126] After agreeing to a cease-fire with Israel in 1949, the Arab states forcibly expelled 900,000 Jews from their lands, all of which Israel absorbed. This figure does not include the flow of European displaced persons following World War II.

The United States welcomed refugees from Vietnam, Cuba, and even the Iran–Iraq war to the point that there are thought to be about 3.5 million Arab US citizens today, and it is increasing by roughly 100,000 per year. The Arab states need to do the same with the Palestinian refugees and the question of "right of return"[127] would quickly vanish.

The late Egyptian leader Gamal Abd al-Nasser said, "The return of the refugees will mean the end of Israel."[128] The Arabs need to discard what they believe to be their trump card in favor of doing the humanitarian thing of helping their fellow Arabs. They must dismantle these terrorist incubation centers and grant the refugees real homes instead of only transitory housing.

Land for peace should no longer be an option until a legitimate representative of the Palestinian people is raised. The current Palestinian populace comprises a brainwashed people. These are the ones who danced in the streets when news of the attacks of September 11 reached their towns and villages. These are the people who raise their children to become suicide bombers and dress their sons as guerilla fighters with toy automatic weapons, while having their daughters dip their hands in liquid symbolizing Israeli blood.[129] These are the people who celebrate Israeli deaths because of suicide attacks as Jewish doctors treat Arab casualties from those same attacks. We must find a way to reverse the cycle of this rabid anti-Semitism in the Palestinian territories.

Until a legitimate, non-terrorism-tainted Palestinian leadership emerges, there is no single person or even recognized leadership with whom Israel can negotiate. Intervention is needed to develop such a group and reverse the propagation of hatred in Palestinian-controlled areas. This is not a role for Israel or even the United States to assume. Instead, it should be handled in cooperation with an Arab partner such as Jordan, or basically the same plan Israel and Jordan were working on in the late 1980s.

Second, we need to fervently fight the racism of anti-Semitism and anti-Zionism. This hatred is the fuel that breeds, feeds, and spreads terrorism and suicide bombers. The United States should not financially bolster, nor should it supply weapons to, nations that regularly broadcast anti-Semitic television programming or endorse anti-Semitic literature.

The war on terrorism is a battle for hearts and minds, but only God can touch a person's heart and change it. While taking these steps politically would be a tremendous move toward a return to truth as a governing principle in the US, such steps will likely never be taken without an almost overwhelming return to God in our nation. Presently, though, the US remains contaminated with relativism and humanism—falsely thinking that our money, education, and charm will suffice.

In Acts 1:8, what is often called the Great Commission, Jesus told the disciples "you shall be witnesses to Me in Jerusalem, and in all Judea and Samaria, and to the end of the earth" (NKJV). Sadly, this Great Commission has become the Great *Omission*. Christ's love is no longer taught in Judea and Samaria (the area of the West Bank) as God had intended. If we are to reverse the hatred that fuels Palestinian terrorism, then we need to return to God's initial instructions to the church.

I believe that the way we handle this war on terrorism will greatly determine where the United States ends up during the events of the book of Revelation, especially in how we react from here on out to the battle terrorists are fighting to control Jerusalem. Is America headed for a great awakening and a revival? Or are we headed for the rude awakening of discovering our confidence in our place in the world has been misplaced?

Prophecy also indicates that we are ultimately heading toward an event that will dwarf the impact of 9/11, and could either bring about the end of our nation, or its salvation. To answer that question, we must first come to grips with what became the greatest moral issue of the twentieth century and has proliferated in the twenty-first.

CHAPTER 18

THE MENACE OF ANTI-SEMITISM

The voice of thy brother's blood crieth unto me
from the ground.

(GENESIS 4:10 KJV)

f God's hedge of protection had been removed from a nation founded on principles of the Word of God to the point that the Civil War erupted, what can we expect to happen if we tolerate the racism of anti-Semitism? This satanic philosophy has resurfaced today from the ashes of the fires that began in Nazi Germany in the 1920s and '30s.

The Jew-hatred that arose between the World Wars has increasingly found a home in today's Arab nations, and indeed is having a rapid rebirth in Europe and North America. History records that Germany was not the only nation in Europe that disliked the Jews. And, while anti-Semitism was for a time buried under the guilt of the

Holocaust, it was not extinguished. Nearly seven decades after the Holocaust, it has reemerged. Yet today hatred of the Jews has turned to the broader hatred of the nation of Israel. Jew-hatred now hides behind the politics of those countries that oppose Israel.

This was made painfully clear by comments in the Washington Times from a member of the House of Representatives elected from Minnesota in 2018:

> Rep. Ilhan Omar [Democrat from Minnesota and a Somali-American Muslim] told a Jewish congresswoman Sunday [March 3, 2019] that their constituents didn't elect either woman to have allegiance to a foreign country.
>
> Rep. Nita Lowey, New York Democrat, called Saturday on Ms. Omar to retract her comment made at a Wednesday event about those who "'push for allegiance to a foreign country," referring to Israel, a remark widely condemned as an anti-Semitic trope.
>
> "I am saddened that Rep. Omar continues to mischaracterize support for Israel. I urge her to retract this statement and engage in further dialogue with the Jewish community on why these comments are so hurtful," wrote Ms. Lowey.
>
> But Ms. Omar. . .one of the first two Muslim women to be elected to Congress, essentially doubled down

in her reply, despite Ms. Lowey having specified that "accus[ing] Jews of dual loyalty" was one of these "anti-Semitic tropes."...

Rep. Eliot Engel of New York and Foreign Affairs Committee chairman, called Friday for Ms. Omar to retract and apologize for the "vile anti-Semitic slur," referring to the dual-loyalty charge....

The Minnesota Republican Party reiterated its call Saturday for Ms. Omar to be removed from the House Foreign Affairs Committee.

"It appears Democrats are losing their patience, but enough is enough," said Minnesota GOP chairwoman Jennifer Carnahan in a statement. "It is time for Omar to be removed from the Committee here and now."[130]

Sadly, an avowed Muslim might be expected to make such misinformed statements, but what of oft-elected congresswoman Maxine Waters of California? In March 2018, Waters was photographed in a warm and welcoming embrace with Nation of Islam leader Louis Farrakhan. The photo was taken at an event during which Farrakhan defended the actions of PA suicide bombers as being understandable. The Anti-Defamation League labeled the NOI leader the "leading anti-Semite in the United States."[131]

Journalist Laurie Goodstein wrote in an article for the *New York Times*:

"I'm not a Chicken Little who's always yelling, 'It's worse than it's ever been!' But now I think it's worse than it's ever been," said Deborah E. Lipstadt, a professor of Holocaust history at Emory University in Atlanta and the author of a planned book on anti-Semitism.

Ms. Lipstadt said she did not wish to be seen as alarmist, because in some ways "things have never been better" for Jews in America.

But she likened anti-Semitism to a herpes infection that lies dormant and re-emerges at times of stress. It does not go away, no matter how "acculturated" Jews have become in America . . .[132]

Newspapers around the world are noting the rise and new openness of anti-Semitism exemplified by remarks of prominent men and women. These remarks differ little from those of Hitler's Nazi Minister of Propaganda Paul Joseph Goebbels on, of all dates, September 11—but in 1937, not 2001:

Who are those responsible for this catastrophe? Without fear, we want to point the finger at the Jew as the inspirer, the author, and the beneficiary of this terrible catastrophe: look, this is the enemy of the world, the destroyer of cultures, the parasite among the nations, the son of chaos, the incarnation of evil, the ferment of decomposition, the visible demon of the decay of humanity.[133]

This doctrine of accusing the Jews of responsibility for virtually all the world's ills is resurfacing today in very similar language in the halls of European government, academia, and the media, and with worldwide distribution over the Internet. Of course, if all these ills are deemed to be because of the Jews, the next logical step would be to begin shutting them out of positions of power, taking away what they own, and boycotting their businesses—identical to the first steps Hitler took in 1933. Sadly, today's world, and especially those Arab countries that won't even allow Jews within their borders, is not far behind Hitler's gospel of "redemptive anti-Semitism" as he expressed it in 1922: "My first and foremost task will be the annihilation of the Jews. . .until all Germany has been cleansed."[134]

Just as this traditional anti-Semitism sought to deny Jews their rights as individuals in society, anti-Zionism today attacks the collective Jewish people as a nation. Just as Jews were exploited as scapegoats for their host countries' problems, Israel is being singled out today as the root of the world's evil. Thus, the events of the UN's World Conference on Racism in Durban, South Africa, in August of 2001. As far as the delegates there seemed to be concerned, racism would be a thing of the past if but one nation, Israel, could be eliminated. The most recent example of this was Israel's November 2003 General Assembly draft resolution calling for the protection of Israeli children from Palestinian terrorist attacks—the first resolution introduced by Israel to the UN since 1976—which was tellingly soundly rejected by the assembly's Social, Humanitarian, and Cultural Committee, even though ironically a similar resolution to protect Palestinian children had passed just weeks before.

So-called political opposition to Israel's policies and simple Jew-hatred has also become completely indistinguishable. A statement such as "the Jews control Washington" is part of the historically anti-Semitic falsehood that the Jews aim to take over the world.

What are the Jews usually accused of? How is it that they have taken "control of the world" by proxy? What are their greatest sins? You have probably been more exposed to such anti-Semitic propaganda than you may have realized. The big three always seem to be: (1) the Jews control the media, (2) the Jews control the money, and (3) the Jews killed Jesus.

Is any of this true, though? Among the wealthiest people in the world, only six percent are Jewish. Who *does* control the money? Well, according to a BBC report, seven of the ten wealthiest heads of state in the world are Arabs; none are Jewish. Neither are the CEOs of any of the world's ten largest companies Jewish.

Do they control the media? Of the ten largest media companies in the world, only one has been run in recent years by a Jew—the Walt Disney Company—hardly a pro-Israel propaganda machine. Of the major newspapers in the US, only two are controlled by Jews—the *New York Times* and the *Boston Globe* (whose owners arguably think of themselves more as Americans than Jews and regularly run anti-Zionist articles). In Europe, much of the media is government run, and none of the government officials directing them are Jewish.

Did the Jews kill Jesus? Read your Bible. The Sanhedrin had to go to the Romans to have Jesus killed. It was the Romans who nailed Jesus to the cross and the spear of a Roman soldier that pierced His side. What of the angry mob that called for His death? I have stood in the courtyard where that happened, and you could not fit more than a hundred people inside it. The Sanhedrin would have probably rallied at least half that number. That is a pretty small sampling for which to blame an entire race of people![135] Plus, that was an awfully long time ago. No one holds the young Germans of today responsible for the Holocaust, and that was less than a century ago. How can we hold the Jews of today responsible for that indescribable act some two thousand years ago? You might as well hold the Italians responsible for the destruction of Jerusalem, because Titus was a Roman! Besides, it was the sin of all humankind that hung Jesus on the cross, not just that of only the Jews.

While anti-Semitism is assuredly on the rise in Europe, nowhere is it more vehemently expressed today than in the Arab nations. Syrian defense minister Mustafa Tlas's 1983 book, *The Matza of Zion*—an Arab variation on the medieval Christian blood libel—accuses Jews of baking Passover matzah with the blood of Muslim children. It has just been reprinted. "Sucking the blood of Arabs" has been aired repeatedly in the Arab media, for example, by Palestine Liberation

Army Col. Nadir al-Tamimi on Al Jazeera television on October 24, 2000. The official Syrian daily *Tishrin* frequently accuses Israel of somehow fabricating the Holocaust. It should also be recalled that Nazi Colonel Adolf Eichmann's sadistic deputy, Alois Brunner, found safe haven in Syria.

Former Iranian president Mahmoud Ahmadinejad was infamous for his anti-Israel diatribe. On January 11, 2006, Avner Shalev, the chairman of Yad Vashem, Jerusalem's Holocaust Museum, warned the world about the irresponsibility of Ahmadinejad's Holocaust denial statements and his call to "examine in-depth this myth."

> "Recent trends in Iran represent a clear feature of current anti-Semitism—the ties between Islamic radicals and Holocaust deniers," Shalev said in a statement. "Iran has embraced such charlatans as David Irving."
>
> Revisionist historian Irving lost a libel suit in a British court against writer Deborah Lipstadt and Penguin books. Lipstadt called Irving one of the world's most dangerous "Holocaust deniers" in her 1994 book, "Denying the Holocaust."
>
> "Sham historians" such as Irving have been totally discredited by the West but have found a "responsive audience" in Iran, "where senior officials have called the factual events of the Holocaust 'a matter of opinion,'" said Shalev.

Shalev noted that the United Nations recently recognized the importance of remembering the Holocaust "as a safeguard against the breakdown of the basic human values that underpin our civilization."[136]

As noted, Iran has never renounced its official state policy that Israel needs to be eliminated. Along with Hezbollah, Hamas, ISIS, and Islamic Jihad, the Islamic Republic of Iran must also be included among those who obstinately refuse to accept Israel's sovereignty.

Holocaust denial is a frequent theme in the Arab media, with the *Palestine Times* writing of "God's lying people" who are "the Holocaust worshippers,"[137] and the Palestinian Authority's TV channel: "No Chelmno, no Dachau, no Auschwitz, only disinfecting sites. . .the lie of extermination." The PA mufti of Jerusalem, Sheikh Sabri Ikrama, explains away the Holocaust by stating: "It is not my fault that Hitler hated the Jews. Anyway, they hate them just about everywhere."[138] Other Muslim clerics call upon worshipers in the mosques to "have no mercy on the Jews, no matter where they are, in any country. . .wherever you meet them, kill them."[139]

In another obscene and unfathomable denial of the Holocaust, Palestinian Authority spokesmen describe Israel as a "racist country that uses the same method of ethnic cleansing that Nazi Germany used against the Jews." The Jews are presented as "wild animals," "robbers," "avaricious," and "thieves" whose end will come as the will of Allah. A typical caricature in one of the official PA newspapers shows a dwarf with a Star of David, his face copied from the face of the Jew in the Nazi weekly tabloid, *Der Stürmer*, printed during the World War II years with the caption: "The disease of the century." Another cartoon shows an Israeli soldier barbecuing Arabs, taking them off the grill, and eating them one by one with relish.[140]

Esti Vebman, an expert on anti-Semitism from the Institute for the Study of Anti-Semitism and Racism at Tel Aviv University, has been following anti-Semitism in the Palestinian Authority and Arab world for years. University of Hamburg academics have concluded that many Palestinian young men today revere Adolf Hitler as a hero. It has long been noted that *Mein Kampf*, Hitler's anti-Semitic diatribe in book form, is still a bestseller in many Arab countries. And it is no surprise that the official media sources in the PA frequently compare the activities of the Israeli government to those of the Nazis. Benjamin Netanyahu, while serving as Israel's prime minister, has been portrayed as a Nazi and described as "a Zionist terrorist who is worse than Hitler."

Washington Times columnist Cal Thomas posed an intriguing comparison between President Trump and Prime Minister Netanyahu and the investigations targeting both pro-Israel leaders. Thomas concludes:

> As David M. Weinberg wrote in The Jerusalem Post in 2017, "An overwhelming majority of Israelis ascribes the last decade of stability and triumph to Netanyahu's

leadership. He may not be the ultimate paragon of virtue—what politician is? But his prudence and professionalism have best served Israel's strategic needs." Compared to the survival of Israel, the charges brought against Mr. Netanyahu are small potatoes. . . .

The point is not to excuse bad behavior in leadership, but to examine their policies to see if they promote the general welfare. In the cases of Mr. Netanyahu and Mr. Trump, they have.[141]

Incredibly, Sif Ali Algeruan of the London-based newspaper *Al-Hayat al-Jedida* wrote of the Holocaust, "It was a good day for the Jews, when the Nazi Hitler began his campaign of persecution against them." He continued:

They began to disseminate, in a terrifying manner, pictures of mass shootings is directed at them, and to invent the shocking story about the gas ovens in which, according to them, Hitler used to burn them. The newspapers are filled with pictures of Jews who were mowed down by Hitler's machine guns, and of Jews being led to the gas ovens. In these pictures they concentrated on women, babies, and old people, and they took advantage of it, in order to elicit sympathy towards them, when they demand financial reparations, contributions and grants from all over the world. The truth is that the persecution of the Jews is a myth, that the Jews dubbed "the tragedy of the Holocaust" and took advantage of, in order to elicit sympathy towards them.[142]

Palestinian terrorists practice a form of anti-Semitism that combines the Nazi dehumanization of Jews with glorifying their murders supposedly for the sake of peace and a Palestinian state. While some European countries have come a long way in facing their past and taking steps to ensure that anti-Semitism will never again become official policy, the Arab world has done nothing to douse the flames of Jew-hatred within their own borders.

CHAPTER 19

Intifada:
Insurrection

You will not fear the terror of the night,
nor the arrow that flies by da. . . .

(PSALM 91:5 ESV)

S ince the beginning of the first intifada on December 6, 1987, and then the second in September 2000, Israel has been subjected to being delegitimized in a worldwide campaign by the media and international forums by various political leaders and intellectuals. Extremists on both the Left and Right have joined together in hatred of the Jewish state. This has resulted in a dramatic increase in anti-Semitic incidents, including numerous physical assaults on Jews. Attacks on Israel's legitimacy have been accompanied by strikes on Jewish targets throughout the world, but particularly in Europe.

Anti-Semitic incidents have included bombings of synagogues and Jewish schools, vandalism and desecration of Jewish cemeteries, death threats and unprovoked violence against Jews, including murder. These hate crimes against Jewish individuals and institutions are often disguised as "anti-Zionist" actions.

Journalist Bari Weiss wrote an article for the *New York Times* on the resurgence of anti-Semitism:

> Anti-Semitism, though, isn't just a brand of bigotry. It's a conspiracy theory in which Jews play the starring role in spreading evil in the world. While racists see themselves as proudly punching down, anti-Semites perceive themselves as punching up.
>
> The Israeli writer Yossi Klein Halevi put it elegantly: "What anti-Semitism does is turn the Jews— the Jew— into the symbol of whatever a given civilization defines as its most loathsome qualities." When you look through this dark lens, you can understand how, under Communism, the Jews were the capitalists. How under Nazism, the Jews were the race contaminators. . . .
>
> European Jews must now contend with this three-headed dragon: Physical fear of violent assault, often by young Muslim men, which leads many Jews to hide evidence of their religious identity. Moral fear of ideological vilification, mainly by the far left, which causes at least some Jews to downplay their sympathies for Israel. . . .

A large number of physically violent acts committed against Jews in Europe are perpetrated by radical
Muslims. The incidents at the top of this article were not
carried out by far-right goons but by Islamists, most of
them young and some of them immigrants. . . .

Now add a third ingredient to this toxic brew: the
fashionable anti-Semitism of the far left that masquer-
ades as anti-Zionism and anti-racism.[143]

According to a CNN poll released in 2018, one in four Europeans
is anti-Semitic. One-third of those polled knew little or nothing about
the Holocaust. Another stunning revelation by the pollsters:

Americans do not fare any better. A survey carried out
[in early 2018] found that 10% of American adults were
not sure they'd ever heard of the Holocaust, rising to one
in five millennials. Half of all millennials could not name
a single concentration camp, and 45% of all American
adults failed to do so.[144]

France, with its large Muslim minority, stands out as the country
where the greatest number and most serious anti-Semitic incidents
have occurred in comparison with other countries. These include:
the physical attack and harassment of Jews all over that country, the
torching of synagogues, the desecration of cemeteries, along with

threats and dissemination of radical anti-Semitic and anti-Israel propaganda.

In 2012, a Jewish school in Toulouse was targeted, and four individuals, including three children, were murdered. In 2015, a kosher grocery was targeted by a young jihadist; four people inside the market were killed. In 2017, a Jewish woman in France was pushed to her death from a third-floor apartment by her Muslim neighbor. Perpetrators have come mainly from among young North African Muslim immigrants.

It should be noted that many, if not most, of these attacks were the result of organized action rather than spontaneous mob activity or vandalism. These ambushes are nothing but blatant manifestations of anti-Semitism involving incitement to attack Jews everywhere.

In other European countries, especially those with large Muslim populations, there have been countless serious physical onslaughts on Jews, in addition to verbal harassment, graffiti, and cemetery desecrations. Jewish community facilities have been targeted, with Jews being physically attacked in Belgium. Universities throughout Europe have become active centers of anti-Semitic and anti-Israel propaganda and threats. In Britain, Jews have been attacked and synagogues and other of their community facilities desecrated.

Numerous anti-Semitic incidents have occurred in the Scandinavian countries, especially Denmark and Sweden, whose governments have been extremely critical of Israel. In Eastern Europe and

Russia, anti-Semitic activities mostly take the form of propaganda and demonstrations. In Russia, many Jews have been injured, with synagogues and other Jewish facilities damaged. One Russian innovation has been the placing of booby-trapped signs with anti-Semitic slurs along highways. They explode when someone tries to remove them. These signs have caused one fatality and numerous injuries and have led to several copycat incidents in Ukraine.

Prominent Italian journalist Oriana Falacci strongly denounced the double standard practiced in Europe today:

> One standard for the Jews and another for Christians and Muslims, one *vis-à-vis* Jewish blood that has been spilled and another *vis-à-vis* other blood. And there is the lack of proportion between attacks on Israel, which are not political criticism but saturated with anti-Semitic terms, and what Israel actually does.[145]

An Israeli historian, Professor Robert Wistrich has noted that it is radical Muslims and not necessarily white Europeans that are leading the present wave of anti-Semitism. The Islamic world has imported anti-Semitism from Europe and "converted it to Islam" as part of the Israeli–Palestinian conflict, then exported it back to Europe and the West in general by means of the Muslim dispersion and anti-West and anti-globalization elements.

Regarding the renewed blood libels of this century, Wistrich concluded:

Arab governments are doing nothing against these fabrications, and in essence legitimize them in order to protect themselves from the wrath of their own embittered citizens, deprived of democracy, freedom of speech and basic human rights.

Against this background it is clear how millions of Muslims are prepared to believe every falsehood, including the blowing up of the World Trade Center by the Mossad.

This "Semitic" anti-Semitism is especially threatening when it is on a mission from Allah, and the 1979 revolution in Iran against the "Great Devil" (America and the "Crusader" West) and the "Jewish-Zionist Devil" bears witness to this.

This is total war, because it is mainly a religious war. Antisemitism of this kind has diverted the Jihad from its original objective and turned into a death cult.[146]

This growing trend is gradually becoming not an echo but an amplification of what happened in pre-World War II Germany. While cries against the Jews grew louder in Germany, the rest of the world simply shrugged with comments such as: "Oh, I don't think that is emblematic of all the Germans." It didn't matter if it was or not; their silence arguably made many accomplices in the murders by such "non-representative" Germans.

Are we any less guilty if we stand quietly and let the cry to kill Jews grow among Arabs and in Europe? How far do we, as a Christian nation, need to let such blatant hatred go before we do something about it? My feeling is that it has already gone too far.

There is perhaps no better sign that the spirit of antichrist is on the rise than this reemergence of rabid anti-Semitism. Satan will, of course, hate Jews first, and then Christians, because they were the first to enter a covenant with God. And we as a nation can be no less guilty for being silent about racism toward Jews. We must realize, as did Thomas Jefferson, that God's "justice cannot sleep forever." My dear friend Isser Harel once said to me, "Hitler first killed Jews, and then he killed Christians. Our cultures and our democracies are the root of the rage. If we're right, they are wrong."

September 11, 2001, was without question a tragic day in American history. It was a physical manifestation of a battle that had been lost weeks, months, and possibly years before because of a lack of fervent prayer. Osama bin Laden had been verbally attacking America for years, but the church was asleep. The demonic powers that were influencing him needed to be fervently confronted through the power of prayer—as in the time of Daniel.

Praying for the peace of Jerusalem is not praying for stones or dirt; stones don't weep or bleed. It is praying for God's protection over the lives of the citizens of Jerusalem. It is praying for revival. It is praying for God's grace to be poured out on the Bible land and all over the Middle East—prayer that demonic powers will be defeated by holy angels in a battle that cannot be seen with the natural eye. The late Mother Teresa was a prayer warrior who once told me she prayed daily for the peace of Jerusalem according to Psalm 122:6. She told me, "Love is not something you say, it's something you do." I believe that with all my heart.

The pastor of Corrie ten Boom's grandfather went to him and told him that his church was going to pray for the peace of Jerusalem. It inspired the Ten Boom family to begin praying weekly. That continued until the Nazis imprisoned several members of the Ten Boom family. The House of Israel is in a state of terror now as it was when the Ten Booms began their prayer campaign. They need the Lord to answer them in their day of terror. They need the God of Jacob to defend them. They need help from the sanctuary and strength out of Zion.

It is time for us to wake up, but will that awakening be a great awakening or a rude one? Which have we been as a nation: a blessing or a cursing to Israel?

CHAPTER 20

WHAT IS OUR
NATION'S FUTURE?

He will judge between the nations and will settle
disputes for many peoples. They will beat their swords
into plowshares and their spears into pruning hooks.
Nation will not take up sword against nation, nor will
they train for war anymore.

(ISAIAH 2:4 NIV)

For more than three decades, I have watched Islamic terrorism heading, like a whirlwind, toward our shores. America
is plunging headfirst into a lake of fire, and many are not
fully aware of it. The hour is too late to tiptoe through the tulips. After
9/11, it has become time to shout this message from the housetops: If
America is to be saved, saintly, moral, God-fearing Americans must
wake up, and wake up now!

The prophet Jeremiah said:

I appointed watchmen over you and said, "Listen to the sound of the trumpet!" But you said, "We will not listen." (Jeremiah 6:17 NIV)

According to the ancient prophet Ezekiel:

The word of the Lord came to me: "Son of man, speak to your people and say to them: 'When I bring the sword against a land, and the people of the land choose one of their men and make him their watchman, and he sees the sword coming against the land and blows the trumpet to warn the people, then if anyone hears the trumpet but does not heed the warning and the sword comes and takes their life, their blood will be on their own head. Since they heard the sound of the trumpet but did not heed the warning, their blood will be on their own head. If they had heeded the warning, they would have saved themselves. But if the watchman sees the sword coming and does not blow the trumpet to warn the people and the sword comes and takes someone's life, that person's life will be taken because of their sin, but I will hold the watchman accountable for their blood.'" (Ezekiel 33:1–6 NIV)

President Trump took office determined to halt the influx of those who would target America, both from within and without.

The Liberal Left has attempted to foil his efforts seemingly at every turn. In January 2017, the president signed an executive order barring immigration for at least ninety days from seven Muslim countries—Syria, Iraq, Iran, Libya, Somalia, Sudan, and Yemen. This move was designed to give his administration time to develop more thorough screening programs to detect terrorists. These efforts were thwarted by a liberal judge in the state of Washington whose decision called Trump's move "unconstitutional." Sadly, the voices "crying in the wilderness" have yet to be overridden by those of the watchmen whose duty it is to blow the trumpet of warning.

The sad news is that preachers in America are, by and large, not crying out. I hear hardened, secular commentators, ungodly politicians, and abrasive talk show hosts crying out in support of the Liberal Left agenda, but Christians too often remain complacent, their voices silent.

I fear that America is receiving perhaps its final call to repentance. God is now judging this nation in the same way He has judged every nation that has rejected His call and challenged His prophetic plan.

Jesus prophesied:

> "Just as it was in the days of Noah, so also will it be in the days of the Son of Man. People were eating, drinking, marrying and being given in marriage up to the day Noah entered the ark. Then the flood came and destroyed them

all. It was the same in the days of Lot. People were eating
and drinking, buying and selling, planting and building.
(Luke 17:26–28 NIV)

The inhabitants of Sodom and Gomorrah enjoyed the same prosperity as Noah's society. Ezekiel wrote:

This was the iniquity of thy sister Sodom, pride, fullness
of bread, and abundance of idleness. (Ezekiel 16:49 KJV)

They had no idea that the good times were God's final mercy
call before destruction. God judged Sodom, yet Sodom had no Bible.
America is the Bible capital of the world, with an abundance of
churches. If anyone should know what is going on, we should.

I am no prophet, but I say with Amos:

"I was neither a prophet nor the son of a prophet, but
I was a shepherd, and I also took care of sycamore-fig
trees. But the LORD took me from tending the flock and
said to me, 'Go, prophesy to my people Israel.'" (Amos
7:14–15 NIV)

I challenge you to search the ancient Scriptures, and to look up
the words *judgment, nations,* and *curses.* You will surely see that God
is not a respecter of nations; that mighty America is in big trouble.

King Josiah was only eighteen years old when God stirred his
heart over something the king had read in the Scriptures. Suddenly,

the young ruler saw that his nation had offended Almighty God and was heading toward destruction. He cried out, "God's wrath is being stored up against us" (see 2 Kings 22:11–13). Josiah truly repented and led his nation back to God.

For those who say, "America is immune; it will not happen here. There are too many godly people in America," I say, "Remember Israel!" Down through the ages, God destroyed Jerusalem and the temple again and again. There is a prophetic line drawn over which a nation may not cross; when it does, God says, "Enough!"

Many believe that the events of September 11 were not a curse. I can assure you, every family that experienced the pain of that devastating day felt wretched as they lost loved ones. That day of infamy was certainly not a blessing! The fanatics who carried out that attack were religious to the extreme, but I can assure you, there is nothing peaceful about their brand of religion.

Where are those who weep for America, who grieve for her sins of arrogance? Millions of Christians have closed their eyes to what is happening in the land of the Bible. Even some preachers are telling jokes in the pulpit, and mocking those who are weeping over the attempt by some of America's leaders to stick their fingers in the apple of God's eye. (See Zechariah 2:8.)

Read the words of Zechariah concerning the nations that touch Jerusalem:

On that day, when all the nations of the earth are gathered against her, I will make Jerusalem an immovable rock for all the nations. All who try to move it will injure themselves. . . .

Then the clans of Judah will say in their hearts, "The people of Jerusalem are strong, because the LORD Almighty is their God." On that day I will make the clans of Judah like a firepot in a woodpile, like a flaming torch among sheaves. They will consume all the surrounding peoples right and left, but Jerusalem will remain intact in her place. . . .

On that day I will set out to destroy all the nations that attack Jerusalem. And I will pour out on the house of David and the inhabitants of Jerusalem a spirit of grace and supplication. They will look on me, the one they have pierced, and they will mourn for him as one mourns for an only child, and grieve bitterly for him as one grieves for a firstborn son. (Zechariah 12:3, 5–6, 9–10 NIV)

On that day his feet will stand on the Mount of Olives, east of Jerusalem, and the Mount of Olives will be split in two from east to west, forming a great valley, with half of the mountain moving north and half moving south. . . .

This is the plague with which the LORD will strike all the nations that fought against Jerusalem: Their flesh will rot while they are still standing on their feet, their eyes will rot in their sockets, and their tongues will rot in their mouths. (Zechariah 14:4, 12 NIV)

What happens when a nation is cursed? God's hand of protection is lifted, the powers of hell given free reign. God forgive anyone who does not see the warning signs! Even today's weather patterns seem to bear out these forewarnings. There is not a person living who can recall such days of disastrous floods and tinder-dry forests that have caused the ignition of countless fires of devastating proportions. At the same time, our winters have grown colder than any seen in modern times, while the wicked heat of the summer takes a rising toll each year. The warnings of this country's falling away from God's protection and guidance seem to be everywhere we look.

That is why I mentioned 2 Chronicles 7:14 in the introduction. It is an extremely hope-giving scripture, but its context is in the midst of a warning for Solomon. Look for a moment at the entire passage:

Thus Solomon finished the house of the LORD and the king's house; and Solomon successfully accomplished all that came into his heart to make in the house of the LORD and in his own house.

Then the LORD appeared to Solomon by night, and said to him: "I have heard your prayer, and have chosen this place for Myself as a house of sacrifice. When I shut up heaven and there is no rain, or command the locusts to devour the land, or send pestilence among My people, if My people who are called by My name will humble themselves, and pray and seek My face, and turn from their wicked ways, then I will hear from heaven, and will forgive their sin and heal their land. . . .

"But if you turn away and forsake My statutes and My commandments which I have set before you, and go and serve other gods, and worship them, then I will uproot them from My land which I have given them; and this house which I have sanctified for My name I will cast out of My sight, and will make it a proverb and a byword among all peoples.

"And as for this house, which is exalted, everyone who passes by it will be astonished and say, 'Why has the LORD done thus to this land and this house?' Then they will answer, 'Because they forsook the LORD God of their fathers, who brought them out of the land of Egypt, and embraced other gods, and worshiped them and served them; therefore He has brought all this calamity on them." (2 Chronicles 7: 11–14, 19–24 NKJV)

Solomon was being warned. And given our condition today, this is valuable advice. America has idols worse than any manmade stone edifice Solomon could have erected: idols of relativism and greed. With them we have made the laws and compassion of God seem meaningless. We have turned our backs on Him by accepting as normal such abominations. God said if we did that, we would be given over to the reprobate minds that perform such acts. (See Romans 1:21–32.) If that is the case, how far are we from acquiescing to a burgeoning New World Order?

CHAPTER 21

THE PRICE OF PROSPERITY

For the love of money is the root of all kinds of evil. And
some people, craving money, have wandered from the
true faith and pierced themselves with many sorrows.

(1 TIMOTHY 6:10 NLT)

God sent us the prosperity of the 1920s to show that He loves us, but we still didn't listen, so He sent us the Depression as an increasing attempt to inspire us to "call on His Name, humbling ourselves and praying, seeking his face, and turning from our wicked ways." But we did not. Thus, the world turned its back on the Jews, and Hitler's genocidal extermination machine closed in on them. Few acted to help until it was too late. A third of the world's Jewish population—six million men, women, and children—were lost with little hope of salvation.

Look around: We are going through much the same cycle today. The prosperity of the 1990s made us even more selfish than we were in the decades before. September 11 and its aftermath hit us far worse than the stock market crash on Black Tuesday of 1929.

What was one of the main causes of the Depression? A new concept that had been introduced at that time called "buying on credit." The entire nation had borrowed to buy things. The economy soared because of increased consumer spending, and when the debts were called in, too few had the cash to pay. America lapsed into the Depression, and then World War II.

America had enjoyed prosperity in the '90s, but terrorists struck on September 11, 2001, and then a recession followed. Since that time, our country has been drawn into conflict after conflict—Iraq, Afghanistan, North Korea, with the looming prospect of another Cold War with Russia, and possibly a confrontation of some sort with Iran. And again the Jews hang on the edge of a precipice as anti-Zionism arises the world over. As the US and Great Britain have been the only nations with enough moral backbone to confront terrorism, so we are also the only nations that can stand up and defend Israel. We didn't in the 1920s and 1930s. Will we do it now?

Isaiah 24:6 declares: "Therefore a curse consumes the earth; its people must bear their guilt. Therefore earth's inhabitants are burned up, and very few are left" (NIV).

Does God fight nations? Yes, He does. Zechariah 14:2–3 states that He will fight all nations that come against Jerusalem. Why would we not allow the only democracy in the Middle East to join us in fighting Iraq? It was simply because we feared the anti-Semitic nations in the area; those who hate Israel, and are afraid they will withhold the oil that lubricates our economy.

President Abraham Lincoln saw the Civil War as the judgment of God upon a prejudiced nation. In a similar context, in 1917 the Balfour Declaration outlined the reestablishment of a Jewish homeland in Palestine, what would be a prophetic and miraculous event. Not only did the U.S. State Department reject these plans, the government caved in to anti-Semitic pressure and passed a major act restricting immigration in the 1920s.

The irony is that Hitler did not come into power until 1933, and yet an immigration policy to keep Russian Jews out of America would be used also to keep out Germans, Poles, and Jews from other nations who were attempting to escape Hitler's "Final Solution." The door had been resolutely shut before Jews even had a chance to knock!

Founded in 1865, the Ku Klux Klan reached its zenith in 1920. The '20s saw those feared hooded "White Knights" sweep across the South like a plague, thanks to the support of such anti-Semitic figures as automotive magnate Henry Ford, who also financed a massive reprinting of the fictitious *Protocols of the Learned Elders of Zion*.

I am firmly convinced that the judgment of God fell upon America over this nation's anti-Semitic plague. The government seemed to coldly close its heart and ears to the cries of six million Jews—over a million of whom were children.

The stock market crashed on Black Tuesday, October 29, 1929. America went from what had been an amazing prosperity to becoming an economic dust bowl as the plague of the Great Depression swept across the land.

However, God had been moving to capture America's attention for more than a century before this tragedy, through what was called the Great Awakening. The movement was led by such evangelists as Jonathan Edwards, George Whitefield, and Gilbert Tennent. But America's heart remained hardened.

Just as Abraham Lincoln proclaimed that the Civil War was God's judgment for the bigotry behind slavery, the Great Depression was surely God's judgment for the bigotry of anti-Semitism that was buried in the souls of many Americans. Seeds of that same anti-Semitism that fed and fueled the Holocaust are alive and well in twenty-first century America, no matter how dormant they seem to recently have been.

A battle is being waged between darkness and light, Babylon and Jerusalem. This is a sure sign that Jesus is coming soon! The Bible says: "From the tribe of Issachar, there were 200 leaders of the tribe with their relatives. All these men understood the signs of the times and knew the best course for Israel to take" (1 Chronicles 12:32 NLT).

God is calling today to those who understand the times. For more than four decades I have seen this battle coming and have been crying out. The vast majority of Christians laughed in disbelief. But that laughter stopped on 9/11.

The battle has not been won. Like a tidal wave, judgment is heading to America. Only the remnant that hears what the Spirit of God is saying can stop this coming slaughter. America is cursing what God has blessed (Israel). Does the Bible reveal what will happen to a nation that does this? A thousand times, yes! Has America's future been revealed? A thousand times, yes!

Satan hates the Jews and must stop Israel before the Messiah returns to end his reign. Prophecy declares that Jerusalem will be united and in Jewish hands when Messiah comes, but Satan's goal is to divide Jerusalem and stop the prophetic clock that will seal his doom.

We are living in onerous days, when men's hearts fail them for fear! The Bible tells us to be like the wise virgins, not the foolish ones, and to prepare for His coming. (See Matthew 25.) The Bible says we can know the season and times, even if we don't know the day or the hour. We are in the last days. Look up, for our redemption draws near!

Neither you nor I can remain silent. The Scriptures call upon us to speak out. (See Isaiah 62:1.) The battle being fought over Jerusalem is not political—it is prophetical. It's not a foreign policy battle—it is a heavenly battle! The rebirth of Israel was not an unexpected gift from God Almighty—it was prophesied to happen. America's very existence, however, *is* a gift from God Almighty!

America cannot win a battle of defiance against God—no one can! People of the world's greatest superpower will wake up one day in total shock, because of our pride and arrogance. We need, instead, to shake ourselves so that we are ready for that day rather than letting it catch us sleeping.

The church in America, by and large, does not fear God. The Bible warns in Revelation, chapter 22, over and over: "Behold, I am coming quickly!" Too many pastors mock the message of the coming of the Lord and fail to preach it from their pulpits. They overlook the prophetic words of Revelation 22:16 that Jesus is the root and offspring of David. Polluted prophets in the pulpits of America are deceiving the sheep, leading them to the slaughter with their demon-inspired doctrines.

God's eternal covenant with Israel is mocked. Too many of our religious leaders fill their Sundays with the unscriptural doctrines of man while rejecting Israel, yet they hold in their hands a Bible written by Jews who all understood the prophetic truths concerning Israel. These pastors, priests, and rabbis beheld with horror-filled eyes the events of 9/11, but weeks later went back to sleep, dumbing down their congregations with messages from mere mortals rather than from the Holy Word of God.

Today's New Age doctrine from hell feeds Jew-hatred and is robbing the church of its eternal purpose: The Great Commission of being a witness in Jerusalem, Judea, and Samaria; and of hearing God—instead of blindly cooperating with the powers of darkness intent on destroying America and Israel.

The curses of Deuteronomy 28 are heading full speed toward America, and the blessings set forth in that same chapter are being snatched away from our land by an angry God who hears the cries of the more than sixty-one million aborted children murdered in

America, all in the name of self and freedom. That computes to approximately 4,000 abortions per day, or one child every twenty seconds. Some states have even opted to permit gruesome and unthinkable partial-birth abortions:

> Partial-Birth Abortion is a procedure in which the abortionist pulls a living baby feet-first out of the womb and into the birth canal (vagina), except for the head, which the abortionist purposely keeps lodged just inside the cervix (the opening to the womb). The abortionist punctures the base of the baby's skull with a surgical instrument, such as a long surgical scissors or a pointed hollow metal tube called a trochar. He then inserts a catheter (tube) into the wound, and removes the baby's brain with a powerful suction machine. This causes the skull to collapse, after which the abortionist completes the delivery of the now-dead baby.[147]

Second Thessalonians 2:11–12 reminds us:

> For this reason God will send upon them a deluding influence so that they will believe what is false, in order that they all may be judged who did not believe the truth, but took pleasure in wickedness. (NASB)

Jesus mentioned deception as one of the last signs before His return. The book of Revelation describes a day when countless billions of people will be deluded by the spirits of demons. (See Revelation 16:12–16.) They choose human favor over the favor of the Lord, wanting to sit next to "great men" in their nation's capitols rather than sitting next to Jesus in the New Jerusalem; fearing that if they rock the boat by speaking the truth their names will be erased from their earthly leaders' list, rather than fearing that their name might be removed from the Lamb's Book of Life.

Yes, we are living in the end times, and Israel is God's alarm clock! The nations are enraged over this bone in their throat: Israel. (See Revelation 11:16–18 NASB.) Tiny Israel is God's bait to entrap an arrogant, God-despising world, shaking its fist in the face of Holy God; preferring to boast over rebuilding the doomed Tower of Babel, eternally cursed by God rather than rebuilding the tabernacle of David by blessing Israel.

> The Lord will go out and fight against those nations, as he fights on a day of battle. On that day his feet will stand on the Mount of Olives. (Zechariah 14:2–4 NIV)

> The ancient Jewish prophets saw the day we are living in and clearly warned that God would defend Israel and would guard Israel. (See Zechariah 12:8–9.)

> "Blessed is he who watches, and keeps his garments, lest he walk naked and they see his shame." And they

gathered them together to the place called in Hewbrew, Armageddon. (Revelation 16:15–16 NKJV)

Why must the church stand with Israel? Because God does. It is part of the church's eternal purpose—and even a promise of mighty power is made if the church would fulfill the Great Commission regarding Jerusalem, Judea, and Samaria.

This is the midnight hour. If God's remnant sleeps, America as we know it will perish! If we choose instead to wake up and be the church again that God called us to be, the hope we have before us is far greater than anything we have seen in the past.

I'm telling you the truth—Jesus is coming back, and He is coming back soon! Just how ready we are for that day will make all the difference in eternity.

CHAPTER 22

HOPE FOR A RESTLESS WORLD

I am thy fellowservant, and of thy brethren that have

the testimony of Jesus: worship God: for the testimony

of Jesus is the spirit of prophecy.

(REVELATION 19:10 KJV)

f the church worldwide will stand up as the light Jesus intended her to be, the politics of nations will right themselves. Legislation can't change people's hearts, but the touch of God can! It is more important to have a nation that prays, and equally desirable to have a president who prays.

Donald Trump grew up in Jamaica Estates, a Queens neighborhood populated by many Jews. He and his family were Presbyterian by church affiliation, and perhaps some of his can-do attitude can be attributed to the early sermons of their pastor, the late Dr. Norman

Vincent Peale of Manhattan's Marble Collegiate Church, and the minister's popular philosophy of the "power of positive thinking."

Even before clinching the nomination of the Republican Party, Trump announced the formation of an Evangelical Advisory Board. The purpose of the group was outlined in a statement from the candidate:

> "I have such tremendous respect and admiration for this group and I look forward to continuing to talk about the issues important to Evangelicals, and all Americans, and the common sense solutions I will implement when I am President."[148]

In the multitude of attempts by the Liberal Left to vilify President Trump, it is rare to see an objective article written or news story aired about the 45th commander-in-chief. Kid gloves are in short supply with this president. No wonder Trump so often uses the term "fake news" when referring to the media.

Despite a booming economy, a much lower unemployment figure, and a stock market that exploded 31 percent following President Trump's election, the Liberal Left continues to castigate him. Lies and rumors about him have been unrelenting. Few realize that in his first year in office, the president implemented significant tax cuts and brought North Korea's leader to the table (not once but three times). During the third meeting in the DMZ between North and South Korea, Mr. Trump became the first sitting president to ever set foot in North Korea. Past presidents Jimmy Carter and Bill Clinton each visited North Korean dictator Kim Jong-Il in 2009. Trump also ended the North American Free Trade Agreement, or NAFTA, substituting a much more equitable pact. The president has had two (Conservative) Supreme Court Justices confirmed while making an impressive number of other Conservative judicial appointments.

Since taking office, President Donald J. Trump's family has been under unconscionable and unending attacks by the Liberal Left, including even the Trumps' youngest and most vulnerable member of the family. Why? The answer is partly because of Trump's worldview. Simply put, his vision is one of moral clarity regarding good versus evil. Liberals are generally moral relativists; they reject absolute standards of good and evil, right and wrong.

In the Liberal Left worldview, man is capable of perfection, human nature is on a path toward enlightenment, and the concept of original sin is primitive, at best. Secular humanists make excuses for evil, or worse, deny that it even exists, and coddle evil by refusing to confront it. Previous Liberal Left administrations reinvented men such as Yasser Arafat as peacemakers, giving them the facade of freedom fighters, not terrorists.

In Donald Trump's worldview, America is under attack only because she is a Christian nation, just as Israel is under a never-ending attack because she is a Jewish nation. The Liberal Left mocks Judeo-Christian beliefs as simplistic and ignorant because these modern-day humanists do not believe evil truly exists; that even malevolent people are basically good, and that it's better to talk and show tolerance than to take a definitive, moral stand.

Today, the battle of good versus evil is being fought from within this nation. Too many Liberals actually hate the thought of an America of which a conservative president dreams. Many despise Israel, the Bible, and Christians in general. They subject Conservatives to scorn, ridicule, and discrimination. There is no attack on American culture more deadly than the secular humanists' attacks.

The dumbing down of America continues, and all in the name of political correctness and a new godless globalism. America, the noble experiment, is today under near-constant siege. A tidal wave of evil is sweeping across our nation. Self-injuring, spirit-destroying, conscience-searing practices are being supported by the Left as never before.

One must wonder, then, if the liberal, secular humanists' hatred for all things conservative could pass Natan Sharansky's "town square test." He wrote in his book *The Case for Democracy: The Power of Freedom to Overcome Tyranny & Terror:*

> Can a person walk into the middle of the town square and express his or her views without fear of arrest, imprisonment, or physical harm? If he can, then that person is living in a free society. If not, it's a fear society.[149]

Just as the fig tree blooms to indicate that summer is near, so the signs of the times we are seeing today indicate that Jesus is preparing

His return, and soon! The biblical mention of the fig tree is the prophetic depiction of the flowering of modern-day Israel.

As He said to His disciples in the book of Luke:

> "Now when these things begin to happen, look up and lift up your heads, because your redemption draws near. . . . But take heed to yourselves, lest your hearts be weighed down with carousing, drunkenness, and cares of this life, and that Day come on you unexpectedly. For it will come as a snare on all those who dwell on the face of the whole earth. Watch therefore, and pray always that you may be counted worthy to escape all these things that will come to pass, and to stand before the Son of Man." (Luke 21:28, 34–36 NKJV)

Let no one mislead you about the times in which we live. If the parable of the fig tree and the signs of Matthew 24 are not enough, look at one last mile marker given by the prophet Daniel: the increase of travel and knowledge.

Daniel accurately foretold the kingdoms and governments that would follow ancient Babylon's disappearance from the world scene in Daniel 2:31–45. Many of his prophecies have been fulfilled, his writings constituting the cornerstone of biblical prophecy. Daniel described a key characteristic of the end times, the period leading up to the return of Jesus Christ to earth, in terms of man's pursuit of knowledge:

"But you, Daniel, shut up the words, and seal the book until the time of the end; many shall run to and fro, and knowledge shall increase." (Daniel 12:4 NKJV)

While Daniel's prediction of "many shall run to and fro" could easily be interpreted as the "rat race" of modern society, most Bible scholars interpret it as the rapid increase and the speed of travel. Comparing today's world with that of even two hundred years ago when travel by train at speeds of sixty miles an hour was an incredible feat, now we fly in jumbo jets that can reach perhaps 600 miles an hour—or even the now-sidelined Concorde that reached speeds of a mind-boggling 1,350 miles per hour. What would Daniel have thought of these modern conveyances if we could transport him here in a time machine? I think he would definitely be looking at the skies for Christ's return!

The rate of man's knowledge has grown beyond our comprehension, as well. Years ago scientists actually set out to measure the rate of expansion of man's "knowledge database," to put it in modern technological terms. They assumed that all scientific knowledge accumulated by the year AD 1 equaled one unit of information. They estimated that the amount of knowledge man acquired had doubled to two units over the next 1,500 years. But it only took 250 years for man's knowledge to double to four units. From 1750 until 1900, a period of 150 years, knowledge doubled yet again. And throughout the twentieth century the rate continued to increase, with the result that it now takes only one to two years for our knowledge database to double once more. Think about that for a moment: Everything we know about the latest scientific developments will double in less than two years!

Encyclopedias and textbooks are out of date almost as soon as they're in print. Doctors, engineers, physicists, and researchers are forced to specialize, limiting their concentration to a narrow area of knowledge. Even in our own daily lives it's almost impossible to keep up with the current flow of information. Is it any wonder we often feel that we need an advanced degree just to operate the latest gadget: iPhone, laptop, or iPad, or some yet-to-be-developed device?

Not only does this knowledge explosion indicate that we are living in the end times, the *type* of knowledge man has acquired is absolutely mind-boggling. Things that were in the realm of science fiction only a few years ago are now a reality (think of wristwatch communication or pocket-sized computers or self-driving vehicles). Our government, not to mention the average citizen, is caught woefully unprepared to deal with the moral and ethical implications of some of these scientific advances.

The "brave new world" that science fiction writers imagined just a decade or two ago is here. It's a world in which man has decided to be his own creator via the practice of cloning. Ironic, isn't it, that millions of unborn babies have been cavalierly aborted while at the same time scientists are cloning human life in a laboratory?

I can't help but think that at some point—perhaps soon—God will intervene to stop mankind's mad pursuit of attempting to create life on its own terms. We are building nothing less than a technological tower of Babel. In place of ancient Babylon's worship of astrology and the heavens, modern man worships science and technology. The end result is the same: mankind seems bent on usurping God's role as Creator. And at some point, the Creator will say, "Enough!" and put a stop to man's folly.

The season of Christ's return is definitely near!

> The Spirit and the bride say, "Come." Let anyone who hears this say, "Come." Let anyone who is thirsty come. Let anyone who desires drink freely from the water of life. He who is the faithful witness to all these things says, "Yes, I am coming soon!" Amen! Come, Lord Jesus! (Revelation 22:17, 20 NLT)

The right of Conservatives in America to express their views without fear of retaliation is frequently challenged and slowly eroding. It is time we stand with President Trump and with moral clarity to ensure that we in America are not our own worst enemy!

PEACE TO PROSPERITY

A VISION TO IMPROVE
THE LIVES OF THE
PALESTINIAN AND ISRAELI
PEOPLE

The following information from the
Trump Peace Plan is from the website

https://www.whitehouse.gov/peacetoprosperity.

The full document of the Peace Plan can be
accessed at this location as well.

OVERVIEW

The White House is pleased to share President Trump's Vision for a comprehensive peace agreement between Israel and the Palestinians.

This Vision is the most realistic solution to a problem that has plagued the region for far too long.

It creates a path to prosperity, security, and dignity for all involved. If the parties can agree on this framework as a basis for negotiations, the potential for both the Israelis and the Palestinians and the region is unlimited.

POLITICAL FRAMEWORK

Palestinians and Israelis alike deserve a future of peace and prosperity: A realistic two-state solution will protect Israel's security, fulfill the aspirations of self-determination for the Palestinian people, and ensure universal and respectful access to the holy sites of Jerusalem.

This Vision would achieve mutual recognition of Israel as the nation-state of the Jewish people and the future state of Palestine as the nation-state of the Palestinian people—each with equal civil rights for all its citizens. The plan designates defensible borders for the State of Israel and does not ask Israel to compromise on the safety of its people, affording them overriding security responsibility for land west of the Jordan River. For Palestinians, the Vision delivers significant territorial expansion, allocating land roughly comparable in size to the West Bank and Gaza for establishing a Palestinian State. Transportation links would allow efficient movement between Gaza and the West Bank, as well as throughout a future Palestine. The plan does not call for uprooting any Israelis or Palestinians from their homes.

ECONOMIC FRAMEWORK

Generations of Palestinians have lived without knowing peace, and the West Bank and Gaza have fallen into a protracted crisis.

Yet the Palestinian story will not end here. The Palestinian people continue their historic endeavor to realize their aspirations and build a better future for their children.

With the potential to facilitate more than $50 billion in new investment over ten years, *Peace to Prosperity* represents the most ambitious and comprehensive international effort for the Palestinian people to date. It has the ability to fundamentally transform the West Bank and Gaza and to open a new chapter in Palestinian history—one defined, not by adversity and loss, but by freedom and dignity.

These three initiatives are more than just a vision of a promising future for the Palestinian people—they are also the foundation for an achievable plan.

If implemented, *Peace to Prosperity* will empower the Palestinian people to build the society that they have aspired to establish for generations. With the support of the international community, this vision is within reach. Ultimately, however, the power to unlock it lies in the hands of the Palestinian people. Only through peace can the Palestinians achieve prosperity.

1. UNLEASHING ECONOMIC POTENTIAL

Peace to Prosperity will establish a new foundation for the Palestinian economy, generating rapid economic growth and job creation.

This part of the plan will create a business environment that provides investors with confidence that their assets will be secure by improving property rights, the rule of law, fiscal sustainability, capital markets, and anti-corruption policies.

Opening the West Bank and Gaza

The plan will reduce constraints on Palestinian economic growth by **Opening the West Bank and Gaza** to regional and global markets. Major investments in transportation and infrastructure will help the West Bank and Gaza integrate with neighboring economies, increasing the competitiveness of Palestinian exports and reducing the complications of transport and travel. To complement these investments, this plan will also support steps to improve Palestinian cooperation with Egypt, Israel, and Jordan, with the goal of reducing regulatory barriers to the movement of Palestinian goods and people.

Constructing Essential Infrastructure

Essential infrastructure is needed for the Palestinian people and their businesses to flourish. This plan will facilitate billions of dollars of investment in the electricity, water, and telecommunications sectors, increasing generation capacity while creating efficient transmission and distribution networks. The applicable authorities will receive training and assistance to manage this infrastructure and to increase competition to keep costs low for consumers.

Promoting Private-Sector Growth

Following the adoption of key policy reforms and the construction of essential infrastructure, *Peace to Prosperity* envisions extraordinary private-sector investment in entrepreneurship, small businesses, tourism, agriculture, housing, manufacturing, and natural resources. The goal of early-stage investment will be to remove constraints to growth and to target key projects that build momentum, generate jobs, and increase gross domestic product (GDP). From the father working in his shop to support his family, to the young college graduate building her first company, Palestinians working throughout the private sector will benefit from this plan.

A lasting peace agreement will ensure a future of economic opportunity for all Palestinians.

Strengthening Regional Development and Integration

Peace to Prosperity encourages *Strengthening Regional Development and Integration*, creates new opportunities for Palestinian businesses, and increases commerce with neighboring countries. This vision will boost the economies of Egypt, Israel, Jordan, and Lebanon and reduce trade barriers across the region. Increased cooperation between trading partners will support companies in these countries, which are seeking to develop international business, particularly in the West Bank and Gaza. The plan will help the Palestinian private sector capitalize on growth opportunities by improving access to strong, neighboring economies.

2. EMPOWERING THE PALESTINIAN PEOPLE

Peace to Prosperity will unlock the vast potential of the Palestinian people by empowering them to pursue their goals and ambitions. This part of the vision will support the Palestinian people through education, workforce development, and an improved quality of life.

Enhance the Quality of the Education System

Enhancing the Quality of the Education System in the West Bank and Gaza will ensure no Palestinian is disadvantaged by inadequate educational opportunity. This vision supports the development and training of Palestinian educators while expanding access to educational opportunities to underserved communities and demographics. Other projects will help encourage educational reforms and innovation. By providing financial incentives to support the development of improved academic standards and curricula, this plan will help turn the West Bank and Gaza into a center of educational excellence.

Strengthen Workforce Development Programs

Peace to Prosperity will *Strengthen Workforce Development Programs*, reducing unemployment rates and increasing the occupational mobility of the Palestinian workforce. By supporting apprenticeships, career counseling, and job placement services, this vision will help ensure Palestinian youth are fully prepared to enter the job market and achieve their professional goals. Additional projects will help employed workers receive the training they need to enhance their skills or change careers. Ultimately, this plan will ensure that all Palestinians have access to the tools they need to compete in the global economy and take full advantage of the opportunities offered by this vision.

Transform the Palestinian Healthcare Sector

Peace to Prosperity will provide new resources and incentives to *Transform the Palestinian Healthcare Sector* and ensure the Palestinian people have access to the care they need within the West Bank and Gaza. This vision will rapidly increase the capacity of Palestinian hospitals by ensuring that they have the supplies, medicines, vaccines, and equipment to provide top-quality care and protect against health emergencies. Other funds will help improve services and standards in Palestinian healthcare facilities. Through targeted investments in new facilities, educational opportunities for medical staff and aspiring healthcare professionals, and public awareness campaigns to improve preventative care, the plan will significantly improve health outcomes throughout the West Bank and Gaza.

Improve the Quality of Life

Peace to Prosperity will support projects that *Improve the Quality of Life* for the Palestinian people. From investments in new cultural institutions to financial support for Palestinian artists and musicians, the plan will help the next generation of Palestinians explore their creativity and hone their talents. It will also support improved munici-pal services and the development of new public spaces across the West Bank and Gaza. These developments will help turn the West Bank and Gaza into a cultural and recreational center to the benefit of all Palestinians.

3. ENHANCING PALESTINIAN GOVERNANCE

Peace to Prosperity encourages the Palestinian public sector to pro-vide the services and administration necessary for the Palestinian people to have a better future. If the government realizes its potential by investing in its people and adopting the foundational elements identified in this plan, job growth will ensue and the Palestinian people and their economy will thrive.

This vision establishes a path that, in partnership with the Palestinian public sector, will enable prosperity.

Transform the Business Environment

The strategy for reform will help the Palestinian public sector *Transform the Business Environment* by improving private property rights; safeguards against corruption; access to credit; functioning capital markets along with pro-growth policies and regulations; and certainty and predictability for investors that result in economic growth, private-sector job creation, and increased exports and foreign direct investment. Just as the Japanese, South Korean, and Singaporean governments rose to meet the daunting challenges their societies faced at critical times in their respective histories, so too can the Palestinian leadership chart a new course for its people. The plan identifies and addresses the requirements for developing human capital, igniting innovation, creating and growing small and medium businesses, and attracting international companies that will invest in the future of the West Bank and Gaza.

Build the Institutions

Building the Institutions of the Palestinian public sector and enhancing government responsiveness to the people is critical. Through this plan, government attention will be directed to increase judicial independence and grow civil society organizations. A stronger court system will better protect and secure the rights and property of the citizens. More government transparency will help foster trust from Palestinians—and outside investors—that court decisions are made fairly, contracts are awarded and enforced honestly, and business investments are safe.

Improve Government Operations

Peace to Prosperity will *Improve Government Operations* and the provision of services to the Palestinian people. In line with successful private-sector models, the Palestinian public sector must strive to be fiscally stable, financially independent, caring to its workers, and efficient in providing services to its citizens. The vision will work to eliminate public-sector arrears and implement a budgeting and tax plan that promotes long-term fiscal sustainability, without the need for budget support or donor funds. It will also assist with the adoption of new technologies that can provide Palestinian citizens the ability to directly request and access government support and services. The plan will offer new training and opportunities for civil servants to improve their productivity, help prepare them to meet governance challenges, and make it easier for them to perform their jobs. And, finally, this vision aims to provide government services at low cost and high-efficiency, which will facilitate private-sector growth.

PRESIDENT DONALD TRUMP'S EXECUTIVE ORDER ON COMBATING ANTI-SEMITISM

The following information, issued December 11, 2019, is from

https://www.whitehouse.gov/presidential-actions/ executive-order-combating-anti-semitism.

By the authority vested in me as President by the Constitution and the laws of the United States of America, it is hereby ordered as follows:

Section 1. Policy. My Administration is committed to combating the rise of anti-Semitism and anti-Semitic incidents in the United States and around the world. Anti-Semitic incidents have increased since 2013, and students, in particular, continue to face anti Semitic harassment in schools and on university and college campuses.

Title VI of the Civil Rights Act of 1964 (Title VI), 42 U.S.C. 2000d et seq., prohibits discrimination on the basis of race, color, and national origin in programs and activities receiving Federal financial assistance. While Title VI does not cover discrimination based on religion, individuals who face discrimination on the basis of race, color, or national origin do not lose protection under Title VI for also being a member of a group that shares common religious practices. Discrimination against Jews may give rise to a Title VI violation when the discrimination is based on an individual's race, color, or national origin.

It shall be the policy of the executive branch to enforce Title VI against prohibited forms of discrimination rooted in anti-Semitism as vigorously as against all other forms of discrimination prohibited by Title VI.

Sec. 2. Ensuring Robust Enforcement of Title VI. (a) In enforcing Title VI, and identifying evidence of discrimination based on race, color, or national origin, all executive departments and agencies (agencies) charged with enforcing Title VI shall consider the following:

> (i) the non-legally binding working definition of anti Semitism adopted on May 26, 2016, by the International Holocaust Remembrance Alliance (IHRA), which states, "Antisemitism is a certain perception of Jews, which may be expressed as hatred toward Jews. Rhetorical and physical manifestations of antisemitism are directed toward Jewish or non-Jewish individuals and/or their property, toward Jewish community institutions and religious facilities"; and

> (ii) the "Contemporary Examples of Anti-Semitism" identified by the IHRA, to the extent that any examples might be useful as evidence of discriminatory intent.

> (b) In considering the materials described in subsections (a)(i) and (a)(ii) of this section, agencies shall not diminish or infringe upon any right protected under Federal law or under the First Amendment. As with all other Title VI complaints, the inquiry into whether a particular act constitutes discrimination prohibited by Title VI will require a detailed analysis of the allegations.

Sec. 3. Additional Authorities Prohibiting Anti-Semitic Discrimination. Within 120 days of the date of this order, the head of each agency charged with enforcing Title VI shall submit a report to the President, through the Assistant to the President for Domestic Policy, identifying additional nondiscrimination authorities within its enforcement authority with respect to which the IHRA definition of anti-Semitism could be considered.

Sec. 4. Rule of Construction. Nothing in this order shall be construed to alter the evidentiary requirements pursuant to which an agency makes a determination that conduct, including harassment, amounts to actionable discrimination, or to diminish or infringe upon the rights protected under any other provision of law.

Sec. 5. General Provisions. (a) Nothing in this order shall be construed to impair or otherwise affect:

> (i) the authority granted by law to an executive department or agency, or the head thereof; or

> (ii) the functions of the Director of the Office of Management and Budget relating to budgetary, administrative, or legislative proposals.

> (b) This order shall be implemented consistent with applicable law and subject to the availability of appropriations.

> (c) This order is not intended to, and does not, create any right or benefit, substantive or procedural, enforceable at law or in equity by any party against the United States, its departments, agencies, or entities, its officers, employees, or agents, or any other person.

DONALD J. TRUMP

THE WHITE HOUSE :: DECEMBER II, 2019.

ENDNOTES

1   Teddy Kollek and Moshe Pearlman, *Jerusalem, Sacred City of Mankind* (Israel: Steimatzkâ Group, 1987).

2   "Jerusalem," http://en.wikipedia.org/wiki/Jerusalem.; accessed March 2013.

3   Toi Staff, "Full text of Netanyahu's speech at the opening of the US Embassy in Jerusalem," *Times of Israel*, May 14, 2018, https://www.timesofisrael.com/full-text-of-netanyahus-speech-at-the-opening-of-the-us-embassy-in-jerusalem/; accessed February 2019.

4   "Cyrus the Great: Cyrus II, Kourosh in Persian, Kouros in Greek," *Iran Chamber Society*, September 11, 2019, http://www.iranchamber.com/history/cyrus/cyrus.php; accessed December 19, 2018.

5   Andrew Silow-Carroll, "Who is King Cyrus, and why did Netanyahu compare him to Trump?" *Times of Israel*, March 8, 2018, https://www.timesofisrael.com/who-is-king-cyrus-and-why-is-netanyahu-comparing-him-to-trump/; accessed February 2019.

6   Vice President Pence Remarks to Christians United for Israel Conference, https://www.c-span.org/video/?462373-1/vice-president-pence-addresses-christians-united-israel-conference&start=31; accessed July 2019.

7   Ibid.

8   Ariel Sharon, https://www.azquotes.com/author/13410-Ariel_Sharon; accessed February 2019.

9   "U.S. Shale vs. OPEC Oil Price War: Who Will Win?" UPFINA, June 19, 2017, https://upfina.com/u-s-shale-vs-opec-oil-price-war-who-will-win/; accessed February 2019.

10 Abu Mazen (Mahmoud Abbas), from the official journal of the PLO, *Falastin el-Thawra* ("What We Have Learned and What We Should Do"), Beirut, March 1976.

11 Tom Robbins, "The Lesson: Incident at the Towers, 1993," *New York Daily News*, December 9, 1998 in Richard Miniter, *Losing Bin Laden: How Bill Clinton's Failures Unleashed Global Terror* (Washington, D.C.: Regnery Publishing, Inc., 2003), 19.

12 Miniter, *Losing Bin Laden*, xvi, xix. (Insert added.)

13 Gary McCullough, "Chamberlains vs. Churchills," *Standard Newswire*, http://www.standardnewswire.com/news/582657.html; accessed July 2019.

14 Ibid.

15 Daniel Pipes, "Islam means Peace, but hear what Muslim Clerics said in their Friday Sermons in Mosques," *Daniel Pipes Middle East Forum*, http://www.danielpipes.org/comments/64956; accessed February 2019.

16   "Bin Laden, millionaire with a dangerous grudge," *CNN.com*, September 27, 2001, http://edition.cnn.com/2001/US/09/12/binladen.profile/; accessed February 2019.

17   Barry Strauss, "Trump And Israel," *Hoover Institution*, May 29, 2019, https://www.hoover.org/research/trump-and-israel; accessed June 2019.

18   Elliott Abrams, "Trump's Statesmanlike Speech in Riyadh," *National Review*, May 21, 2017, https://www.nationalreview.com/2017/05/trump-saudi-arabia-speech-statesmanlike/; accessed February 2019.

19   Jack Moore, "Trump: Iran's 'Bad Behavior' in the Middle East Demands a New Response From the U.S.," *Newsweek*, October 7, 2017, http://www.newsweek.com/trump-set-announce-new-responses-irans-bad-behavior-middle-east-680057; accessed February 2018.

20   "Iran begins nuclear fusion studies," *TehranTimes*, July 25, 2010, http://www.tehrantimes.com/news/223584/Iran-begins-nuclear-fusion-studies; accessed February 2018.

21   Benjamin Netanyahu, personal interview with Mike Evans, August 2006.

22   Statement for the Record Worldwide Threat Assessment of the US Intelligence Community Senate Select Committee on Intelligence, Daniel R. Coats, Director of National Intelligence, May 11, 2017, https://www.hsdl.org/?view&did=801029; accessed February 2018.

23   Statement for the Record Worldwide Threat Assessment of the US Intelligence Community, Daniel R. Coates, Director of National Intelligence, February 13, 2018, https://www.dni.gov/files/documents/Newsroom/Testimonies/2018-ATA---Unclassified-SSCI.pdf; accessed October 2018.

24   "Vice President Pence Remarks to Christians United for Israel Conference," C-SPAN, July 8, 2019, https://www.c-span.org/video/?462373-1/vice-president-pence-addresses-christians-united-israel-conference&start=31; accessed July 2019.

25   "Bolton vows Washington to increase pressure on Iran until Tehran ends nuclear program," MENAFN, July 9, 2019, https://menafn.com/1098738499/Bolton-vows-Washington-to-increase-pressure-on-Iran-until-Tehran-ends-nuclear-program?src=Rss; accessed July 2019.

26   Ibid.

27   "PM Netanyahu speaks with Pastor John Hagee at the CUFI Conference in Washington," Israel Ministry of Foreign Affairs, July 8, 2019, https://mfa.gov.il/MFA/PressRoom/2019/Pages/PM-Netanyahu-speaks-with-Pastor-John-Hagee-at-the-CUFI-Conference-in-Washington-8-July-2019.aspx; accessed July 2019.

28   See Appendix 1.

29 "US to hold Bahrain economic conference to launch Middle East peace plan," *The Guardian,* May 19, 2019, https://www.theguardian.com/world/2019/may/19/us-bahrain-economic-conference-middle-east-peace-plan; accessed June 2019.

30 Hanan Ashwari, "The 'ultimate deal'? For Israel, maybe. We Palestinians will never accept it," *The Guardian,* July 19, 2018, https://www.theguardian.com/commentisfree/2018/jul/19/ultimate-deal-israel-palestine-peace-middle-east; accessed June 2019.

31 https://www.whitehouse.gov/peacetoprosperity/; accessed June 2019.

32 Vice President Pence Remarks to Christians United for Israel Conference, C-SPAN, July 8, 2019, https://www.c-span.org/video/?462373-1/vice-president-pence-addresses-christians-united-israel-conference&start=31; accessed July 2019.

33 Kelsey Dallas, "'I will never let you down': Trump expresses support for faith groups in National Prayer Breakfast speech," *Deseret News,* February 7, 2019, https://www.deseretnews.com/article/900054604/i-will-never-let-you-down-trump-expresses-support-for-faith-groups-in-national-prayer-breakfast-speech.html.

34 Martin Luther King, Jr. (1929–68), US clergyman and civil rights leader. *Strength to Love,* pt. 4, ch. 3 (1963).

35 Yossef Bodansky, *The High Cost of Peace: How Washington's Middle East Policy Left America Vulnerable to Terrorism* (Roseville, CA: Forum, 2002), 9–10.

36 https://www.azquotes.com/quote/1584782; accessed February 2019.

37 Sarah Begley, "Donald Trump's Full Speech to AIPAC," *Time,* March 21, 2016, http://time.com/4267058/donald-trump-aipac-speech-transcript/; accessed October 2018.

38 "Congress & the Middle East: Jerusalem Embassy Relocation Act, (October 24, 1995)," *Jewish Virtual Library,* https://www.jewishvirtuallibrary.org/jerusalem-embassy-relocation-act-october-1995.

39 "President Clinton Administration: Press Conference with Israeli PM Ehud Barak (July 15, 1999)," *Jewish Virtual Library,* https://www.jewishvirtuallibrary.org/president-clinton-press-conference-with-israeli-pm-ehud-barak-july-1999; accessed October 2018.

40 "Congress & the Middle East: Jerusalem Embassy Relocation Act (October 24, 1995)," *Jewish Virtual Library,*

https://www.jewishvirtuallibrary.org/jerusalem-embassy-relocation-act-october-1995; accessed October 2018.

41 http://secureisrael.com/embassy.htm; accessed October 2018.

42 Rabbi Aryeh Spero, "President Trump Fulfills Prophecies and Moves Our Embassy to Jerusalem," *American Thinker,* May 13, 2018, https://www.americanthinker.com/articles/2018/05/president_trump_fulfills_prophecies_and_moves_our_embassy_to_jerusalem.html#ixzz5VKaYrVmq; accessed November 2018.

43 President Donald Trump's speech recognizing Jerusalem as Israel's capital, *NBC News,* Dec. 6, 2017, https://www.nbcnews.com/politics/white-house/read-trump-s-full-speech-jerusalem-today-i-am-delivering-n827111; accessed January 2018.

44 Secretary of State Mike Pompeo, "The U.S. and Israel: A Friendship for Freedom," U.S. Department of State, July 8, 2019, https://www.state.gov/the-u-s-and-israel-a-friendship-for-freedom/; accessed July 2019.

45 David B. Barrett and Todd M. Johnson, *World Christian Trends AD 30–AD 2200: Interpreting the Annual Christian Megacensus* (Pasadena, CA: William Carey Library, 2001), 243–244. According to the totals of the chart on these pages, about 6 million Christians died as martyrs to their faith out of the 40–55 million killed during World War II.

46 Stuart Taylor, Jr., "The Rage of Genocidal Masses Must Not Restrain Us," *The Atlantic,* October 1, 2001, https://www.theatlantic.com/politics/archive/2001/10/the-rage-of-genocidal-masses-must-not-restrain-us/378037/; accessed February 2019.

47 *The Guardian Data Blog,* https://www.theguardian.com/news/datablog/2010/feb/28/deadliest-earthquakes-strongest-data; accessed February 2019.

48 Barrett and Johnson, 229.

49 Kate Shellnut, "80% of Americans Believe in God. Pew Found Out What They Mean," *Christianity Today,* April 25, 2018, https://www.christianitytoday.com/news/2018/april/we-believe-in-god-what-americans-mean-pew-survey.html; accessed February 2019.

50 This list is from Mark Hitchcock, *Is America in Bible Prophecy?* (Sisters, OR: Multnomah Publishers, 2002), 27–28, though I have changed some of the scripture references to verses that more clearly represent his points.

51 Thomas Jefferson, "Commerce between Master and Slave," 1782; available online at https://patriotpost.us/documents/173.

52 Rev. Dan White, "President Trump Restores America as a Christian Nation," January 22, 2017, https://danwhite5868.wordpress.com/2017/01/22/president-trump-restores-america-as-a-christian-nation/; accessed February 2019.

53 *Holy Trinity Church v. United States,* 143 U.S. 457, 465 (February 29, 1892).

54 Ibid., 471.

55   David Barton, *The Bulletproof George Washington* (Aledo, TX: WallBuilders Press, 1990), 35, 44, 50, 57.

56   Peter Grose, *Israel in the Mind of America* (New York: Alfred A. Knopf, 1984), 5.

57   George Washington. "Letter to Jews of Newport, Rhode Island," 1790, in Kenneth R. Timmerman, *Preachers of Hate: Islam and the War on America* (New York: Crown Publishing Group, 2003), xi.

58   Franklin Graham, "From Franklin Graham: Is the Handwriting on the Wall for America?" Billy Graham Evangelistic Association, May 1, 2016, https://billygraham.org/decision-magazine/may-2016/from-franklin-graham-is-the-handwriting-on-the-wall-for-america/; accessed July 2019.

59   Michael Feldberg, "John Adams and the Jews," *My Jewish Learning*, https://www.myjewishlearning.com/article/john-adams-and-the-jews/; accessed February 2019.

60   Ibid.

61   Some scholars believe that Isaiah 18 refers to Cush—Egypt as we know it today. Though Pastor McDonald may have misinterpreted this scripture, his call to action was still a godly one. It was the first step in the American conscience toward supporting the rebirth of the nation of Israel.

62   Grose, 9.

63   Ibid., 15.

64   Ibid.

65   Ibid., 20.

66   https://en.wikipedia.org/wiki/Lockheed_Martin_F-35_Lightning_II#cite_note-9jul2013-23; accessed November 2018.

67   Jackson Richman, "Trump approves largest-ever aid package to Israel, sets up showdown with Turkey over F-35s," *Jewish News Syndicate*, August 13, 2018, https://www.jns.org/ndaa-signed-by-trump-confirms-aid-to-israel-delays-sale-of-jets-to-turkey/; accessed November 2018.

68   Sean Savage, "Why is Washington seeking to block the sale of F-35 fighter jets to Turkey?" *Sun Sentinel*, June 4, 2018,

http://www.sun-sentinel.com/florida-jewish-journal/fl-jjps-turkey-0613-20180604-story.html; accessed November 2018.

69   Ibid.

70   Heather Naert, U.S. Department of State, Washington, D.C., May 17, 2017, https://www.state.gov/r/pa/prs/ps/2017/05/270923.htm; accessed November 2018.

71   Chris Mitchell, "Turkey Punishes Israel for Hamas Border Attacks, Netanyahu Ties Erdogan to Terrorism," *CBN News,* May 16, 2018, http://www1.cbn.com/cbnnews/israel/2018/may/turkey-punishes-israel-for-hamas-border-attacks-netanyahu-ties-erdogan-to-terrorism; accessed November 2018.

72   Elad Benari, "Erdogan: Hamas is not a terrorist organization," *Israel National News,* May 16, 2018, http://www.israelnationalnews.com/News/News.aspx/246031; accessed November 2018.

73   "The Recognition of the State of Israel," Truman Library, Eliahu Epstein to Harry S. Truman with attachments re: recognition of Israel, May 14, 1948.

74   "Suez Crisis," *GlobalSecurity.org,* http://www.globalsecurity.org/military/ops/suez.htm; accessed January 2019.

75   David Geffen, "In Appreciative Memory of JFK," *Jerusalem Post*, October 27, 2010, https://www.jpost.com/Features/In-Thespotlight/In-appreciative-memory-of-JFK; accessed January 2019.

76   John Fitzgerald Kennedy, Inaugural Address, January 20, 1961, https://www.jfklibrary.org/learn/about-jfk/historic-speeches/inaugural-address; accessed November 2018.

77   Herbert Druks, *John F. Kennedy and Israel* (Westport, CT: Greenwood Publishing Group, Inc., 2005), 139.

78   Walter Z. Laqueur, "Kissinger & the Yom Kippur War," *Commentary Magazine,* September 1974, https://www.commentarymagazine.com/articles/kissinger-the-yom-kippur-war/; accessed December 2018.

79   Seymour M. Hersh, *The Samson Option: Israel's Nuclear Arsenal and American Foreign Policy* (New York, NY: Random House, 1991), 224–226.

80   Ibid., 223.

81   Seymour M. Hersh, *The Price of Power: Kissinger in the Nixon White House* (New York: Summit Books, 1983), 234.

82   Jason Maoz, "Nixon: The 'Anti-Semite' Who Saved Israel," *Jewish Press*, August 3, 2005, http://www.jewishpress.com/indepth/front-page/nixon-the-anti-semite-who-saved-israel/2005/08/03/; accessed January 2019.

83   Keith Koffler, "Obama Wildly Cheered by Reform Jews," December 16, 2011, white house dossier; http://www.whitehousedossier.com/2011/12/16/obama-wildly-cheered-reform-jews/; accessed January 2019.

84   "Zionism, Nixon-style," *The Jerusalem Post* editorial, December 12, 2010; http://www.jpost.com/Opinion/Editorials/Article.aspx?id=199133&R=R6; accessed January 2019.

85   J. J. Goldberg, *Jewish Power: Inside the American Jewish Establishment* (New York: Basic Books, 1997), 158.

86   Chaim Herzog, *Living History* (New York: Pantheon Books, 1996), 182.

87   Oswald Chambers, https://www.christianquotes.info/images/oswald-chambers-quote-ordinary-people-extraordinary-purpose/#ixzz5fteJ5eHu; accessed February 2019.

88   Howard Norton and Bob Slosser, *The Miracle of Jimmy Carter* (Plainfield, NJ: Logos Books, 1976), 93.

89   Jay Nordlinger, "Jimmy Carter, Apologist for Arafat," *National Review*, October 16, 2002, http://www.freerepublic.com/focus/f-news/1768654/posts; accessed December 2018.

90   Yasser Arafat, *Brainy Quote*, https://www.brainyquote.com/quotes/yasser_arafat_178960; accessed December 2018.

91   Gore Vidal, *Imperial America: Reflections on the United States of Amnesia* (New York: Nation Books, 2005), 72.

92   Elizabeth Stephens, *US Policy towards Israel: The Role of Political Culture in Defining the 'Special Relationship,'* (Chicago: Sussex Academic Press, 2018), 201.

93   "U.S. Presidents & Israel: Quotes About Jewish Homeland & Israel," *Jewish Virtual Library*, March 23, 1982, http://www.jewishvirtuallibrary.org/jsource/US-Israel/presquote.html#4; accessed January 2019.

94   Dr. David R. Reagan, "Yitzhak Rabin," http://www.raptureforums.com/IsraelMiddleEast/yitzhakrabin.cfm; accessed September 2018.

95   Oren Liebermann, Michael Schwartz and Rob Picheta, "Israel announces new Golan Heights settlement named 'Trump Heights,'" CNN, June 17, 2019, https://www.cnn.com/2019/06/17/politics/trump-heights-golan-settlement-us-israel-scli-intl/index.html; accessed July 1, 2019.

96   Mitchell G. Bard, "George W. Bush Administration: Deconstructing Bush's Middle East Strategy," *Jewish Virtual Library*, http://www.jewishvirtuallibrary.org/jsource/US-Israel/deconstruct.html; accessed January 2019.

97   "Why Obama 'hates' Israel," *Rabbi Pruzansky's Blog*, November 23, 2010; http://rabbipruzansky.com/2010/11/23/why-obama-%E2%80%9Chates%E2%80%9D-israel/; accessed January 2019.

98   Mike Pompeo, American University, Cairo, Egypt, January 10, 2019.

99   https://en.wikipedia.org/wiki/United_Nations_Security_Council_Resolution_2334; accessed January 2019.

100 Lawrence Myers, "Why They Hate Trump So Much," *Townhall*, July 5, 2017, https://townhall.com/columnists/lawrencemeyers/2017/07/05/why-they-hate-trump-so-much-n2350469; accessed November 2018.

101 Benny Avni, "Obama's hypocrisy when it comes to interference in our politics," *New York Post,* December 29, 2016, https://nypost.com/2016/12/29/obamas-hypocrisy-when-it-comes-to-interference-in-our-politics/; accessed November 2018.

102 Toi Staff, *Times of Israel*, Bill Clinton admits he tried to help Peres beat Netanyahu in 1996 elections, April 4, 2018,https://www.timesofisrael.com/bill-clinton-admits-he-tried-to-help-peres-beat-netanyahu-in-1996-elections/; accessed November 2018.

103 Chris Pandolfo, "What is 'Antifa'? And why is the media so reluctant to expose it?" *Conservative Review*, April 19, 2017, https://www.conservativereview.com/news/what-is-antifa-and-why-are-the-media-so-reluctant-to-expose-it/; accessed November 2018.

104 George Soros, "Remarks delivered at the World Economic Forum, Davos, Switzerland, January 25, 2018," https://www.georgesoros.com/2018/01/25/remarks-delivered-at-the-world-economic-forum/; accessed November 2018.

105 Michael Steinberger, "George Soros Bet Big on Liberal Democracy. Now He Fears He Is Losing," *New York Times Magazine*, July 17, 2018, https://www.nytimes.com/2018/07/17/magazine/george-soros-democrat-open-society.html; accessed November 2018.

106 Dennis Prager, "George Soros and the Problem of the Radical Non-Jewish Jew," February 26, 2007, https://www.creators.com/read/dennis-prager/02/07/george-soros-and-the-problem-of-the-radical-non-jewish-jew; accessed March 2019.

107 Anna Porter, *Buying a Better World: George Soros and Billionaire Philanthropy* (Toronto, Ontario, Canada: Dundurn Press, 2015), 32.

108 Liel Leibovitz, "Soros Hack Reveals Evidence Systemic Anti-Israel Bias," *Tablet*, https://www.tabletmag.com/scroll/210826/soros-hack-reveals-evidence-of-systemic-anti-israel-bias; accessed March 2019.

109 Greg Richter, "Dershowitz: Hunting Trump Will Come Back to Bite Dems," *Newsmax,* June 19, 2017, https://www.newsmax.com/Politics/Alan-Dershowitz-Democrats-political-injustice/2017/06/19/id/796994/; accessed March 2019.

110 Guy Millière, "Muslim Invasion of Europe," *Gatestone Institute,* October 22, 2015, https://www.gatestoneinstitute.org/6721/muslim-invasion-europe; accessed February 2019.

111 Mortimer B. Zuckerman, "Graffiti on History's Walls," *U.S. News & World Report* vol. 135, no. 15 (November 3, 2003), 47–48.

112 Michael Reagan, "Congress doesn't want to solve immigration issue," *New Jersey Herald,* February 19, 2019, https://www.njherald.com/20190219/congress-doesnt-want-to-solve-immigration-issue#; accessed February 2019.

113 Besheer Mohamed, "New estimates show U.S. Muslim population continues to grow," *Pew Research Center,* January 3, 2018, http://www.pewresearch.org/fact-tank/2018/01/03/new-estimates-show-u-s-muslim-population-continues-to-grow/; accessed February 2019.

114 Seymour M. Hersh, *The Samson Option: Israel's Nuclear Arsenal and American Foreign Policy* (New York, NY: Random House, 1991), 9.

115 Bodansky, 568.

116 Elliott Abrams, "Stop Supporting Palestinian Terror," *National Review,* April 17, 2017; https://www.nationalreview.com/magazine/2017/04/17/taylor-force-act-congress-palestine-terrorism/; accessed November 2018.

117 Bassam Tawil, "Palestinians: Welcome to the World of Western-Funded Terrorism," *Gatestone Institute,* December 19, 2016, https://www.gatestoneinstitute.org/9601/palestinians-western-funded-terrorism; accessed November 2018.

118 Julie Stahl, Chris Mitchell, "Palestinian Leader Swears 'By Allah' to Keep Paying for Terrorism: 'Pay to Slay' Tops Agenda," *CBN News,* October 4, 2018, http://www1.cbn.com/cbnnews/israel/2018/october/palestinian-leader-swears-by-allah-to-keep-paying-for-terrorism-pay-to-slay-tops-agenda; accessed November 2018.

119 Ibid.

120 "House Passes Taylor Force Act," December 5, 2017, https://foreignaffairs.house.gov/press-release/house-passes-taylor-force-act/; accessed November 2018.

121 From the author's personal transcript of conference speeches.

122 Ibid.

123 Ibid.

124 Mortimer B. Zuckerman, "Graffiti on History's Walls," *U.S. News & World Report* vol. 135, no. 15 (November 3, 2003), 47–48.

125 Dr. Alex Safian, "Why Palestinians Still Live in Refugee Camps," *Camera,* August 14, 2005, https://www.camera.org/article/why-palestinians-still-live-in-refugee-camps/; accessed March 2019.

126 Zuckerman, 48.

127   The Palestinian right of return is the political position or principle that Palestinian refugees, both first-generation refugees and their descendants, have a right to return and a right to the property they themselves or their forebears left behind or were forced to leave in what is now Israel and the Palestinian territories, as part of the 1948 Palestinian exodus, a result of the 1948 Palestine war, and due to the 1967 Six-Day War; https://en.wikipedia.org/wiki/Palestinian_right_of_ return; accessed March 2019.

128   Zuckerman, 50.

129   Dore Gold, *Hatred's Kingdom: How Saudi Arabia Supports the New Global Terrorism* (Washington D.C.: Regnery Publishing, Inc., 2003), 246.

130   "Muslim Ilhan Omar continues to assail Jews in Congress," *Washington Times*, March 4, 2019, http://www.gopusa.com/muslim-ilhan-omar-continues-to-assail-jews-in-congress/; accessed March 2019.

131   Tyler O'Neil, "Dem. Rep. Maxine Waters Greets Anti-Semite Louis Farrakhan With Open, Loving Arms," *PJ Media,* March 20, 2018, https://pjmedia.com/video/watch-dem-rep-maxine-waters-greets-anti-semite-louis-farrakhan-with-open-loving-arms/; accessed March 2019.

132   Laurie Goodstein, "'There Is Still So Much Evil': Growing Anti-Semitism Stuns American Jews," *New York Times*, October 29, 2018, https://www.nytimes.com/2018/10/29/us/anti-semitism-attacks.html; accessed March 2019.

133   *Der Parteitag der Arheit vom 6 bis 13 September 1937: Offizieller Bericht uber den Verlauf des Reichsparteitages mit samtlichen Kongressreden* (Munich, 1938), p. 157, in Friedlander, *Nazi Germany and the Jews,* 184–185.

134   Gerald Fleming, *Hitler and the Final Solution* (Berkley: University of California Press, 1984), 17, in George Victor, *Hitler: The Pathology of Evil* (Dulles, VA: Brassey's, 1998), 123.

135   Phyllis Chesler, *The New Anti-Semitism: The Current Crisis and What We Must Do About It* (San Francisco, CA: Jossey-Bass, 2003), 218–223.

136   Julie Stahl, CNSNews.com Jerusalem Bureau Chief, "Iran to Host Holocaust Deniers Conference," January 12, 2006, http://www.genocidewatch.org/images/Iran-12-Jan-06-Iran_to_Host_Holocaust_Deniers_Conference.pdf; accessed March 2019.

137   *Palestine Times* No.114 (December 2000).

138   *Associated Press* (March 25, 2000).

139   Ahmad Abu Halabiya, "Friday sermon in Gaza mosque on October 13, 2000," broadcast live on Palestinian Authority TV.

140 Hitler is a Youth Idol, Mein Kampf is a Bestseller, (Various articles from http://www.mfa.gov.il/MFA/Archive/Articles/2000/Hitler+is+a+Youth+Idol-+Mein+Kampf+is+a+Bestseller.htm,) https://sitamnesty.wordpress.com/2010/02/24/hitler-y-est-une-idole-des-jeunes-mein-kampf-un-bestseller/; accessed March 2019.[[web site no longer available]]

141 Cal Thomas, "Bibi and Trump agonists," *Washington Times*, March 4, 2019, https://www.washingtontimes.com/news/2019/mar/4/trump-and-netanyahu-policies-matter-more-than-pers/.

142 Ibid.[[This is not from the previous article. Please provide correct info.]]

143 Bari Weiss, "Europe's Jew Hatred, and Ours," November 29, 2018, *New York Times*, https://www.nytimes.com/2018/11/29/opinion/antisemitism-europe-jews.html; accessed March 2019.

144 Richard Allen Green, "CNN poll reveals depth of anti-Semitism in Europe," https://www.cnn.com/interactive/2018/11/europe/antisemitism-poll-2018-intl/; accessed March 2019.

145 *Courierra de la Sera* (April 12, 2002).

146 Robert Wistrich, "Muslim Antisemitism," *Reason, Liberty, & Culture,* http://www.sullivan-county.com/id3/cairo.htm; accessed March 2019.

147 Partial-Birth Abortion Q & A, *National Right to Life,* https://www.nrlc.org/archive/abortion/facts/pbafacts.html; accessed July 2019.

148 Nick Gass, "Trump's evangelical advisory board features Bachmann, Falwell," *Politico,* June 21, 2016, https://www.politico.com/story/2016/06/trump-evangelical-advisory-board-224612; accessed March 2019.

149 Natan Sharansky, *The Case for Democracy: The Power of Freedom to Overcome Tyranny & Terror* (New York: PublicAffairs, 2004), 40–41.

BOOKS BY: MIKE EVANS

Israel: America's Key to Survival

Save Jerusalem

The Return

Jerusalem D.C.

Purity and Peace of Mind

Who Cries for the Hurting?

Living Fear Free

I Shall Not Want

Let My People Go

Jerusalem Betrayed

Seven Years of Shaking: A Vision

The Nuclear Bomb of Islam

Jerusalem Prophecies

Pray For Peace of Jerusalem

America's War:The Beginning of
    the End

The Jerusalem Scroll

The Prayer of David

The Unanswered Prayers of Jesus

God Wrestling

The American Prophecies

Beyond Iraq: The Next Move

The Final Move beyond Iraq

Showdown with Nuclear Iran

Jimmy Carter: The Liberal Left and
    World Chaos

Atomic Iran

Cursed

Betrayed

The Light

Corrie's Reflections & Meditations

The Revolution

The Final Generation

Seven Days

The Locket

Persia: The Final Jihad

GAMECHANGER SERIES:

GameChanger

Samson Option

The Four Horsemen

THE PROTOCOLS SERIES:

The Protocols

The Candidate

Jerusalem

The History of Christian Zionism

Countdown

Ten Boom: Betsie, Promise of God

Commanded Blessing

BORN AGAIN SERIES:

Born Again: 1948

Born Again: 1967

Presidents in Prophecy

Stand with Israel

Prayer, Power and Purpose

Turning Your Pain Into Gain

Christopher Columbus, Secret Jew

Living in the F.O.G.

Finding Favor with God

Finding Favor with Man

Unleashing God's Favor

The Jewish State: The Volunteers

See You in New York

Friends of Zion:Patterson &
   Wingate

The Columbus Code

The Temple

Satan, You Can't Have My
   Country!

Satan, You Can't Have Israel!

Lights in the Darkness

The Seven Feasts of Israel

Netanyahu (a novel)

Jew-Hatred and the Church

The Visionaries

Why Was I Born?

Son, I Love You

Jerusalem DC (David's Capital)

Israel Reborn

Prayer: A Conversation with God

Shimon Peres (a novel)

Pursuing God's Presence

Ho Feng Shan (a novel)

The Good Father

The Daniel Option (a novel)

Keep the Jews Out! (a novel)

Donald Trump and Israel

TO PURCHASE, CONTACT: orders@TimeWorthyBooks.com
P. O. BOX 30000, PHOENIX, AZ 85046

MICHAEL DAVID EVANS, the #1 *New York Times* bestselling author, is an award-winning journalist/Middle East analyst. Dr. Evans has appeared on hundreds of network television and radio shows including *Good Morning America, Crossfire* and *Nightline,* and *The Rush Limbaugh Show,* and on Fox Network, *CNN World News,* NBC, ABC, and CBS. His articles have been published in the *Wall Street Journal, USA Today, Washington Times, Jerusalem Post* and newspapers worldwide. More than twenty-five million copies of his books are in print, and he is the award-winning producer of nine documentaries based on his books.

Dr. Evans is considered one of the world's leading experts on Israel and the Middle East, and is one of the most sought-after speakers on that subject. He is the chairman of the board of the ten Boom Holocaust Museum in Haarlem, Holland, and is the founder of Israel's first Christian museum located in the Friends of Zion Heritage Center in Jerusalem.

Dr. Evans has authored 93 books including: *History of Christian Zionism, Showdown with Nuclear Iran, Atomic Iran, The Next Move Beyond Iraq, The Final Move Beyond Iraq,* and *Countdown.* His body of work also includes the novels *Seven Days, GameChanger, The Samson Option, The Four Horsemen, The Locket, Born Again: 1967,* and *The Columbus Code.*

✦ ✦ ✦

Michael David Evans is available to speak or for interviews.
Contact: EVENTS@drmichaeldevans.com.